A TIFFANY'S CHRISTMAS

FESTIVE READING COLLECTION

HOLLY GREENE

A TIFFANY'S CHRISTMAS

A FESTIVE NYC ROMANCE STORY

CHAPTER 1

*T*here was nothing quite like Christmas at Tiffany & Co.

Year upon year, Naomi was captivated by the magic of the iconic NYC jewelry store. Even before she stepped inside, the beautifully intricate and captivating holiday windows transported her to another world, filled with festive glamor and wonder.

A real-life fairytale, right there on Fifth Avenue.

And once she stepped through those revolving doors and came out the other side, the everyday hustle and bustle of Manhattan melted away and she was in wonderland.

Holly Golightly was right; nothing bad could truly ever happen at Tiffany's.

And for Naomi, only good things had.

Her mom used to work as a store assistant at the flagship store, and as a little girl, Naomi would come here to visit Amelia while she worked.

At Christmastime there was simply no better place to be than by the glittering display counters, watching her mom help customers chose their perfect purchase.

She couldn't in a million years afford some of the items she sold, but that was never a concern. Her mom just loved making other people happy, and helping to find a gift that was just right for that special someone was enough to make her day, every day.

Sadly Amelia was no longer around to do that, but by returning here every year during the holidays Naomi felt like she was holding on to that childhood memory, and keeping it alive.

Now, she looked at surrounding spruces adorned with Tiffany's signature little blue boxes, each standing as a regal centrepiece for each of the central display cases on the ground floor. Illuminated lighting and additional silver and robin's egg-colored blue baubles completed the look to perfection.

Wreathes, similarly decorated in inimitable Tiffany's style, lined the walls of polished wood and dark green marble interspersed between the panels.

This year, a huge Tiffany-blue advent calendar stood sentry at the front entrance, and Naomi could only guess at the luxurious treasures to be revealed beneath each door throughout the Christmas countdown.

'You really would've loved this year's décor Mom,' she whispered to herself as she strolled casually along the glass display cabinets, marveling at the stunning jewelry.

But Naomi was never there to shop. She just came to remember.

And in a way, continue the tradition her parents had started when she was a just a toddler. She still remembered clinging excitedly to her dad's hand as every year he spirited her through the doors of the store's glittering wonderland, before heading straight toward her mother's post.

After the visit, the two of them would stroll further up the street as far Rockefeller Center, taking in the famed Fifth avenue holiday displays along the way.

There, father and daughter would some spend time gliding on the ice before enjoy steaming hot chocolate and gawping in wonder at the mammoth Christmas tree.

Reliving that same tradition every year (albeit alone) was pretty much all Naomi needed to make this time of year perfect.

And these days she felt she needed it more than ever.

Christmas was supposed to be a time of kindness, joy and compassion, but there was little of that in the air this year.

As an *NYCTV News Today* reporter, she should know. It was Naomi's job to find interesting local news to share with the city, but recently her stories were getting bleaker and bleaker.

She didn't want to spend another second thinking about muggings and officer-involved shootings, and she'd had more than enough of burglaries and attacks. To say nothing of politics.

It was Christmas week and Naomi just wanted something escapist and inspiring.

Tiffany's was exactly that.

There were so many good memories here. It was far more than just a store. Time spent within these walls helped shape her life in more ways than one.

In a way, it had inspired her career. The stories her mother used to impart about her work days, so many tales of romance and joy behind those famous little blue boxes, had lit a fire under Naomi's own fascination with finding the extraordinary within the ordinary, and partly the reason she'd become a specialist in human interest stories.

Today, the store ground floor was filled with shoppers seeking out Christmas gifts in time for the big day next week.

Naomi glanced at an elegant woman nearby whose neck was adorned with vintage fur stole. Her silver hair was pinned up in a neat french twist, and large pearl earrings dangled from her wrinkled ears.

She reminded her of a character from one of those old musicals she and her mother loved to watch, and Naomi hummed to herself as she moved on, watching people jauntily swinging the store's signature blue bags.

She spied a little girl with big chocolate curls round her ears and a bright red woollen hat on her head, holding her father's hand, scampering behind him as he strolled along the glass display cases.

The child looked a lot like Naomi when she was about that age, though her own hair was considerably longer now and her eyes hazel while the little girl's eyes were blue.

Time goes by so fast.

She still couldn't believe that in a few short months she'd be saying goodbye to her thirties and hello to her forties.

She loosened her green-check scarf as she stopped to look at a beautiful gold necklace with a twist knot pendant. It was beautiful and exactly the kind of thing she would choose for herself.

If I could afford it...

Still, Naomi was more than content to just look and admire the exquisite piece, until just out of her peripheral vision, something caught her attention.

A man was coming through the revolving doors. He was tall, tanned, and very handsome with dark brown hair and a concerned look on his face - but it wasn't so much his distinguished appearance than his harried, uncertain expression that had caught her eye.

That and the fact that he'd come *in* with a Tiffany's bag, not out, which alerted her to the fact that something was off.

In fact he was so focused, that unlike anyone else who entered the store, he didn't pause to admire the unmissable advent calendar, nor check out any of the displays; he just kept striding past counter after counter.

Her journalist radar well and truly pinging, it wasn't long before Naomi was doing the same.

Intrigued, she followed along as a Tiffany's assistant clad in a formal attire, pointed him in the direction of the elevators at the back of the shop floor - and quick as you like, Naomi hurried her pace toward the already retracting doors.

CHAPTER 2

'Wait!' Naomi called out, stepping in behind the man just before the doors closed.

She flushed a little as the elevator attendant smiled a greeting.

'Which floor are you visiting today?' he asked politely and she repeated what she'd heard the man utter just as she stepped inside. 'Fourth, please.'

Arriving at that floor, they both stepped out, the man graciously allowing Naomi to depart first, despite his obvious haste.

He then headed directly toward the Guest Services desk, while she meandered idly between the shelves, pretending to look at one item or another, as she drew closer.

There was a display of leather wallets just a couple of feet away from the desk, just close enough for her to listen in without being obvious.

'May I help you?' a smiling store assistant asked from nearby, and Naomi cursed inwardly behind her smile.

'I'm good, thanks. Just browsing.'

'Of course. Let me know if you need anything.'

She'd missed his opening gambit at the desk, but noticed that the man was gesturing toward the bag, while the Guest Services lady looked on with a puzzled frown.

The assistant then opened the bag and withdrew the contents; the store's unmistakable blue box; this one elongated and rectangular.

But instead of the also-typical Tiffany white satin ribbon and bow, this was wrapped in holiday red; a more festive deviation for this time of year, Naomi knew.

'I'm sorry, sir, but I'm afraid I can't help you,' she heard the assistant say. 'If there was a receipt I'd be able to check the system, but without one, there's just no way of telling ...'

'But there has to be *some* way of finding out who lost it,' the man was insisting. 'It's could be very valuable and likely intended as a Christmas gift.'

A lost gift....? Now well and truly intrigued, Naomi drifted even closer.

'Please ... is there maybe a list of items sold yesterday that you could check against ... see if something might correspond to a box this size? Someone is surely missing this and I'd really like to get it back to its rightful owner.'

The assistant did well to hide her incredulous expression. 'I'm sorry, sir, but that really is impossible. A great majority of our jewelry purchases come in boxes this size, and of course we have so many such sales coming up to the holiday season ...'

A heavy sigh. 'Which means opening the box wouldn't really help us either, though I'd really like to avoid that if I could...' he muttered, his voice trailing off, as he struggled to figure out what to do next.

The assistant smiled politely. 'I'm so sorry we can't help, but I'm sure the owner will come back once they've realized they've left it behind,' she offered and he nodded despondently.

Naomi's heart raced as her mind began figuring out the basics of the situation.

And she recognized an opportunity.

'Excuse me …' She stepped closer to the desk just as the man was walking away, and he and the Tiffany's assistant both turned to looked at her. 'Sorry to interrupt, but I couldn't help but overhear your conversation,' she explained, indicating the box and bag. 'Something's been lost?'

The man's green eyes widened with interest, and some reserve too.

'Might you be the owner?' he asked cautiously.

'Oh no, I'm afraid not,' she told him. 'I just thought I might be able to help.'

'Really? How so?'

She extended her hand. 'My name's Naomi Stewart and I'm a reporter with *NYCTV News*.'

'Oh I thought I'd seen you before,' the Tiffany's assistant called out warmly. 'I love your segments.'

Naomi smiled. 'Thank you.' She fell into step beside the man as he walked away. 'If you let me know the circumstances, perhaps I might be able to help you find the owner, Mr…'

'Ricci. My name is Raymond Ricci. I just don't see how,' he replied, though she could tell that thanks to the assistant's recognition, he was no longer quite so suspicious of her. 'Someone left their Christmas shopping behind in a café. Not exactly a thrilling news story.'

'Well, that depends on how you look at it,' Naomi said, ambling alongside him as they headed back to the elevators. 'Somebody out there is surely missing it, or perhaps might not yet have even realized they've left it behind - or where. I was thinking that maybe you might consider making a public appeal via our news channel? If *NYCTV* could help find the owner and reunite them with the gift in time for the holidays, it would make for a wonderful feel-good segment.'

'But anyone could claim to be the owner,' Raymond questioned.

'And I don't even know what the box contains. To say nothing of the fact that whatever's inside is none of my business; it's just lost property from my café.'

'You own the café it was left in?'

'Yes, one of my wait staff found it beneath a table yesterday, and brought it straight to me. We were hoping that someone would've come back for it by now, but nobody has. I don't want something so potentially valuable laying around my premises, so I thought I'd come to Tiffany's to see if they could shed any light. But there was no receipt in the bag, so we're all still in the dark.'

His brow wrinkled and Naomi couldn't help but notice that he really was very handsome. Those arresting green eyes really stood out against his strong jawline and sallow skin.

"I'm pretty sure I can weed out any time-wasters. We have a nose for that in my line of work,' she explained with a grin. 'Comes with the territory.'

He nodded. 'OK, so if I were to do this ... how would you want to work it? I'd really love to find the owner as soon as possible.' Raymond looked at her and she also noticed the determination in his piercing gaze. 'It's Christmas week after all.'

'Actually, I think the timing will only enhance people's eagerness to get involved,' she told him, eagerly. 'We can filter the calls through the station and I can question responders before presenting any leads to you. Let me help you with this, so you can focus on your business Mr Ricci. I've been looking for a feel-good Christmas segment. Goodness knows this city needs it.' She smiled brightly. 'What do you say?'

He looked thoughtful for a moment, then an acquiescent smile spread across his face. 'I guess we can give it a shot - what have we got to lose? And please, call me Raymond.'

'Great,' Naomi grinned happily, eager to get cracking. 'I already have a couple ideas about how to frame the story so as to weed out time-wasters. But first, I need you to help me set the scene by laying out exactly how you came to find the gift and where. Do you have time to maybe grab a coffee somewhere?'

'Sure,' Raymond replied with a smile. 'I know just the place.'

CHAPTER 3

*H*e led Naomi straight to the 'scene of the crime'; a cosy traditional Italian café called Caffe Amore, located on a quiet little corner between Fifth and Madison.

Simple in décor with polished wood and black and white tiled floors, patrons were enjoying food on checkered cloth-covered tables and wrought-iron chairs sipping coffee, or indulging in some very appealing-looking sweet treats.

Behind the old-style glass-fronted cabinets was a seemingly endless variety of freshly-made pastas, sandwiches and pastries, as well as a gelato fridge.

On the walls, Naomi noticed some very old photographs of the place down through the years, signifying a family-run establishment that had lasted through the ages.

The café was warm, inviting and full of character, the kind of place anyone would be happy to while away the hours, and she immediately understood how someone could get so comfy and cosy here that they'd easily lose track of time, let alone belongings.

Raymond led her to a small table for two by the window and sat down across from her, setting the Tiffany's bag on the table between them.

Naomi unwrapped her scarf from around her neck, set her coat on the back of her chair, then took out her phone and put it on the table, ready to record their conversation.

He signaled to a waitress. 'Coffee? And maybe something to eat while you're here?' He indicated the display cabinet. 'Go ahead. Pick whatever you want, tiramisu, cannoli ...'

'You shouldn't say that,' Naomi joked. 'I can eat a *lot*.'

He raised an eyebrow. 'I like a woman who enjoys her food.'

She met his gaze as her heart fluttered a little in her chest. He was *very* handsome, and her first instinct about his Italian heritage was obviously correct.

But she was here for a story, not a date. She needed to remember that.

She decided on coffee and traditional cannoli, and got straight down to the specifics, getting all the details she needed to lay the groundwork for the news segment and appeal.

But when the cannoli arrived and she took her first bite of the delicate almond pastry, Naomi almost forgot to focus on his words.

'Oh my, this is ... incredible,' she said, as the creamy mascarpone filling permeated her senses. 'I've had cannoli downtown, but this is something else.'

Raymond chuckled; a deep, rich rumble that she liked. It reminded her a little of her dad's laughter.

'My own recipe,' he told her proudly, before adding with a wink. 'Sicilians do it better.'

Naomi could have sworn he was flirting with her and couldn't deny that she quite enjoyed the prospect. But then she reminded herself that Raymond Ricci was Italian, so of *course* he was. Flirting was practically in his blood; it had nothing to do with her.

Did it?

'So, back to the story ...' she said, swallowing hard.

CHAPTER 4

$\mathcal{T}$he following day, everything was set.

Naomi pressed her lips together to spread lipstick evenly over them as she checked her reflection.

'You truly are a magician, Jill,' she commented to the make up artist.

'Honey, if all of my clients had your face to work with, every job would look this good,' Jill mused. The petite redhead had started working for the station a month after Naomi joined five years before.

Since then they'd become best-friends, and Jill was the only artist she allowed to do her makeup.

'Stop, you flatter me.'

'No, I enhance you. That's what a good makeup artist does.' Jill began to pack away her kit. 'And I really hope you get to the bottom of this mystery. It's such a great idea for a story. Really Naomi, with your looks and knack for sniffing out leads, you really should be on CNN or something.'

'You know I'm happy here,' she replied.

It was the same discussion they'd been having for years. Jill thought she could do better. Naomi was content with what she had, though one day, she'd really like to get the behind the camera and produce.

And she didn't want to do hard news either. Human interest stories were her thing.

'Is Mr Ricci here?' she asked turning in the revolving make-up chair. She was dressed in a tasteful jade green suit with a red-button down on the inside and white pearl earrings. Her dark-brown curls were pinned up in a messy bun, with tendrils framing her face, and her TV makeup glow and understated.

'You mean Romeo? I'm heading down now to give him a touch-up on set,' Jill said with a wink. 'You sure you know how to pick the guys too - he is *hot*.'

'Stop it, it's not like that,' Naomi insisted, but there was no mistaking the fact that Jill was right. The main player in her latest news story was indeed hot.

Which could only serve to increase the public response to it.

IN STUDIO, Naomi weaved between cameras and stepped over large cables on the way to her position.

Raymond was already in place, and looked nervous as she approached. His foot bounced repeatedly and his hands were flat on his knees.

He combed his fingers through his dark hair, first smoothing it back and the next minute ruffling it afresh.

She smiled a little, remembering how nerve-wracking her first time on camera had been, but it was cute to see such a confident man so out of his comfort zone.

The set for this segment was festively decorated with plastic gingerbread men in white-trimmed clothing, and green and red 'sugar drop' eyes. The border was trussed up with candycane-colored trim to represent roof shingling, along with a 'blazing' fire in the corner and a cheery Christmas tree in the corner to top it all off.

'You'll be fine,' Naomi reassured Raymond as she took her place across from him.

'I have never been this nervous in my life,' he admitted. 'I can't keep still.'

'I know what's like. Believe me. Try to think of this as just a conversation between the two of us, like yesterday in your café. Forget the cameras. You just concentrate on me.' She smiled. 'I'll get you through this in one piece. I promise.'

He took a deep breath. 'I just hope it works,' he said, indicating the Tiffany's bag sitting on a small table in front of them.

They'd decided to show viewers the bag, but not the contents. One element of Naomi's plan to weed out any time-wasters.

'I know you do. So do I. That's why we're here after all.' She placed a hand on his. 'You'll be fine.'

'Of course he will!' Jill interrupted exuberantly. 'He's got you.' The make-up artist turned to Raymond. 'I'm Jill and I'm going to touch you up.'

'Excuse me...?'

Naomi had to laugh at his expression.

'Nothing much, just a little powder to cut down on the shine.' Jill smirked. 'Trust me honey, a face like yours doesn't need much enhancement.' She turned to wink again at Naomi, who tried not to blush.

Raymond just shrugged. 'Whatever you say.'

CHAPTER 5

*M*inutes later, the segment was underway.

'Today, I have in-studio, a real-life Santa Claus of sorts,' Naomi smiled to the camera before turning to Raymond. 'Mr Ricci, thank you for being with us on *NYCTV News Today*.'

'It's my pleasure.'

'We're so happy to have you with us. But maybe start by telling us why are you here?'

His nerves suddenly forgotten, Raymond went on to tell the story of how the Tiffany's bag had been left behind in his Manhattan business. Again, upon Naomi's advice, they had agreed to leave out many of the specifics, such as the location and indeed the name of the café - so as to ensure that they could weed out the time-wasters and correctly identify whomever came forward. Only the true owner would be able to fill in the blanks.

Naomi raised the Tiffany bag to the camera for viewers to see, while Raymond outlined what they had agreed to share.

'I thought the owner might come back for it, but a day later nobody had, so I went to Tiffany's to see if I could maybe track someone down that way. I didn't open the box and I don't want to.

After all, it's meant for someone special. It wouldn't be right to open some else's gift.'

Then Naomi faced the camera. 'When we at *NYCTV News Today* heard about Raymond's predicament, and his heartfelt determination to have the gift returned to its rightful owner, we had to help. That's why today we are appealing for that person - or anyone who might have more information - to contact us here in studio so that we can ensure that you, or your special someone, is reunited with this wonderful gift in time for Christmas. The number to call is on your screen now. *NYCTV News* will remain closely involved in the hunt all the way, and will of course keep you advised of what we hope will be a happy ever after to this story. Thank you for watching. I'm Naomi Stewart.'

'And we're out.'

At the edge of the set, her producer flashed two thumbs up and Naomi turned to Raymond, who looked relieved.

'That wasn't so bad.'

'Told you I'd make it easy on you.'

'You were right,' he said, meeting her gaze. 'You really do have a way of making people feel like there's nobody else in the room.'

As he said this, her heart skipped a beat, but then she reminded herself that he was talking about her talent as an interviewer, nothing more.

The sound team came up to remove their mics as Naomi and Raymond got to their feet.

'How long do you think before people start calling?' he wondered.

'Knowing these things, I'm pretty sure the phone's already hopping,' she told him. 'You were great on camera.'

'Thank you so much for doing this. I appreciate your help. I don't know what I would have done if I hadn't bumped in to you - in Tiffany's I mean.'

'You're welcome,' she said with a soft laugh. 'And like the story goes … nothing bad ever happens there. Let me walk you out. It can get pretty confusing out back.'

She started to lead him away from the set and Raymond followed. 'You know, I never even asked why you were there that day.'

Naomi shrugged. 'Revisiting old memories,' she admitted simply, and when he looked confused she decided to tell him about her parents, and how going there every Christmas was her way of remembering.

'Kind of tradition, I guess. Like that slogan they have on their stuff; 'Return to Tiffany's.' I keep returning there every year to remember.' Then she laughed self-consciously, realizing how stupid it all must sound.

But Raymond looked thoughtful. 'No, I get it,' he said quietly, looking sideways at her. 'Family traditions are so important, especially at this time of year. And for what it's worth, I think your folks would be very proud.'

CHAPTER 6

*T*he response to the slot was immediate and unprecedented.

Calls started to flood in to the station from people insisting they were the ones who'd lost the gift and wanted to get it back.

It was easy to tell from the get-go which were the frauds based on Naomi's three main criteria: either the timing was wrong, they couldn't identify the location as Caffe Amore, or the fact that the box in question was not the traditional Tiffany's square-shaped 'little blue box' but long, rectangular and wrapped with a red ribbon instead of white.

But they did get one early response that seemed genuine, and when Naomi went to check it out in person, her producer insisted on sending a cameraman to the woman's home to capture the happy moment live, just in case.

'And the Italian guy too if you can swing it. The camera loves him.'

Naomi couldn't argue with that, and for his part Raymond had also been insistent about making sure they had the right person before handing the gift over.

. . .

Now they climbed the steps of the Brooklyn apartment, the camera guy bringing up the rear.

'Do you really think this could be it?' Raymond asked.

'I hope so.'

'I still can't believe the response,' he continued, shaking his head. 'It's great, but who knew so many people could be so dishonest?'

She sighed. 'I wish I could say I'm surprised, but I'm not. I've been working in news for a long time now and I've learned not to expect too much.'

'Saves you the disappointment, huh?'

Naomi shrugged. 'I've gotten used to the depressing stuff, but still, you always need to try to find the light.' She smiled. 'That's why this whole thing drew me in. It was a chance to showcase something good, when lately all we've been getting is the bleak and dreary. I wanted to give New Yorkers something to feel good about - especially at this time of year, a holiday story to make them smile.'

'You're really passionate about this, aren't you?'

Their eyes met and again, there was something in the way Raymond looked at her that made her breath catch.

'Of course. As are you.' She chuckled and tucked an imaginary strand of hair behind her ear. 'Shall we go in?'

He nodded, and the three continued on up the steps.

A woman opened the door on the second knock. She was a tall, slender brunette in her mid thirties with a gap between her front teeth.

Her makeup was flawless and her clothes stylish, but not expensive designer-wear.

'Please, come in,' she invited, and Naomi noted that she seemed far more interested in the cameraman, than the prospect of recovering her lost belongings. 'Oh. I didn't know there'd be cameras. Maybe I should change my clothes...'

'Don't worry, there's no rush just yet,' she assured her. 'Lots of time for that if you'd like, but first we need to ask you a few questions.'

The interior was tasteful, but sparsely decorated. If she had to guess, Naomi would bet the woman didn't own it, and from the lack of furniture, couldn't afford to.

'Please have a seat. Can I get you something to drink?' she asked as they walked into the living area. 'Juice, tea or coffee?'

'I'm good,' Raymond replied.

'Me too,' Naomi agreed.

The woman's name was Belinda Brooks, and from what she'd already shared with the station she'd been to Caffe Amore on the correct date and time. It was a promising start but they needed specifics before they went any further.

'Belinda, can you tell us more about your visit to the café that day?' Naomi began.

'It was morning, closer to noon really. I was in Tiffany's over on Fifth to pick up a present for my mother. She turns seventy on Christmas Eve and I wanted to get her something special.'

'That's wonderful. Happy Birthday to your mom,' Naomi enthused warmly.

'Thanks. I'll tell her that when I give it to her,' Belinda responded. 'I spent a lot of time there picking it out. I wanted to be sure it was the perfect gift.'

'Of course. Would you mind telling us what it was that you bought?'

The woman frowned then. 'I thought you said on the news that you didn't open the box? So how would you know what was in there?' She looked at Raymond through narrowed eyes. 'Did you open my mom's present?'

'No,' he interjected quickly. 'Of course not. Like I said, I didn't want to intrude on anyone's privacy. But I'm sure you understand that we need to be sure it's being returned to the right person.'

'Right,' Belinda replied with a nervous laugh. 'Understandable I guess. So it was ... a leather purse,' she said, after a beat.

Naomi's spirits sank. 'A purse?' she repeated.

She shared a glance with Raymond, who looked somewhat crestfallen.

'Yes.'

But Naomi didn't give anything away. 'That is a wonderful gift for your mom.'

'I know. So when can I have it back?' Belinda questioned, glancing at the camera. 'Do you wanna do that now? I really should get changed first…'

'We just have to check a couple more things,' Raymond replied before Naomi had a chance to intervene. 'You understand I'm sure, that we'll need to verify a few things.'

Belinda's brow wrinkled infinitesimally. 'And how would you go about that, may I ask?'

'Well, we've gotten everything we need for the moment. Someone from the studio will be in touch soon.' She stood up.

'But when?' the woman insisted forcefully, getting to her feet too. 'Coming from Tiffany's it wasn't cheap, you know. I need to get it back and you have no right to keep it from me. Who do you think you are?'

Raymond placed a gentle hand on her arm and his voice was velvety soft as he spoke. 'Don't worry, we'll ensure your mother has a great birthday, Belinda. Why don't you take her down to the café? I'll reserve a table and arrange a special birthday surprise.'

'You would? Thank you … she'd love that. She loves Caffe Amore, we both do.'

'It would be my pleasure to have you both as my guest.'

Naomi marveled at how calmly he'd disarmed a potentially confrontational situation in the loveliest way.

He really was a nice guy.

The three left the apartment, and no one said anything until they were back out on the street and the camera guy had taken off.

'That was a nice thing you did back there,' Naomi began.

'I recognized her,' Raymond said. 'She comes in to the café every now and again. Never buys much, just a coffee and sits alone with it for hours on end. Get the sense that she doesn't have much money, but is desperate for mom's approval, hence the desire for the gift.'

She looked at him. 'I got that too. About the approval thing I mean. But you were very kind, not only for not calling her out about the gift, but helping her do something special for her mother's birthday.'

He shrugged. 'Happy to.' Then he sighed deeply. 'Not looking good though, is it? Only a few more days left till Christmas.'

'Hey, you and I are on a mission remember? We won't be easily deterred.' Naomi held up her hand for a high five, trying to raise his spirits. 'And we're going see this story through to the end.'

He grinned back. 'To the end,' he agreed, holding his hand up to meet her palm, and as he pulled away accidentally entangled her fingers in his.

Blushing hard, she dropped her hand quickly and fished out her phone.

'So what next then?' Raymond asked. 'Any more promising leads for us to chase down?'

Naomi scrolled through the messages from the production team. 'Lots more, but only time will tell as to whether or not they're promising. I'll go through these at home later,' she told him.

'Or we could go through them together back at the café?' Raymond suggested, with an irresistible smile. 'Food's on me.'

'DID YOU ALWAYS LOVE TO COOK?' Naomi asked later, when Caffe Amore had closed for the day, and it was just her and Raymond out back in the kitchen.

It was late by the time they'd gone through the latest batch of responses to the appeal, so he'd insisted on making her dinner. 'How did that happen?'

'My mom.' Raymond wiped his hands on an apron and planted his huge hands on the stainless steel counter top. 'When I was young I was always in the kitchen with her. I was her 'little helper" he explained. 'My siblings were all a lot older than I was. I was, will we say, an unexpected arrival. The closest, my brother, is ten years older than me.'

Naomi almost choked on her red wine. 'Ten?'

He nodded. 'Yes. My folks thought they were through with children when Mom got pregnant again. She actually though she was starting the menopause but nope - there I was.'

'Wow. That's amazing,' Naomi laughed. 'I don't know what I would do if that happened to me. I think I'd be too shocked to even react.'

'You want children?' he asked, his incredible green gaze focused on her. Again, she felt her stomach flip.

'Yeah, I do,' she replied honestly. 'I always wanted to be part of a bigger family. Don't get me wrong, I had an amazing childhood.

My mom and dad were wonderful, the best parents you could ask for. They were amazing really, my dad in particular used to talk about always trying to finding the magic in every moment, the extraordinary in the everyday.' She smiled. 'Like I told you before, Mom worked at Tiffany's and she used to say that there was a story behind every little blue box. It's why I wanted to get so involved in your story. And ..."

Naomi bit her lip and Raymond raised a curious eyebrow. She sighed. 'I guess now would be a good time to come clean about how I actually did get involved. That day... when you asked why I was there in Tiffany's, I didn't quite tell you the truth. The part about being there to remember my parents was true, but it's not exactly the whole story ...'

She went on to admit that she'd seen him come in to the store, and had purposely followed him up to the Fourth Floor.

When she'd finished, Raymond guffawed.

'I *knew* there was something off. It was a bit too convenient that a news reporter "just happened" to overhear my predicament.' He shook his head, chuckling still. 'Wow; you really do have a nose for a story, your folks taught you well. Clearly we have a lot in common in that regard,' he winked, kneading pasta dough - his mom's recipe.

"So, yeah, it was just me, and as an only child, we get all the attention.' Naomi smiled. 'I wanted siblings but they weren't coming, so I decided that when I got older I'd aim to have a big family of my own.'

'And how is that plan coming along?' He returned to the stove and a sizzling sound filled the air.

'Ha...not so well,' She took another long gulp from her glass. 'My last relationship was a complete disaster. Incompatible doesn't even begin to describe us.'

He raised an eyebrow. 'So how come you got together in the first place?'

'Desperation? Delusion? Pick any 'D."

He frowned. 'I don't understand. Why would someone like you be desperate?'

She raised an eyebrow. 'You know, you're asking some very serious questions now. Which one of us is the reporter again?'

He smiled. 'Sorry. I'm a curious guy.'

Naomi shrugged. 'I guess I work a lot,' she admitted. 'The job means long hours, conferences and having to travel all around the city at any hour … you name it, and as a business owner I'm sure you can imagine how that is. It doesn't always leave a lot of time to date. When I met my last boyfriend it was at a speed-dating thing that a friend invited me to for a charity she worked at. He was nice, and pretty decent looking. So I took a chance. Problem was he wasn't a lot of fun.'

'Sorry it didn't work out.'

'It was for the best. I want the right person. I don't just want anyone. I made a mistake, but at least it wasn't one I had to live with for the rest of my life.'

'Rest of your life?'

'If I'd married him, I mean.'

'You were engaged?'

Naomi laughed. 'No! Thankfully we never got that far.'

A LITTLE WHILE LATER, Raymond began to plate the food. She'd seen everything he'd prepared and was eager to try the finished product.

It was a new recipe he was testing out for the café, and she was going to be the first person to try it.

Turned out that Raymond had based the entire menu at Caffe Amore round his own recipes. There was nothing on it that he hadn't concocted himself. Even the cannoli.

'But do you want to get married?' he asked as he set the pasta bowl on the countertop in front of her and sprinkled herbs over huge chunks of bison meat, something she'd never tried before. But Naomi wasn't afraid to try new things.

She picked up some food but the fork slipped from her hand, and she leaned from the barstool to catch it, but underestimated just how far it had dropped. The next thing she knew she was starting to topple over and let out a yelp as she began to fall.

Naomi fully expected to collide with the floor but to her surprise, Raymond's strong hands were suddenly there to catch her.

She still stumbled over but it wasn't nearly as bad as it would have been.

He cradled her in his arms for a beat as she looked up at him with a racing heart. Then she righted herself and stood back, swallowing hard.

'I … do,' she muttered.

His brow furrowed. 'What?'

'I do … want to get married - someday,' she blabbered, her heart thundering, as she tried to cover up her embarrassment.

Raymond smiled and took a seat alongside her. 'Me too.'

CHAPTER 8

*W*ork for Naomi had tripled since the segment.

There was so much interest in, not just the gift, but the story too. The slot had since been syndicated to a couple of networks outside of the city, and when that happened, even more responses flooded in.

Her producer, Patrick was over the moon.

'I think you've found your niche,' he commented happily, as she sat in his office, reading over the terms of the new contract she'd just been offered.

'Are you serious?' Naomi stared up at him. 'You're going to allow me to produce a couple of segments too?'

The money element didn't matter so much, and though it wasn't a minor increase, it wasn't what was most important.

She just wanted the opportunity to tell more stories. Thanks to Raymond's lost gift, Patrick was finally giving her that chance and it felt like a dream come true.

He smiled and the light reflected off the bald spot on the top of his head.

'If all goes well when your next contract comes up for negotiation we might add even more. I know you've always wanted to produce. You certainly have the talent, and if it was up to me I'd have made you a producer already. But now the guys upstairs have seen what you can do too. Merry Christmas, Naomi.'

She got to her feet and promptly threw her arms around him. 'Thank you!'

'You're very welcome,' Patrick laughed. 'Now go get me another great story for your next segment.'

'Yes, sir.'

Naomi was still walking on air as she strode from her boss's office back to her desk.

She picked up her phone to check her messages and her smile grew even larger when she saw that there was one from Raymond.

Meet me at the place you'll find the Food of Love.

Naomi frowned. Caffe Amore. She'd made that very joke about the place the other night at dinner.

Why did he want her to meet him there? Then a thought struck her; had the person who'd left the bag behind finally returned?

She hurried out to the street to catch a cab, then to her surprise noticed a horse-drawn carriage outside her building, with a curious sign on the side door.

It said: '*Naomi, your carriage awaits.' Raymond.*

Wondering why he figured anyone would ever want to take a carriage ride through the middle of Manhattan, she clambered aboard all the same. The driver seemed to know where to go too.

What on earth are you up to Raymond?

WHEN THEY REACHED the café she saw him waiting outside.

'What's all this?' Naomi asked.

'Since things have been so busy lately, I thought you might be in as much of a need of a break as I am.' He looked at his watch. 'And given it's lunchtime I figured you might have an hour or so to spare.'

His gaze was intense but gentle. It made her stomach feel as if hummingbirds were fluttering around inside it.

What are you doing? This is supposed to be a news story, not a romantic one.

CHAPTER 9

'OK. But why all this?' she indicated the horse and carriage.

'You're the reporter - figure it out,' he said coyly. 'What's colorful yet evergreen? Come with me to the place where it's closest to the sky.'

'OK I think I get it. Are you making me do some kind of ... scavenger hunt?' Delighted by the prospect, she thought for a moment. 'Colorful and evergreen.... the tree at Rockefeller?'

Raymond got in beside her and all too soon they arrived at their destination, just in time to see a large group caroling beneath the towering Christmas tree.

'OK, is there another clue?'

'Of course. Now we go to a place where you're likely to fall, yet most likely to fly.'

She thought again for a moment. 'Hmm ... this one's a little trickier, but I think I got it.' She smiled and looked down upon the ice rink. 'I'm thinking we'll need some skates?'

'Wow, you're good! Come on then.'

Raymond led her out onto the ice by both hands, just like her dad used to. She didn't need any help, she was a decent skater, but there was something about him leading her that felt right. It was a confusing feeling, but she loved it.

They glided out to the middle of the rink. He was a good skater and it wasn't long before he was spinning and twirling around her.

'Okay, showoff,' Naomi teased as she tried to keep pace.

He skated up and they stood face-to-face. 'You should practice more. I can show you a thing or two.'

Her cheeks grew hot. 'Maybe I'll take you up on that.'

'Naomi,' he said as hands gently reached for her waist. 'I know this might be strange, and we haven't known each other long, but I really enjoy spending time with you.'

Her heart almost stopped. He smiled and she smiled back and for a moment she felt like a teenager again.

But then her phone rang and recognizing the ring tone as Patrick's, she pulled it out of her pocket, really wishing she didn't have to break the spell.

Still, she couldn't ignore her producer. 'Hey Patrick. What's up?'

Naomi's eyes widened she heard the words coming through, and automatically she turned to look at Raymond. 'You're sure?'

Hanging up, she grabbed his hands in delight. 'Guess what? I think we've finally found our person.'

CHAPTER 10

The guy in question, Dominic Anderson, was back at the station, waiting.

He'd seen the syndicated news segment the day before on a sister channel in Connecticut, and had travelled down from Rhode Island to claim the gift.

'Do you really think he's the one?' Raymond queried as he and Naomi hurried into to the studio.

'He got everything right; the name of the café, the box, the ribbon ... and he seems very determined. Patrick said he refused to go anywhere until he saw me personally.' She smiled encouragingly. 'I really hope so.'

'Me too,' Raymond reached for her hand and quickened his pace. It matched the beating of her heart as she rushed along beside him.

They reached Patrick's office where inside, Dominic was waiting for them. He stood up immediately.

'Naomi Stewart.'

'Hello,' she said with a smile, extending her hand and he shook it. 'And this is Raymond.'

'Nice to meet you,' Dominic replied. 'I recognize you from the

TV slot. And from Caffe Amore, of course.'

Raymond eyes widened in mutual recognition. 'And now I recall your face from that day. You ordered a second cannoli.'

Dominic's smile grew wide. 'I was hoping you'd remember me.'

Naomi took a deep breath. This was their guy, she knew it. But still, she needed to get the formalities out of the way.

'Okay, Dominic, let's get down to specifics. What time of day were you at the café?'

'The morning of the 18th. I had some Christmas shopping to do, and I stopped at the café for a break from the crowds. I was there when I got a call from my mom. My brother was involved in an accident back home in Rhode Island and taken to hospital. I just left without thinking to grab a cab to take me back to Grand Central. My brother was the only thing on my mind. I left my shopping on the floor next to my table. I was right at the window by the door, looking out onto the street.'

Naomi's eyes drifted to Raymond. He had even given them the correct table.

'Please, tell me what I need to do to get it back. I had no idea where I'd left it, I thought maybe in the back of a cab, or on the train … and I've been going out of my mind calling all the cab companies. It's an engagement ring for my girlfriend, you see. I'm planning a Christmas proposal.'

Now her heart sank. He'd got everything right so far - except the box.

An engagement ring would not have been wrapped in a rectangular box and red ribbon. The distinctive packaging was all part of Tiffany & Co's legendary little blue box experience.

She turned to look at Raymond, who hadn't appeared to notice the discrepancy. He looked just as excited as Dominic, and now she didn't know how to broach the subject.

She looked at Patrick, who raised his eyebrows in confusion.

When Naomi remained silent, Dominic sat up.

'Oh, and I have the receipt,' he offered suddenly. He reached into this pocket and pulled out a small piece of paper, handing it to Raymond. 'Man, I was so sure I'd never get it back, and after all the trouble I went to - to make it a surprise, I mean. Then my mom told me there was a TV story about a Tiffany's gift lost in New York, so I watched it and realized you were talking about me. I came back down as soon as I could. I've spent the past few days in the hospital with my brother.'

'How is he?' Raymond asked, ever courteous.

'He'll make it. He'll have a long journey but the doctors expect him to make a full recovery.'

'I'm happy to hear that,' Naomi stated. Then she took a deep breath. 'But Dominic, there's just one problem … the box…' She noticed Raymond's gaze on her and hated to be the one to pull the plug on the excitement.

'Oh that's right!' Dominic laughed uneasily then. 'You guys didn't open the box, did you? So maybe you don't believe me that it was an engagement ring.' He was chuckling now. 'Like I said, I really wanted this to be a surprise, so I asked the guy at Tiffany's to wrap the little blue box in a *bigger* blue box, if that makes sense. So when I give it to Anna - my girlfriend - on Christmas morning, she won't suspect a thing.'

Naomi exhaled a laugh. 'Oh my gosh. Amazing!' She turned to Raymond who was laughing too. 'Dominic, I think you truly are our guy.'

He looked like he might burst with relief.

'Thank you. Thank you so much. I was afraid I'd have to jump through all kinds of hoops and wouldn't be able to get it back in time for Christmas. We've all been through such a tough time lately, and so I really wanted to do something memorable.'

The wheels were turning in Naomi's brain as she thought of something.

'Dominic, I know you went to a lot of trouble already, but how would you feel about making your proposal even *more* memorable for your girlfriend?'

'How so?'

'Well, have you ever thought of doing so on national television?' She turned to look at her producer, who was smiling like a Cheshire cat.

Dominic's eyes grew large and his jaw slackened. 'Are you serious?'

'Totally,' Patrick enthused. 'We'd be so honored to be part of your proposal and make it something you and your fiancée will never forget.'

Naomi smiled at Raymond.

'And I know our viewers would really love to see how this story ends.'

CHAPTER 11

A buzz of excitement raced through the studio on Christmas Eve.

It reminded Naomi why she'd started working TV news in the first place; to be a part of magical, feel-good stories like these.

And this had the potential to be one of the nicest she'd ever uncovered.

'Everyone ready?' she asked, passing through the set on her way to make-up.

'All good to go,' Patrick replied. 'This really was a genius find, Naomi.'

'It couldn't have come together better if we planned it,' she commented smiling.

She and Raymond had hardly had a chance to speak since Dominic had come to claim the gift, but Naomi was pretty sure he'd be here today to see everything through to the end.

That fact that she hadn't heard from him since stung a little, but she tried her best to ignore the feeling and concentrate on the task in hand.

'So are the happy couple here yet?'

'Dominic just got out of make-up,' the production assistant informed her.

'OK, everyone, take your places!' Patrick bellowed. 'It's showtime.'

NAOMI WALKED onto the set and waited for the sound team to wire them all up. She smiled at Dominic as he joined her on the chair opposite.

'Ready?' she winked and he nodded, swallowing hard.

'Good morning New York,' Naomi declared once the cameras began to roll. 'Today, in this very special *NYCTV News* report, we return to the story of the New York café owner, Raymond Ricci, whose act of generosity launched our search for the owner of a Tiffany's gift left behind in his - aptly named it seems … ' she added with a chirpy smile, 'Caffe Amore. And we're so happy to report that there's been a major development; we at *NYCTV News Today* have indeed managed to track down the owner! And you'll soon see, as we conclude this happy journey, that there's even more to this Christmas tale. But first let's meet our elusive shopper, Mr Dominic Andersen. Dominic, welcome to the studio.'

'Thank you. It's …uh…great to be here.' He gulped nervously.

'We're all so happy to finally find you. The response to our appeal was incredible, so it was quite the search,' Naomi informed her audience. 'Some promising leads and interesting stories, but only one true possibility. And Dominic here was so determined to get back his Tiffany's prize - which he'd intended as a Christmas gift for a very special someone - that he didn't just call the station. He came down here from Rhode Island to see us in person. Dominic, tell us the story in your own words.'

'I was desperate,' Dominic said, going into detail about how he'd come to lose the gift, and then about finding it again. And the unique elements that only he would know; the packaging, the timing and of course, Raymond's café.

Then he turned to look toward his girlfriend, who was standing at the edge of the set, looking on. 'There was something special I needed to do this Christmas, and that gift was a major part.'

Naomi smiled. 'That's right. There's still another twist to come in this Christmas tale. 'Anna, can you come and join us on set?'

As intended, Dominic stood up and escorted his now-visibly startled girlfriend onto the set. Then Naomi got to her feet to greet a shell-shocked Anna, while he reached for the rectangular Tiffany box on the table between their chairs.

'Folks, Anna had no idea she'd be on camera today, so forgive her if she's a little bit speechless right now,' she explained. 'Welcome Anna.'

Naomi looked on smiling, as Dominic opened the rectangular box to reveal the smaller, traditional little blue ring box from within, and his girlfriend sucked in a suitably theatrical breath.

'Anna,' he began, getting down on one knee, while everyone else on set looked on. 'I love you. I've loved you every day since we met. I know it's taken a while, and that you thought maybe this would never come, but today is the day. Please, make me the proudest and happiest man in the world by agreeing to be my wife?'

Anna had no words. Tears rolled down her cheeks as she reached for her boyfriend and embraced him, her head nodded fervently.

A moment later Dominic was slipping a magnificent Tiffany diamond ring on her finger, while the entire set erupted in feel-good applause.

Naomi turned to the cameras, genuine tears of emotion in her eyes.

She was delighted for the couple, but deep down she so wished Raymond could've been here too.

He was such a huge part of this story she couldn't believe he hadn't come along to see it through to the end.

'Well, you just saw it here folks, a Tiffany's Christmas and true fairytale ending, happening right here, right now in Manhattan. I'm so happy we at *NYCTV Today News* were able to bring this heart-warming story to you as it happened, and we're especially honored to have played a part in its happy ending.

We wish Dominic and Anna every happiness. And we wish you - New York - a very Merry Christmas.'

CHAPTER 12

*I*t was wonderful to watch Dominic and Anna walk off set together; her magnificent Tiffany diamond ring on her finger, and the biggest smile on her face.

That moment Naomi decided there would be no more sad stories in her segment.

No more tales of woe and misery.

From now on, she was going to bring nothing but joy and cheer to New Yorkers. She was going to show them that there was still so much good in their incredible, wonderfully diverse city. And it was there to be found in every corner.

She'd already discussed it with Patrick and he'd agreed. Things were going to change for the better.

LATER THAT EVENING, Naomi was curled up on the couch of her apartment sniffling at *It's a Wonderful Life* on TV, when she got a text from Raymond, similar to the one he'd sent the day he'd arranged the horse and carriage to take her to Caffe Amore and onwards to Rockefeller.

Except this one said. *Meet me at Tiffany's.*

Another scavenger hunt? On Christmas Eve?

Naomi couldn't deny that the prospect of such a thing excited her. Or anything involving Raymond for that matter.

When? she replied.

As soon as you can.

CHAPTER 13

S he grabbed a cab and got there within half an hour to find the man who'd barely been out of her thoughts for the last week, standing on Fifth Avenue with a broad smile on his face.

Most of the department stores - including Tiffany's - had now closed for the holidays, so the streets were calm and quiet.

And was it her imagination or was there a hint of snow in the air?

'Hey, Naomi.'

'What's going on?' she asked, shivering a little in the cold. Or was it nervousness? 'How come you weren't there for the broadcast earlier? And what are we doing *here?*" she questioned.

She tucked her hair behind her ears, now wishing she'd bothered to brush it before she came out. Or that she'd hadn't removed her TV make-up.

She must look an absolute mess.

'It's Christmas Eve remember - I couldn't possibly get away from the café today; we were run off our feet. But don't worry, I watched it all on TV. It was wonderful. Well done.'

'Well done you, you mean. It was your story after all.'

'Nope. You were the one who took my petty little problem and turned it into something up-lifting.' He reached into his pocket and took something out. 'And for that, I wanted to say thank you.'

Her eyes widened as she caught sight of yet another Tiffany's blue box.

'Raymond ... what's this?'

'A gift of course,' he stated.

'Well, I can see that,' Naomi sputtered in disbelief. 'But you really shouldn't have.'

Her eyes were still trained on the blue box. What could possibly be inside, she had no idea.

'Open it.' He held out the box to her.

'Raymond ...' she said hesitantly. 'I don't know that I deserve this. I think it might be too much.'

'You do deserve it and it's not too much,' he countered. 'Because of you, two people got a very happy ending this Christmas. It couldn't have happened without you.' He chuckled. 'You restored my faith in people, you know. There was no way I would have ever found Dominic if you hadn't offered to help me.' His voice softened and he reached for her hand. 'And I'm very glad you did, for more reasons than one.'

Her mind was in conflict and her hands were shaking as she took the box from him. She couldn't believe it. Raymond had actually bought her a gift - and from Tiffany's of all places.

It felt like treasure in her hands.

Naomi stared at the box for several long seconds while she contemplated untying the ribbon.

Finally, she decided to just go for it, and unfastening the bow and opening the box, she pulled out the tiny blue jewelry pouch that lay inside.

Tipping it out to reveal what was inside, her eyes widened when she spied a delicate silver chain and a heart-shaped pendant marked with the famous 'Return to Tiffany's' inscription.

'I remember what you said,' Raymond explained, his voice soft. 'About returning here every year to honor your family tradition.'

Overwhelmed, she looked at him in disbelief, and tears sprang to her eyes. 'This is … amazing. But you shouldn't have.'

'I wanted to,' he said, reaching for her hand again. 'Naomi, I don't think you realize what this time with you has meant to me. You look for the good when people expect bad.'

She swallowed as he placed her hand over his heart. Hers was stampeding with each word he uttered.

'I'm not entirely sure how our lives got entangled for this little adventure, but I'm inclined to think it was for a reason. And it all started right here.' He nodded up at the Tiffany's store.

She smiled, thinking of her parents, their stories and memories and her yearly tradition.

It was as if Raymond had wrapped all of those things up in that single blue box.

'I know.'

He stepped closer.

'I care about you, and I love that you value tradition and memory. And I got you that pendant because I was kind of hoping that you might consider making some new Christmas traditions - with me.'

Now Naomi's cheeks were burning hot. She could hardly look at him as she tried to suppress a grin. She failed miserably and instead decided to just say what she felt.

'I'd … like that a lot.'

His broad grin matched hers. 'Then there really is just one more thing to do. Merry Christmas, Naomi.'

She gasped as Raymond stepped forward and eliminated the space between them, and Naomi only barely got the words out before their lips met, and her eyes closed.

'Merry Christmas.'

CHRISTMAS IN NEW YORK

CHAPTER 1

"*I* still can't believe I'm spending Christmas in New York," Penny laughed, rubbing her hands together to warm them.

A tall slender blonde in fitted light blue jeans and a red puffa jacket, she walked towards the kerb where an awaiting black town car stood with an open door. Her boots left prints in the fresh snowfall.

"Why not? And what better way to spend it - and your birthday too," her best friend Kate replied as they neared the car, elation reflected in her honey-coloured eyes. Her diminutive frame was curvier than Penny's, the reward of motherhood.

Their breaths came in wisps as they spoke, filling the area around them with a quickly-evaporating fog

"Besides, what were you going to do in London all alone?" she added.

"I wouldn't have been alone," Penny defended, but they both knew better.

Penny was a workaholic. She had been ever since her fiancé's death three years before.

It had been difficult for her ever since, being part of a world without Tim. Kate knew that.

Over the years she'd tried her best to pull her friend out of the recesses and back into the sunlight where she belonged, but Penny was stubborn. She always had been.

It had taken desperate measures on Kate's part to get her on the flight over from London.

"So where's Ian?" Penny asked, referring to Kate's husband.

"He's meeting us at home. He has some things to get done before he heads back." Kate's words were punctuated by the slamming of the trunk of the town car.

Penny's single suitcase was securely tucked inside, right next to her son Toby's stroller.

"So what happened to your SUV? I thought you loved that thing," Penny asked as she approached the open passenger door. The vehicle's driver was standing sentinel as her eyes grew large at the sight of the interior of the expensive Lincoln.

"I do, but where we are now makes it difficult for me to find parking. The car comes with Ian's job, we just never had a reason to use it before," Kate answered as both women slid into the backseat one after the other.

The door closed behind them.

The warm scent of vanilla greeted Penny as she slid around making herself comfortable. She wasn't used to being chauffeur driven and she fidgeted in the small space.

There was an ice bucket and two champagne flutes tucked into a holder. The glasses alone must have cost more than her coat. She would have much rather preferred Kate's Range Rover. At least she wouldn't be afraid to break something.

"It's great that you both were able to get the holidays off together. I know last year was a bit of a mess."

"Yeah well, you know how corporate types can be – all work, work, work."

"No I don't," Penny mused lightly. "I always liked the blue collar guys – the kind who work with their hands."

She looked out the window as they pulled away from the airport. As a masseuse Tim had been great with his hands, and very attentive. He always knew when she was tense and was quick to alleviate the problem.

He was a master at working out the knots from her neck and back, not to mention his stellar foot massages. She missed them. She missed feeling pampered and cared for.

Tim had been her entire world. Having been an orphan, Penny wasn't used to having people care for her, but Tim had, he'd loved her through a time when she could barely love herself.

Then he was gone, and everything she'd hoped for died with him.

"I have to pick up Toby from by my mother before we head home," Kate interjected, knowing her friend's thoughts had strayed.

Penny wasn't difficult to read, especially for someone who knew her as well as Kate. The pair had been best friends since kindergarten, both born and raised in a quite suburb of London until Kate had gone to New York to attend university.

It was where she'd met Ian Jarvis, her husband. She was studying interior design and he, finance. The artist and the businessman, an unlikely pair, but the two made it look effortless the way they seemed to read each other's minds.

Now they had a house in Middlesex County, a beautiful two-year-old son and careers they were both proud of.

They were the image of the ideal couple.

"I can't wait to see my godson." Penny offered Kate a bright smile to mask her short trip down memory lane. "I bet he's gotten so big since I last saw him - on Skype wasn't it?"

"Yes, nasty thing. A weak excuse for human contact." Kate wrinkled her nose and Penny felt the tirade even before her friend started. "You know how I feel about those things. All the social media that make us 'closer' to the point that we forget to actually speak to one another. Ten people in a room and they're all glued to their smartphones! No one even bothers to look up. It's ridiculous!"

"I know you hate them Katé, but they do serve a good purpose –"

"I miss the days of conversation. I loved it when people got together for dinner and talked about things that were important – life, future plans. Now it's all posting pictures of the food to Facebook and taking selfies for your Instagram. I swear if it wasn't for my manager demanding I have a social media presence, I promise you'd I'd never twit."

Penny chuckled as she leaned back. "It's tweet Kate. Tweet. You tweet on Twitter."

"Whatever, you know what I mean."

Kate, the anti social media activist was a woman who still wrote in her diary instead of a blog.

She posted letters rather than emails if she had a choice, and painted when the entire world had gone digital. Her best friend was a woman from another time and Penny loved her.

CHAPTER 2

"I thought we were going to your house?" Penny commented, when it became clear that they weren't headed for the usual turnpike.

Toby was snuggled in his car seat between them, fast asleep. His head rose and fell peacefully against his chest.

"Oh no, we're staying in Manhattan at the moment. Didn't I mention that? The house is being renovated and Ian didn't want Toby in all that dust," Kate replied as she sipped from her bottle of Evian.

She wordlessly offered Penny a bottle, which was politely refused. She'd had enough warm liquids on the plane and couldn't hold another.

Penny responded with disappointment. She was looking forward to getting out of the city setting and enjoying some fresh air. London was a concrete jungle she'd been in her entire life.

"Where are we staying then?"

"At the Easton - on the Upper West Side. Ian's company owns a few apartments there and they offered us one."

"Nice. The perks of being a top performer I take it."

"What can I say, he works hard. He's always at the office. I swear if I didn't know I could trust my husband, I'd believe he was cheating, but affairs aren't something I have to worry about."

The confidence in Kate's voice was awe-inspiring. Penny wasn't sure she'd be as confident if the shoe was on the other foot.

Tim hadn't had late nights, but he did have a lot of female clients. She would have been lying if she said that she'd never had a niggling of fear and insecurity when it came to his fidelity – but she was told that insecurity was common for children who'd been raised in the social services.

Insecurity, doubt and fear – the three deadly plagues. Penny had suffered from all of them at some point in her life, insecurity being the worst of the bunch.

When she met Tim she was convinced she didn't deserve to be happy. That people like her didn't get the happy ending.

She'd pushed him away but he wouldn't give up. He pursued her until she relented, earning her trust every step of the way.

He proved to be the best of men – the best man she'd ever known. It was unfair that such a wonderful life should be snuffed out by the callousness of one armed man, who wanted the contents of a supermarket's register.

Tim had been in the wrong place at the wrong time, getting a bottle of wine to celebrate their fourth anniversary. In the blink of an eye, his life came to an end and Penny's beliefs about happy endings were proven true.

"It must be really nice having the life you always wanted. Remember growing up you always said you'd move to New York one day and become a famous designer?" She offered a warm smile of admiration. "You really did it, Kate."

"I'm not famous," her friend countered as they pulled up outside the salubrious apartment building. "But I am happy," she continued, smiling at her sleeping son.

When her eyes returned to Penny they glistened slightly as her voice quivered. "I want you to be as happy, Pen."

"I am –"

"No you're not –"

Their conversation was interrupted as the passenger door was pulled open and their driver stood waiting.

He already had Toby's stroller out and unfolded.

Penny gave Kate a placating look before stepping out of the car. A light snowfall was just beginning and passersby huddled down in their coats and jackets.

She pulled her coat closer around her neck as Kate bundled up Toby.

"We better get inside. I don't want him getting a cold," her friend stated as she held her son to her chest, shielding him from the nipping wind.

CHAPTER 3

*T*he doorman had the door ready upon their approach and Penny followed her friend into the exquisite lobby.

The driver followed behind them like a lost puppy, with Penny's luggage in-hand.

The Easton was a testament to Upper East Side design and elegance. The building had every amenity imaginable and a view to kill for.

Penny was dumbstruck as she was given the tour of Kate's three-bedroom, two-bath apartment. The kitchen looked like something off of the cover of *Better Homes and Gardens*. Her small one-bedroom with pokey fireplace was the ugly stepchild in comparison.

I bet that's real marble. What the hell am I doing here?

Penny was still asking herself that question as she sat in the living room skimming through magazines as Kate got Toby settled down again. He'd woken fifteen minutes earlier and seemed fractious.

"Sorry about that. He can be a bit cranky when he has an accident," Kate commented as she took a seat beside Penny.

They looked at each other in silence, their earlier exchange the proverbial elephant in the room.

Finally Kate broke the discomfort. "Look, you know me. I can't hold my tongue and discretion isn't my strong point so I'm just going to say it."

"Kate –"

"You aren't happy Pen," Kate's eyes began to smart with tears.

Penny felt the sting of panic well-up inside her. She couldn't handle tears, especially not Kate's.

"You haven't been for a long time, and I'm worried about you." She locked her gaze on Penny. "Ever since Tim died you've been a different person. You barely laugh. You don't go out. All you ever do is work. You even stopped calling Tim's parents."

Penny's eyes widened. "How on earth did you know that?"

"Mrs. Walters gave me a call when you stopped returning hers. She's worried about you too Pen. We all are."

"You don't have to worry I'm fine," Penny replied tersely. She hated people talking about her behind her back. "Since when do you and Colleen talk to one another? I don't remember either of you ever doing that when Tim was alive."

"Don't," Kate cautioned, sensing the shift. "Don't make this into some kind of conspiracy. I gave her my number at Tim's funeral. She kept it. When you stopped calling and returning their calls she was worried, so she contacted me. How else was anyone going to know if you were alright? I barely know half the time."

"That's not fair Kate. You know I can't stand to see you cry," Penny blubbered as they embraced.

"I can't help it. I'm just so worried about you and I love you."

"I love you too, and I'm sorry I made you worry. It was just … easier to keep to myself after Tim's death. It didn't hurt so much when there weren't so many reminders of when I was happy."

Kate held her at arm's length. "Tim wouldn't have wanted this. You know that. You need to let yourself be happy again."

"I know," Penny replied as she wiped her cheek with the back of her hand.

"He wouldn't have wanted you to stop living."

The two women fell into another embrace, the comfort of their friendship easing away the tension of the years of imposed emotional distance.

They were still sniffling when Ian and his guest arrived.

CHAPTER 4

"So the Junko contract is still pending? I thought Morrissey was pushing that for Christmas? I spent the past six months having no social life to get that done because the company 'needed' the deal to go through ASAP. It's spent the past three weeks on that man's desk. Now you're telling me it's on hold until the New Year?" Mike Callaghan's voice filled the empty corridor as he and Kate's husband Ian, disembarked the elevator.

Each at over six feet tall and with similar wide set jaws and unruly spiked medium brown hair, Ian and Mike could have passed for twins at a distance.

On closer inspection the differences were evident.

Ian's chestnut eyes were set into a slimmer more serious face, though the five o'clock shadow matched Mike's perfectly.

Mike's softer appearance gave him a more boyish look with his blue eyes and dimpled chin.

Ian was wearing his customary tailored grey suit with a navy tie and leather shoes, while Mike was dressed in dark jeans, a light blue buttoned-down and a light grey vest. He wore loafers on his feet and the top button of his shirt was undone.

"I tried to get him to move on it but he's stalling. You should probably drop a hint to Nolan, just to cover yourself," Ian stated as he turned his key in the lock of the apartment.

"Yeah I will. Morrissey has been after me for ages. I don't want him trying to put the fault for the delay on me." He followed Ian into the apartment, both continuing their conversation as they walked into the living room.

"Honey we're home!" Mike joked as he rounded the corner, his slight twang faltering the moment his blue eyes settled on his friend's wife and her guest.

What's she doing here?

"HONESTLY MIKE, the amount of time you spend here people might think you're part of the family," Kate laughed as she stepped towards him, placing a friendly peck on his cheek.

She immediately turned to her husband, giving him his customary smooch.

"Yeah, well it happens when you have no life," Mike joked, glancing in Penny's direction.

"You better get one if you ever intend to make me a godmother some day," Kate retorted, taking Ian's briefcase and setting it aside. She looked at their otherwise empty hands. "I thought you two were bringing home dinner?"

"Don't worry. I called and ordered before I left the office. The delivery guy should get here any second." Ian replied as he promptly removed his tie on his way to their bedroom.

"What did you get?" Kate called after him.

"Chinese," Mike and Ian answered in harmony before Ian disappeared into the other room.

CHAPTER 5

*P*enny watched the cosy display at a distance, suddenly uneasy. She hadn't anticipated there being anyone else at Kate's tonight.

She was hoping for a quiet night with her friends, not a mini dinner party. This trip was definitely not turning out how she planned.

And who was the guy? He looked familiar but she couldn't place him.

"Penny, you remember Mike - Ian's best friend?" Kate noted the blank look she received and elaborated. "He was the best man at our wedding. You remember Penny don't you Mike?"

Him!

For Penny, the memory came rushing straight back.

Ian and Kate were married only a few months after Tim's death, and she'd spent the entire ceremony and reception trying to keep it together for Kate's sake.

She'd tried to avoid people but weddings weren't exactly a time to be recluse. People found you whether you wanted to be found or not, especially men.

Weddings were magnets for needy singles trying to score. Mike had been one of them.

He'd pestered Penny until she'd finally blown up, promptly telling him how little she cared for his callous advances. That was the first and last time they'd spoken.

"Yeah, I think I do," she replied noncommittally.

"Yeah, she's the woman who bit my head off for asking her to dance," Mike chuckled as he flopped down on the couch.

"You deserved it," she snapped, the unpleasant feelings resurfacing.

"Excuse me?" he continued, leaning forward, the corners of his eyes squinting. "I was being perfectly civil. You were the one having a tantrum."

"You call that civil? What - were you raised in a barn? I told you to leave me alone and you kept harassing me –"

"Asking someone if they'd like a drink and for a dance isn't harassing behaviour last time I checked. And yes, I was raised in a barn actually. I grew up on a farm in Minnesota; barns were something we had plenty of."

"Well that explains a lot." Penny was raging ahead full steam, blood rising to her cheeks as her hands clenched at her sides.

How dare he act all innocent and try to make her look like a petulant child?

"Okay you two, time out," Kate interjected, stepping between them, her hands in a makeshift T.

She looked at the equally annoyed faces, "Both of you please keep your voices down," she scolded, as she stifled her own. "Toby is asleep in the other room and I'd like it to stay that way for a while longer."

As if on cue the toddler's voice erupted in a scream and Kate settled a scathing look upon each of them before marching towards the nursery. "Don't let me hear another word from you two," she warned before going to tend to her son.

Penny and Mike exchanged curt looks.

Insufferable.

Annoying.

By the time she rejoined them, Penny had found a spot in an armchair, a magazine occupying her attention, while Mike was flipping through sports channels for something good to watch.

The buzzer rang.

"Great, dinner's here!" Ian stated as he stepped out of the bedroom, smoothing down the front of his polo. "What did I miss?"

Three pairs of eyes settled on him, but no one answered.

CHAPTER 6

*D*inner had been far from spectacular.

Penny and Mike refused to say more than the basic necessities to one another.

Pass the rice. Where's the wontons?

Everyone felt the tension until Penny finally excused herself, citing fatigue from the flight as the culprit.

It wasn't true of course. She just needed space.

She had come to New York with expectations of a dream weekend away from normal life, but so far it was a nightmare.

She loved Kate and Ian and adored their relationship, but being in their home and seeing their family and how easily Mike seemed to fit into the picture, made her realize just how alone her own existence was.

She didn't have anyone to greet her when she got home. Not even a cat. There was no child to cuddle or friend who was part of the family.

She was alone. Her entire world was her work, but it didn't keep her warm at night.

·   ·   ·

WHEN SHE WOKE the next day a delicious aroma welcomed her. She would have wandered out in search of the morsels that were waiting, but the fact that she'd slept in her clothes from the day before was a problem.

She made quick work of a shower, slipping into a pair of red leggings and a cream cashmere sweater before making her way to the kitchen.

"Good morning," she greeted, feeling a bit better after her rest.

"You mean good afternoon," Kate replied as she bounced Toby on her hip. The toddler's face was smeared with some kind of green goo. There were flecks of it in Kate's hair. "It's after one," she added.

"You're kidding? I slept that long? I never sleep that long."

"You never sleep, that's why you needed the rest." Kate wrinkled her nose in Penny's direction. "Lunch is over there," she pointed with her head as she tried to give Toby another spoonful of peas. "I ordered Italian. Thought you'd like it."

Penny chuckled as she poked at the containers of food. "Do you ever think you'll learn to cook?"

"Never. Ian cooks, the maid cleans and I make the place look spectacular. Match made in heaven," she mused.

Penny returned to the comfort of the armchair she'd occupied the night before, folding her leg beneath her. "Where's Ian this morning?" It was Saturday so hardly at work.

"He and Mike went to get the tree. They should be back soon."

Penny huffed. "Is Mike coming over again?" she asked between forkfuls.

"More than likely. He lives one floor down. Why?"

"Nothing," she pouted. A moment later Kate's chuckle got her attention. "What?"

"I was just thinking about you and Mike." She gave Toby another spoon of baby food.

"What about Mike and me?" Penny asked, sitting up.

"Just that you two are so much alike –"

"I am nothing like that guy. He's pigheaded and opinionated.

Can you imagine him suggesting that *I* was acting childish at the wedding? He was the one being an opportunist. Trying to hit on me like that after…"

Kate looked over. "After Tim?" she finished, her voice gentle. "Pen, he couldn't have known that."

Penny remained silent, her food momentarily forgotten.

"We didn't tell anyone about Tim. I know you like your privacy, and I didn't want people…I didn't want you to be uncomfortable, so Ian and I agreed to keep that to ourselves. No one knew."

Still, she remained silent.

"I've known Mike a long time and he's isn't that kind of guy. He'd never take advantage of someone who was vulnerable, especially if he knew. If he wanted to get you a drink or asked for a dance, it's because he wanted to."

She wiped Toby's mouth. He'd had enough for the day. "I'm going to get him cleaned up. I'll be right back."

Penny watched as Kate and Toby went into the other room, leaving her alone with her thoughts.

She'd never considered that Mike's actions may have been anything but unscrupulous. The fact left her unsettled. She was still contemplating it when Ian, and the man himself, arrived with tree in hand – arm.

*H*e couldn't stop thinking about her.

Ever since their verbal tug-o-war Mike couldn't get the thought of Penny from his mind.

The thoughts had escalated to guilt by the time he and Ian returned to the Easton. Ian had explained, though reluctantly, what had instigated Kate's best friend's caustic reaction three years earlier, and why it would have ignited her ire the night before.

Mike knew that pain all too well.

The moment his eyes settled upon her, seated the in same chair as the night before, he wanted to say something, to apologise.

If he had known, if he'd had even an inclining what Penny had been going through at the wedding three years ago, he would have left her alone.

He knew what it was like to have people hovering around you, wanting things from you, when all you wanted was to be alone. Hide.

"Where's Kate?" Ian asked as he and Mike shuffled into the living room with a huge spruce.

"She's cleaning Toby up. Messy lunch." She stood. "Need a hand with that?" she asked, already clearing a path for them, shifting the coffee table out of their way.

She surreptitiously glanced in Mike's direction but said nothing.

"Hey," he murmured as he passed her, helping Ian hoist the tree into place.

"Hi." Her eyes shifted away from him. She returned to her seat.

The next half hour was spent making faces at Toby, while Kate, Ian and Mike tried to get the tree straight in the stand.

"No, it's still leaning." Kate said, tilting her head. "Shift it more your direction, Mike."

"Penny, can you help us out here? Advise my wife that this isn't a show house, it doesn't have to be straight," Ian called from beneath the bows of the blue spruce.

"Not me." She tickled Toby's nose with her finger. "I know better than to get in Kate's way when she's decorating." Penny continued bouncing the toddler on her knee as Ian struck the table with a red plastic hammer.

"Thank you, Penny. Now…more to you Mike."

CHAPTER 8

By the time the decorations were brought out, both men were exhausted and Kate was slightly agitated.

She liked things to be perfect and hated when it wasn't.

The tree wasn't. It bent to the right.

Ian had picked a faulty tree.

"Don't fret Kate. You can't really tell from the way we have it leaning back like that," Penny tried to pacify her, but it was no use.

She would be put out for the rest of the evening. It was one of those things you either loved or hated about Kate; she was a perfectionist.

As they began hanging the finely crafted ornate balls from each of the willowy bows, Penny found herself transported to other Christmases.

There was her first real Christmas, with her foster family, O'Connells. They'd been nice to her while she was in their care. They treated her almost like their own, until it was time for her to go back.

You never got to settle when you were a foster child. You never really had a home.

It wasn't until she met Kate in her last year of primary school, that Christmas began to have a whole new meaning.

She glanced at her friend as a wave of affection wafted over her. Kate had been her one constant in life, a true friend.

So was her family. They had welcomed her into their home and into their lives. Every Christmas, except before they left for New York, she'd spent with them in their Wimbledon home.

As she continued dressing the tree, the last thing Penny expected was to bump heads with Mike. Her forehead collided with his chin.

"Sorry…" they mumbled in harmony, holding each other's gaze for the first time since he'd arrived.

She wanted to say something. She just couldn't. How could she even begin?

Penny didn't want to have to dredge up the past, to explain her behaviour that day – about Tim.

Thankfully she didn't have to.

Mike's eyes twinkled in the sparkling white lights of the tree. He smiled, making the dimples in his cheeks appear. "I …uh… I wanted to apologise for last night. I was a bit of a jerk," he said, kneeling to retrieve the ball she'd let slip from her hand.

Thankfully the soft carpet underfoot had prevented it shattering.

"No, I was being stupid. I'm the one who should apologise –"

"No, I should." Mike's voice lowered. "I didn't know about …" he faltered for the right words. "I didn't know about your loss."

Penny's eyes grew wide. She glanced over Mike's shoulder to where Kate and Ian were quietly discussing where to hang an ornament.

When her gaze returned to Mike's, she found his hadn't moved.

"Don't be mad. Ian told me earlier. He thought I'd understand."

"How could you understand?" Penny's voice echoed the loneliness of the statement.

"Because I do. And I just want to say I'm sorry. For yesterday, and for three years ago."

He handed her an ornament, but said nothing more.

On the other side of the tree, Kate sneezed.

CHAPTER 9

Kate was sick.

The cold she'd been so afraid Toby would get from the winter temperatures, had snuck up on her instead, leaving Ian to tend a very miserable wife and a mewling child who wanted his mother.

It was a little more than the stalwart businessman could handle, having to people vying for his attention.

Penny, seeing his plight, offered to take Toby to the children's playroom downstairs in the building, while Ian tended to the bigger baby upstairs. Kate was never a person who took illness well. While she was the most organised and efficient of people, when sickness struck, she was equally demanding.

"Come on little guy," Penny cooed as she took Toby by the hand and boarded the elevator, pressing the number for the play area.

She watched the numbers on the wall light up as they began to descend. It stopped on the floor below. She stepped aside, pulling Toby towards her, as she waited for the passenger to board. When the doors opened however, she got a surprise. "Mike."

"Hey there!" he greeted with a smile as he boarded, the large doors closing behind him. He looked down at Toby, "Hey buddy.

How're you doing?" he asked, ruffling the little boy's mop of brown curls.

Toby tried to grab his hand in response.

"Where are you two headed?"

He has a nice smile ... Penny found herself thinking as she watched Mike play with her godson.

"Down to the play area," she replied, a strange feeling tickling her insides. She hoped she wasn't coming down with something too. "Kate isn't feeling well this morning so I'm giving Ian some space. What about you? Where're you headed?"

"I was just headed down the street for some coffee, but how about I join you two?" His eyes met Penny's, a smile still tugging at the corners of his lips. "I can keep you company a while."

Did she want company? She wasn't sure. If she did, did she want Mike's? They had somewhat buried the hatchet on their three-year-long misunderstanding, but that didn't suddenly make them friends. Did it?

He wasn't a bad guy, from what little she'd seen of him, and Kate assured her of his character – and her best friend was an excellent judge. However, it still didn't dispel the strange feeling in her stomach. Something akin to a nervous flutter, but Penny didn't get nervous flutters.

Not in a long time.

"Alright," she finally answered, giving Mike the smallest of smiles.

CHAPTER 10

*T*he play area was surprisingly empty when they arrived, but Penny was thankful for it.

"Where is everyone? I was expecting other children to be here. Schools are finished for the holidays," she commented as she let go of Toby's hand and allowed him to wander.

"There probably aren't that many children in this building yet. Besides, the families that do have them usually travel for the Christmas break," Mike replied as he joined Penny at a nearby table, turning his chair to face her.

He couldn't help watching her. Though he tried to be subtle, his eyes kept wandering back to her face.

She was so striking. Her oval face, though nondescript, was enhanced by her large almond-shaped eyes and long lashes.

He watched them flutter against her cheeks as she observed Toby playing in the submarine-shaped apparatus.

She smiled effortlessly as she watched the child.

It was the first time he'd such a smile from her, so relaxed and unguarded. It was beautiful.

He was glad she'd decided to wear her hair back in a ponytail, allowing him to see it.

He hadn't entirely thought this plan through, but the moment he saw her he knew he couldn't let the opportunity slip by him.

Ever since he saw her for the first time, there was something about Penny that captured him. She'd smiled at all the right places, as Kate and Ian exchanged vows, as he watched her from behind Ian's shoulder. She was stunning all dressed in aqua, with her hair swept up in a bun, tendrils framing her face.

He hadn't gotten the chance to say much to her as they processed out of the church, but after, at the reception, he'd tried. He had believed, mistakenly, that her aloofness was due to the fact that she didn't know anyone at the wedding, having only arrived the night before, missing the rehearsal.

He thought she just needed some prodding to help her relax. He hadn't known then what he knew now.

"How's your day been?" he asked gently.

"Good, if you leave out the sneezing and sniffling coming from Kate's room all morning," she joked.

He liked the sound of her laugh.

"Yeah, Kate can be a bit of a whiner when she's sick," he added. "I was there last year when she got a cold about this time. It was the worst. I don't think I'm even that bad," he chuckled.

"How long have you lived here? In the building I mean?" she glanced back at Toby, who was now trying to kiss the fish mural on the wall.

"Pretty much since it opened. The company took two apartments. I was fortunate to get one. Ian was offered, but having a family he opted to take a house outside of the city. Can't say I blame him; I'd probably do the same." He followed her gaze to Toby, but it was only a moment before it returned to her. "What about you?"

"What about me?" Penny asked perplexed.

"Are you the city type? Or more a suburban girl?"

She considered the question. It wasn't something she'd ever been asked before.

"I guess I'm more of a suburban girl," she smiled wistfully.

"What's that about?" Mike asked, curious to find out what could make her smile.

"Oh, I was just remembering something from when I was young?" She looked at him, and after a while of him continuing to sit silently watching her, she continued, her gaze fixed on the distant memory. "I was raised in foster homes. This one family, the O'Connells, were really great." She played with her cuticles as she spoke. "They had this really nice two storey house in the suburbs of London. It was the first time I'd ever been out of the city proper. It was really nice. No traffic and noise, just peaceful nights and a lawn. I'd never seen a lawn before then."

Mike continued to watch her intently, not wanting to interrupt, lost in her memory.

"Out of all the families I lived with, they were my favourite. They treated me like one of their own, and I guess I came to associate that kind of life with suburbia," she chortled. "Kinda silly isn't it?" She turned to look at Mike then, and her breath caught.

She couldn't describe the look on his face. He seemed engrossed in what she was saying. His eyes were settled on her, but not intrusive, as if he was truly listening. Almost like he cared, which was ridiculous.

Mike didn't know her - why would he care? Still, she couldn't help but be transfixed by that look, and for the first time she realised, he wasn't bad to look at.

His eyes were intense, piercing blue. Even with his face still, there was gentleness in his appearance, despite his overwhelming size, seated in a chair built for children.

"You're staring," Mike commented, his dimples showing.

Slightly startled she replied, "So are you."

"I guess I found something nice to look at." A soft snorted escaped him as Penny's face reddened. "Yeah, that was corny," he added.

Penny laughed harder. "Yes, it was." She rose from her seat to collect Toby before he ate one of the fish. Mike followed.

"I was just thinking," he said, standing beside her, waggling his fingers in front of Toby. "You're only here for a few days. You should see the city before the real Christmas rush breaks in. How about I pick you up tomorrow and show you around Manhattan a little?"

Toby stretched out his arms, trying to get from Penny to Mike. She let him go as she considered the invitation. Mike hoisted the toddler above his head, making him giggle, before settling him in his arms.

Penny watched the exchange, which somehow, made her feel more at ease.

"What time?" she asked, laying a gentle hand upon Toby's back.

He smiled. "Lunchtime sound good?"

"I'll be ready."

CHAPTER 11

*C*entral Park was white.

A blanket of snow had fallen overnight, leaving behind a veritable wonderland. The soft powder blanketed everything as far as the eye could see, hanging from tree limbs and obscuring the grass and pathways, leaving only a few naked magnolia trees to contrast the down.

The sun sparkled against the snow, casting the scene in soft light, as families played together and lovers meandered hand-in-hand.

It was magical, and Penny was falling under its spell.

"Not what you were expecting?" Mike mused beside her, as he chewed his hotdog, which came with all the trimmings.

"No, definitely not what I expected," she answered as they walked, their footfalls in synch. "I would never have pegged you for a hotdog kinda guy."

"Gray's Papaya isn't just a hotdog. It's an experience. One everyone who visits New York should have."

Once again a small laugh erupted from some quiet place inside her, which had long lay dormant. It felt good. Really good.

Penny stuffed the last bit of her hotdog into her mouth,

savouring the morsel. Mike had been right, a Gray's hotdog was an experience. She crumpled the remnants into her palm, but halted abruptly as Mike's encircled hers. Her breath hitched and her eyes widened, a slight shiver tracking up her arms.

"Let me." Her fingers unfolded without protest, transferring the wrapper from her hand to his.

A small smirk played at Mike's lips as he turned and tossed the wrappers in a nearby bin. She watched him silently before falling into step with him once more.

They walked in companionable silence, neither feeling the need to break it with conversation. Their steps weaved away and towards each other as they moved further into the park.

"It's like walking in a snow globe," Penny whispered to herself as she took in the beauty around her. Winter in New York was very different from winter in London. She couldn't describe how it made her feel – warm, hopeful. She breathed deeply, holding on to the feeling, determining never to let it go, even when she had to go back home.

"Do you like horses?" Mike's voice interrupted. There was a glint in his eye, a playfulness, as he spoke.

"Never really been around them. Why?" Her brow furrowed gently, even more when Mike grasped her hand and began marching towards a horse and carriage.

He couldn't mean to –

"You will now," he stated.

Penny's stomach flipped, but she didn't resist. Even as he spoke to the driver and offered her a hand to board the all-white buggy, which was lined in red velvet, she didn't protest. Instead, she gripped his hand, looked into his eyes and smiled as she pulled herself up and settled upon the plush bench. Mike was beside her a moment later and they were off.

*T*he moment the horse and carriage moved off Penny felt a thrill run through her. The stately ginger stallion pranced proudly as he pulled, black harness upon his back, his driver bedecked in black top hat and red tails – quintessentially Christmas, a Santa for Central Park, the carriage his sleigh.

"Who are you?" she mused, her head shaking lightly.

"What do you mean?" Mike countered, shifting towards her.

"You took me for a hotdog lunch and now a carriage ride through Central Park. You're like a hero from a Hallmark movie or something." She laughed openly. "I bet you even have the dream life here in New York too."

Penny's laughter would have continued if it hadn't been for the look in Mike's eyes, a sadness.

The lump in Mike's throat rose and fell as he swallowed down the memories. He may have wished for the dream life, but his was far from some pretty composition.

He hesitated to speak, searching Penny's face for the answer, but finding it was something closer to his heart that had the reply. He looked away, focusing his eyes on the bobbing of the stallion's head.

"I didn't always live here Penny. I came out here to live with my uncle when I was thirteen," he paused, then continued. "Like I said, I was raised in Minnesota, a little farm near Wright. Growing up there was wonderful." He smiled, a sad smile.

Penny sat back, listening.

"It was me, my dad, my mom and my brother Nathan. Nathan was a great kid. He was two years younger than I was, and followed me around like a shadow. Everything I did, he had to do to. I fell, he fell. We were always together. My mother would warn me to watch out for him. And I did. I tried to. But I failed."

"You don't have to –" she whispered, her eyes fixed on the way his jaw tensed. She suddenly wanted to sooth that straining muscle with a stroke of her thumb. She resisted.

"It's okay," Mike interrupted, offering a weak smile in compensation. "It was a long time ago."

He didn't turn away, but avoided her gaze nonetheless.

"We were playing near the creek. Running over the rocks and jumping over logs, typical boy stuff. I was having such a great time, I didn't notice the larger than normal splash from behind me. I just kept running. It was a while before I realised I couldn't hear Nathan anymore." His eyes rose to her face. "By the time I did, it was too late. He'd fallen in, hit his head. My parents sent me to my uncle a couple of months after the funeral. They divorced two years later."

He turned, facing her. "When I said understood, about Tim, I meant it. If I'd known that you were going through that, I would have left you alone. All I wanted after Nathan died was for people to stop asking, and just let me be. It's rough when you lose someone you love. Especially when you were powerless to prevent it – change it. I know that feeling. It took me a long time to get over it, as much as you can."

"I'm sorry Mike." The words left her mouth, even before she thought them. Her hand, like her lips, had acted on their own accord, reaching out to hold Mike's as he spoke. "I had no idea."

"Look, this isn't what I brought you out here for," again he offered a smile in recompense. "To share my life's history. I wanted to show you how great life can be, when the sadness fades. And it does Penny. It may take a while, but you learn to live again. To let go and go on." He squeezed her fingers gently. "There are moments like this to be had for you Penny. Carriage rides, great food and pretty decent company," he mused lightly. "But only when you're ready."

She looked at Mike, unable to speak, his words piercing her, and she offered only a smile in return as sounds of the park surrounded them.

The silence that passed between them then, though tinted with some unspoken understanding, recognition of souls who had loved and lost, it sparked with something new.

His hand still holding hers.

CHAPTER 13

"*Y*ou like her."

"What?" Mike asked, over a pot of bubbling root vegetables. Ian and Penny were out Christmas shopping, and Toby was at his grandmother's, leaving him and Kate alone.

"Just stating the obvious," Kate replied as she set the table. "You like her. Penny, you do, admit it. I can tell. I can always tell these things." She adjusted the water goblets, ensuring they were perfectly inline.

Mike smiled as he stirred gravy and tasted the rich brown liquid. "Doesn't really matter, does it?"

"Of course it does. If you like Penny, and she likes you, then there's a chance I can finally get her to move out here. You two can get married and Toby can have a god-brother."

Mike almost choked on the gravy.

"Woah, what are you talking about? Aren't you going a little fast Kate? I mean, Penny doesn't even - "

"Yes, she does. Maybe she doesn't know it yet, but she does. She likes you too."

The speed at which Kate crossed the room and stood beside

him, must have been some kind of record, her manner conspiratorial. Mike wasn't sure what to make of it.

"Kate?" he eyed her warily, checking the roast meat.

"Mike," she smirked. "Since that little carriage ride of yours, I've heard nothing but questions about you. That's the most she's asked about anyone since Tim." She touched his shoulder, turning him squarely in front of her. Her blue eyes were serious. "So, as her friend I have to say this." Their eyes locked. "If you aren't serious about my friend. If you in anyway doubt that you may be interested in her, then walk away now."

"Excuse me?" His brow wrinkled.

"You heard me. Penny is my best friend. She's been inside herself for three years since Tim, and she's finally coming out. I won't let you, or anyone, drive her back in. Understood?" She patted his cheek and grinned. "I love you Mike, as a brother, but I'd castrate you like Lorena Bobbitt if you hurt Penny. Got it."

He nodded his head, shocked.

"Perfect! Now let's have a very Merry Christmas and get you and Penny together, shall we?" With that, she turned on her heel and returned to her table setting, adjusting the knives.

Mike eyed her uncomfortably.

CHAPTER 14

By the time Ian and Penny returned the table was set, the food was ready and the wine was chilling.

"We're back!" Penny sang as she walked into the living room, boxes and bags in hand. "Something smells great."

"Mike's been cooking up a storm since you left," Kate supplied as she sipped her wine, casually flipping through a magazine.

"You mean dinner isn't take out?"

"No," Mike's voice drifted past her ear, the warmth tickling her cheek. "I did everything," he stated as he passed with a basket of hot rolls.

She turned, watching him as he walked over to the table, and despite herself, she smiled.

I have to stop doing that.

She excused herself to put away her purchases, small tokens to take back home and special gifts for Penny, Ian and Toby. When she returned everyone was seated.

The meal was sumptuous, the conversation delightful and the company engaging. They talked and laughed at random, about the beard on the new Macy's Santa Clause to Penny's work with special needs children.

The conversation rolled on at will, the company unguarded. It was the freest she'd felt in a long time, being around people. Mostly Penny stayed to herself. Despite what she had first believed, this trip was turning out a lot better than she'd expected.

By ten o'clock Ian was loading the dishwasher, while Penny and Mike sat beside each other on the carpet, looking through old photo albums.

Kate watched them with satisfaction as she called her mother to check on Toby. Once assured that her son was well and asleep, she put her plan into action.

She yawned exaggeratedly. "Ian, I think we should head to bed now. I'm so tired."

"What? It's only ten –"

"Yes, but I'm sooo tired," she stated, walking over to where he stood and giving him the look. It was one Ian knew well.

"Okay," he stated as he put the last dish in and set the washer. "I guess we're going to bed. Night guys."

He and Kate headed towards the bedroom, while Penny and Mike watched silently as the door closed behind them.

Penny reacted first.

"She isn't very subtle is she?"

Mike chuckled. "Not at all," he replied, his eyes settling on her face. His arm was around her back, resting on the seat of what he'd dubbed her favourite chair, as they poured over photos of her and Kate as children.

"Should I go?" The question was loaded and he knew it. If she wanted him to leave he would, but something in the way she looked at him told him she didn't.

"No," was the gentle response that was interrupted with a demure smile. "I'd like it if you stayed."

"Then I'll stay."

It may have been only seconds that their eyes were engaged, but in those moments, with those words spoken, Mike sensed that there was more in her invitation than simply a few extra minutes. It was an invitation into her life. An invitation he'd gladly accept.

"Can I get you another glass of wine?"

"Sure."

He grabbed her glass and his and made his way to the kitchen to pour them another round. It was a fine merlot, medium bodied – a good year.

As he poured he watched Penny. She'd risen from the floor and stood by the tree, admiring the decorations. He couldn't help but think that she looked liked she belonged there. She shouldn't be going back to London. She belonged in a place like this, having Christmases like this with friends who loved her. She'd been closed-off for so long. He wanted to see her bloom.

"A toast?" He placed a glass in Penny's hand.

"To what?"

"To the end of misunderstandings...and to getting to know each other better."

His eyes sought out the willingness in hers and found it.

"To getting to know each other."

CHAPTER 15

*W*hat was this feeling?

Every day since her arrival in New York, he'd been there. Dinner, decorating or just hanging out on the couch, Mike was there.

But today he wasn't. And Penny couldn't describe the feeling.

He wasn't there at breakfast or at lunch. He wasn't there when they sat down to watch *It's A Wonderful Life* or *A Miracle on 34th Street*, her favourite Christmas movies.

She'd sat in her chair and ate pecan pie and ice cream, while Kate and Ian talked about the menu for Christmas dinner, but she couldn't focus on the conversation or the movies.

When Kate announced the trip to Rockefeller Centre for Christmas Eve skating, Penny felt a moment of excitement, which somehow failed to crescendo.

She loved skating, at least watching skating, since God had granted her two left feet. Still she enjoyed it, even if it was just an observer – though Kate promised she'd change that.

However, she felt better as she dressed – slim fit jeans, a white shirt with a caramel coloured sweater, which matched her boots.

She even hummed as thoughts of Mike danced through her

mind, when Kate said he'd be joining them. Then, just as they were walking out the door, she announced that he wouldn't be coming after all.

Penny hadn't expected to be so disappointed. She hadn't realised she'd wanted to see him as much as she did, until she wouldn't.

As they travelled to the rink she found herself looking out the window hoping to catch a glimpse of him, though she knew it was unlikely. Ian said he'd had something important to do. She wondered what could be so important, but scolded herself for the thought.

Mike wasn't her boyfriend. He could do whatever he liked. He was a grown man. A handsome man. With a voice she couldn't shake and eyes that pierced her soul.

God help her, what was happening?

AT THE RINK, Penny had attempted to remain the polite observer, but Kate wasn't having it. After several laps with Ian, she sought he out, determined to get her on her feet and around the rink.

Ian settled in for what was sure to be an amusing display, leaning against the side for the best vantage point. His determined wife had established that she needed no help and he would happily oblige. He loved her tenacity, even when he knew he'd eventually have to step in.

Kate's efforts to school Penny in the art of ice-skating was more amusing than could've been predicted. They huffed and puffed, groaned and teetered as Kate tried to support Penny's taller frame while leading her.

Penny's feet spread wide while her knees folded in one moment, then slide in front and behind like a scissors the next, while Kate clamoured to keep her upright. Ian folded over with laughter, the fountain illumining his white sweater in blue, purple and orange light.

However, his laughter halted at Kate's exclamation. She'd lost hold of Penny, who was stumbling backwards. He watched powerless, as her feet slid out from under her and flew into the air. Squinting, he anticipated her connection with the ice.

Mortification had settled in long before her feet left the ground.

The second Kate's face began to slip away, Penny knew she was about to take an embarrassing spill. She squeezed her eyes shut awaiting the impact that didn't come.

Then, as if out of nowhere, strong hands gripped her beneath the arms, holding her up, saving her.

"Falling for me, are you?" Mike's smiling face appeared beside hers, his chin nestled in the crook of her neck.

Their warm breaths mingled in air before them as Penny's heart hammered in her chest and she found herself smiling.

He's here.

CHAPTER 16

"*I* thought you weren't coming," she managed as he set her right, turning her to face him.

"Thought I'd surprise you," he smirked. "Looks like you were … attempting to skate."

"Kate was making me. I'm awful and she knows it." Her cheeks flushed.

"Let me."

Her eyes widened in refusal, but the words never had a chance to be uttered. Before she could think, Mike's arm was wrapped around her waist, his hand holding hers for stability while the other rested gently against her stomach, as his body fell into line with hers.

"First trick. Find your centre," he instructed, eyes fixed upon her. The intensity of his gaze caused something in her stomach to flutter. Her heart stuttered as his fingers splayed beneath her ribcage, his grip tightening slightly as he told her to slide her right foot forward slowly.

"That's it," he encouraged.

She wobbled.

"Don't worry, I have you," he added as she squeezed his hand. "Now the left." He smiled. "Good, now the right again."

Penny hardly noticed as they moved away from the side of the rink, where Kate and Ian watched silently.

Her mind was otherwise engaged. Mike was so close.

She could smell his cologne. It was strong but not overwhelming, much like his grip – firm but gentle, cradling her against his body. She'd never paid attention to how strong he was before.

She could feel the curve of his bicep against her back, the solidness of his chest where her arm rested against it, even from under his coat.

She swallowed hard, her face flushing as she took a deep breath.

"Penny…" he said her name and she felt her skin tingle. She liked the way it sounded on his lips.

This was all confusing. The feelings were strange after so long.

"Penny?" he repeated.

"Sorry?"

"I asked if you'd like to have dinner with me tonight," he chuckled at her confusion.

She nodded, unable to reply. His face was right there. All she could see was the curve of his mouth, the way the right side rose slightly higher than the left. How the white lights in the trees reflected like crystals in his eyes.

"I'd love to," she fumbled for words.

"Great. I made a reservation."

The corners of her eyes wrinkled at the announcement. "You planned this?"

"Let's just say I hoped," he replied, gently turning her to face him, their bodies flush. "I was a boy scout. They taught me to always be prepared," he smirked.

"You were a pretty good scout weren't you," her voice trembled.

"Very good."

CHAPTER 17

*T*here were few sights that could compare to the view from the deck of The River Café.

Situated at the base of the Brooklyn Bridge, with the twinkling Manhattan skyline canvassed before you, it was a truly stunning view, especially tonight.

Every building illuminated against a wintery backdrop, each light in the window like a star in the sky, framed by the frosted corners of the restaurant's large windows – it was beautiful, romantic, spectacular.

When he'd made the reservation it was with one hope – that she would agree. It had taken some name dropping and string pulling to get a private table on Christmas Eve at such short notice, but thankfully his work connections had paid off.

Still, it had been a bold move, but necessary.

He'd didn't want to go too fast and push her when she wasn't ready, after all she'd been through, but he didn't have that much time.

Tomorrow was Christmas and two days after that she'd be returning to London.

All he had was now.

Mike had never been a shy man. He was never one to rush either, or be ruled by emotion.

But with Penny, he simply didn't know how to be. Ever since their carriage ride, where he'd told her things he'd never imagined sharing with someone he'd known only a short time, something inside him had changed.

But last night's conversation, and the promise that there could be something more between them, that the pull that yanked at that deep place in his soul, that yearned each time he saw her, could be answered – he couldn't let it go.

He couldn't let her go without at least trying. For reasons he didn't know and didn't care to have explained, he wanted to show all of him.

Everything he'd never done, he wanted to do. He wanted to heal the hurt she still felt, to sooth the pain of her loss, to open her up again. He wanted to peer inside that precious place she'd closed off, the place that cried to be freed each time she smiled, forgetting the past – the place he could lose himself in – or find himself.

Now, seated with her at their table for two, overlooking the black glass of the East River, the lights of Manhattan reflected upon it, their dinner done, he felt bold.

Reaching out his hand, he placed it atop her fingers, watching her face for her reaction. When it came, it lit up someplace deep in his stomach. Her smile was the most beautiful he'd ever seen, lighting up her face and echoing in her eyes. He could see there was still some fear, that this was all strange, almost new to her, but he wasn't deterred.

"I'm glad you came," he smiled, to ease her concerns.

"So am I." Her fingers closed around his.

"This place is amazing, and the view is just…" She looked out, trying to find words to describe it. "It deserves to have poetry written about it or something. I don't have words that could do it justice."

"I know you didn't really want to come to New York for Christmas, but I hope your view of things has changed. At least a little."

"I didn't want to come. If it weren't for Kate being who she is, I definitely wouldn't have, but I'm happy I did. It's been too long since I've seen her or Ian. And Toby. He's a different child since I last saw him. It's like the world moved forward and I got left behind, but being here, in this city, with all of you, has made me see what I've been missing."

He stroked the back of her hand with his palm, urging her to continue.

"Christmas was always favourite time of year. A time I looked forward to despite my circumstances. Kate's family became my family and each year was something I cherished. When I met Tim, and we started having Christmases together, it was like having my own family. When I lost him, I felt as if I lost everything I'd ever hoped for."

Her eyes glistened, and though every reflex wanted to tell her not to go to that place, he knew she had to.

"Everyone told me that things would get better after he died. But none of them had ever lost someone they loved. No one could understand."

He inhaled as she did, needing that calming breath as much as she. Her heart was beautiful, even through the pain.

"Then there was you," she continued. "You were first person I felt understood – that I wasn't alone with those feelings – that there was someone who got it. Me." Her heart quickened as the words flowed free.

"I don't know what it is I'm feeling right now." She squeezed his hand tighter. "This is like a dream, that I don't want to wake up from, and it's scary. I barely know you, but somehow it feels…it feels –"

"Like something you can't explain, but don't want let go of."

Penny stilled, his words reverberating in her mind.

How could he know what she felt? In the past few days, the

more she thought of him, spoke to him, saw him, something had changed inside her.

Some lock that had been rusted, had been broken off, the door opened. She hadn't laughed this much in years. Felt this much in years.

And though it was frightening, though her every sinew told her to run back into that little room where she'd been hiding, protecting herself, for the past three years, there was the part of her that screamed to hold on to what she was feeling now.

Not to let it go. Not to run away but to towards. She didn't know which was more terrifying – the dark, or his light, and the possibility of losing again.

She couldn't breathe.

"Penny, I know what you're feeling right now. I can see it in your eyes." He took a deep breath. "I know it's scary to feel. When I was younger, after my brother's death, I didn't want to feel. I couldn't feel. I tried for a long time to hide. To stay buried. Low to the ground. Alone. But Ian helped me to find my way. He was my friend and encouraged me, and the first time I saw you, I saw something of me in you. I saw the person who didn't want to be seen, who wanted to shy away. That day I reached out hoping to help this beautiful woman I didn't know, not knowing what you were going through, not understanding that you were going through what I had. But even after you tore my ego in two," he smiled. "I couldn't forget you. And now I've had the chance to know you a little. I can't forget you."

Be bold. You only have two days.

"What I'm saying is … I like you. A lot. And it doesn't make sense. But does it have to?"

She was still there. She hadn't run. It spurred him on, even though his words might very well be burying him in her silence. He couldn't stop now. Finally, he said it.

"Let me make this Christmas one to remember."

CHAPTER 18

There were snowflakes dancing on the buildings.

A cathedral of lights of pale blue and white, welcoming you through ornate light gates.

A diva on a cloud above a Taj Mahal with a disco ball roof. Ice castles behind shop windows, illuminated in purple and pink.

A tiny sparkling penguin riding upon a glittering white Lexus. Then there was the reindeer, pulling a sleigh full of robin's egg blue and white-ribboned boxes of varying sizes, large jewelled brooches tucked in between.

Her night with Mike hadn't ended as a typical date would.

There was no dinner and straight back to the house, but a walk along Fifth Avenue, which was a carnival of lights in the middle of the city.

They looked into each window as they shared a bag of roasted chestnuts, purchased from a street vendor dressed as an elf.

Penny had even gotten a free elf hat out of the encounter, when he heard it was a very special Christmas for her – thanks to Mike, of course.

Their gander down Fifth had taken longer than expected, as Penny took her time to admire the hard-work that had been put in to the Christmas windows, and the warm, happy feeling that seemed to emanate from every pane, sucking you into the merriment of the holiday season.

She'd understood then when so many people wanted to be in New York for the holidays. It was like nothing that could be compared to any experience she'd had before.

By the time they got in at two in the morning, with fingers intertwined, she was thoroughly tired, but exceptionally happy.

He hadn't pressed for a kiss. She wasn't sure she was ready for it, but she did grace his cheek with a peck before wishing him goodnight.

It was every woman's dream evening, and even in her sleep, Penny smiled at the memory of it.

CHAPTER 19

"*M*erry Christmas!"

A shout started her awake as a slender body pounced onto the bed beside her.

"What?!" Penny exclaimed, utterly confused.

Kate smiled beside her, a Santa hat on her head and red pyjamas on. "Merry Christmas sleepyhead! You were taking too long to get up so I decided to speed you along." She smirked. "Must have been a good night. I waited up until one before I headed to bed, and you weren't in yet." She looked like the Grinch, the way her smile consumed her entire face.

Penny promptly hid her head beneath the sheets.

"Still sleeping. Come back later." She batted her away.

"Nope. Wake up. It's after ten and you need to help with dinner." She yanked the comforter from Penny's head, ruffling her hair. She moaned in response. "Now come on! The faster you get up, the faster we eat and the faster we get to presents!"

Kate had always been a Christmas Day pixie, flitting here and there, enchanted by every bit of finery she could find. It was utterly endearing and completely annoying all at the same time – especially when all you wanted to do was snooze.

· · ·

IT TOOK ALMOST HALF an hour for Penny to emerge from her bedroom, but once she did she was greeted by the sight of Mike, casually dressed in dark jeans and t-shirt with Frosty the Snowman on it, chopping away at some unfamiliar vegetable.

"Good morning," he greeted her as he tried to suppress a smirk. "You can start over here by me." He tapped the chopping board with his knife, beckoning her.

"What are we doing?" she asked, peering over his shoulder curiously, looking at the piles of different vegetables and spices that enveloped the counter.

Ian was near the oven inspecting a large turkey.

"You and I are dealing with veggies and side dishes. We've got seasoned potatoes, asparagus, candied yams, Brussels sprouts and wild rice on our menu today. Ian's handling the turkey, cranberry sauce, stuffing and everything else. He picked up dessert yesterday, so we've got cherry almond cheesecake, a Yule log and some macaroons."

Penny was dumbfounded. "All that for just the four of us?"

"Not four of us," Kate piped in as she folded napkins on the dining room table. Toby was playing in his playpen quietly. "Our parents usually join us, but this year mine are in Jamaica, so it's just going to be seven of us." She looked up from her work, the grin she'd had early still painted on her face. "We always go big, just like back home. Remember?"

She did.

Christmas was always a production, with the performance happening on the dinner table. Penny always preferred the pre-show cooking in the kitchen however, and spent most of the day there helping out. She rolled up the sleeves on her lavender cardigan.

"Let's get going."

*B*ing Crosby was crooning 'A Marshmallow World' as they settled in around the tree. Anna and Peter, Ian's parents, were seated together on the couch.

Anna was drinking eggnog that she'd brought with her, while Peter and Ian discussed plans for a New Year's football game.

Kate was situated right under the tree with Toby, who was pulling at a silver candy cane ornament.

Mike was packing away the last of dinner. Penny had offered to help but he'd refused, telling her to enjoy herself.

And she had.

She played with her godson, watching him laugh and try to call her 'Auntie Penny' which came out as 'Annie Peeny', which only made her laugh. It was a bit like being a foster child again, surrounded by people she cared for, and who cared for her.

"Gather around everyone. Time for presents!" Kate proclaimed, holding up a large box. Toby clapped.

They each took turns exchanging gifts, cooing and giggling as they unravelled each in turn, showing them off.

Finally it was Penny's turn. First she gave Toby his gift, followed by Kate and Ian. She hadn't planned for Anna and Peter, so their consolation was a large hug each. Finally, there was Mike.

She'd hesitated on whether to get him anything or not, but finally she'd decided that she would. She pulled out the envelope and handed it over to him, their fingers brushing in the exchange, sending a ripple through her stomach.

He had once again found himself beside her on the floor.

The card inside was simple, a note to wish him a merry Christmas, bought the evening after their carriage ride. A thank you for the wonderful day.

She hadn't expected there would be more to add only days later, or that she'd find herself wishing she had something more to give him.

"It's just something small," she explained as he opened it, nervousness causing her stomach to turn.

"Thank you," Mike replied with a smile. "I have something for you," he whispered, concealing his words from the curious ears in the room. "It isn't here though. Meet me tomorrow?"

Penny was perplexed, but more so, she was curious. What could he possibly have for her that would need for them to meet?

"You keep surprising me."

His eyes twinkled. "Good."

CHAPTER 21

*A*nother night of thinking of him.

This time was different however.

Penny kept being plagued by thoughts of returning home tomorrow, her dream self running from the plane that was to whisk her back to her life.

She woke breathless and even more confused. What did it mean? Her life was in London. Everything she cared about was there. Everything she wanted.

Wasn't it?

She only had one day to figure that out – today – tomorrow she was scheduled to board a flight, first thing.

Mike arrived around ten, and the pair spent most of the day talking, lamenting that Christmas Day was over already. Both avoided the ever looming elephant in the room, that was her soon departure.

They left at two, for lunch at Del Frisco's Double Eagle Steakhouse, another unforgettable experience.

The restaurant boasted floor-to-ceiling windows that looked onto Sixth Avenue and Rockefeller Centre.

They shared crab cakes and salad, Mike opted for steak while she had seared tuna, as their main. Lunch was long and full of even more conversation. They talked about the things they wanted in life – a home, family – a place to call their own. They had similar desires they discovered, but neither mentioned what it could mean.

By the time they left it was dark.

As they walked, Penny got the distinct feeling that Mike was stalling, but for what she couldn't imagine. They walked Fifth Avenue again, and she was once more in awe of the lights and displays. She still wasn't sure where they headed, and honestly, she wasn't bothered.

She was having fun and she was going to enjoy it while it lasted.

"What's this?" she asked as they arrived at Radio City Music Hall.

"This," he smiled, "is where we're going."

"The Rockettes? We're going to see the Rockettes Christmas Spectacular?" Her voice was several octaves higher than normal, and her smile brilliant.

Mike offered his arm, hooking Penny's into it. "Let's see the show."

THE SHOWGIRLS SUNG a Christmas medley in harmony and the orchestra played as the curtain rose, illuminated in twinkling white lights.

Then came the first act, a wintery night complete with full moon, glowing white trees and of course the highlight, the dancing Rockette reindeer and a singing Santa.

Penny shook his hand as the jolly soul came into the crowd to greet them.

She was mesmerised, and it only grew the longer they watched.

Mike loved this show, it was one his uncle had taken him to several times as a child.

He knew Penny would love it.

And while the audience watched the show, he watched her. The way she looked on in wonder, the way her smile lit up her face and the lights of the stage reflected in her eyes. He smiled, only because he knew she was enjoying it.

He tried to settle in to do the same, but his eyes kept drifting back to her.

CHAPTER 22

*A*fter, the snow fell lightly as they ambled through Rockefeller Plaza.

"Are we going skating again?" Penny asked, a rush in her veins at the prospect.

"Not this time. In fact I'm going to need you to put this on." He pulled out a silk handkerchief. Penny looked at him puzzled. "Trust me."

She turned and allowed him to blindfold her. The next thing she felt was him leading her, and the distinct sensation of rising. They had to be on an elevator.

The chime as they reached their floor confirmed it. Then she was walking again, gripping Mike's hand to keep her wits about her.

"Now," she felt the knot behind her head loosen. "Look."

Penny's lips parted as she took the sight before her, all of New York laid at her feet, glowing bright.

Central Park looked like a frozen tundra from there, the white of the snow almost overpowering the dark of the trees. She felt as if she were in another world, a happier place with happier people, at least for that moment.

Then she realised they were alone. At the Top of the Rock observation tower.

"Where is everyone?"

"It's just us."

"How –"

"I have my ways."

She smiled, trying to contain the emotions welling inside her. She'd never had anyone do something this amazing for her before. She looked out over Manhattan and then back to Mike, as she tried to decipher what she was feeling.

"Mike, you've made this New York Christmas trip amazing. I've seen and done more now than any other before. Now this. I can't begin to thank you."

He took hold of her hand. "Say you'll come back."

"I don't even want to go." The worlds struck her as she uttered them, the first time she'd said them allowed, admitted what she felt.

Mike squeezed her hand gently, pulling her closer. "Penny?"

"Looking out here, seeing everything … it's like there's a world I could be part of. A world I can't find back in London Everything I had, except for my work, I lost three years ago. I've been holding on to those memories for so long, that I stopped making new ones."

She smiled and turned to him.

"You helped me make new ones, so I guess you did keep you word. This really was a fairytale New York Christmas."

"So don't go."

"I have to."

"No, you don't," he breathed deeply. "Kate would love nothing more than to have you move here. So would I. You said it yourself, there is nothing but your work in London. But you could also work here. You would have family and friends here." He stepped closer. "You can have the life you want, Penny. All you have to do is be open to it."

CHAPTER 23

*H*is proximity was doing things to her heart, making it race, and her stomach flutter.

She listened to his words, each one delving deeper and deeper inside her, to the place that wanted all he was offering.

As his face closed the space between them, her eyes focused only on his lips, she knew if she did this there was no going back.

If she kissed him, she couldn't go back to nothing. Couldn't have all of this just be memories. She'd want more.

Then their lips met.

Cautious at first, Mike allowed her to decide whether she wanted him to continue. When she responded, her fingers curling into the chest of his jacket, he was filled with hope that spilled over.

He wrapped his arms around her, pulling her flush against him, as his lips knew her better, the taste of her mouth sweet.

She did the same, grazing his bottom lip with her tongue before exploring his taste in return.

Both mingling, each growing increasingly more breathless as the kiss continued.

It was dizzying.

When Mike finally broke away, not wanting to push too fast, his pupils were wide with the thrill of their kiss.

He smiled as Penny's head rested against his chest, her soft breaths filling the air around him, her heart beating in tune with his.

"I don't know how to do this … " she whispered.

"You don't have to do it alone. I'll help you figure it - *everything* - out." He pulled her close again. She lifted her head, looking into his eyes. "Say the words, and I promise I will be right there, every step of the way."

He fought the urge to kiss her again, his jaw clenching as he waited for her response.

Penny pressed her head to his chest and tried to breathe.

It was a big decision, which would change her life utterly if she made it.

Could she make such a choice?

She raised her head, determination in her eyes, and kissed him.

He needed no encouragement. Her words were barely audible over the sound of his pulse in his ears, as they melted between their lips.

"I think I know what I want."

He pressed his smile hard against her lips.

Finally they parted, and Mike turned her to the city's skyline, Penny's back pressed against his chest, as his arms wound round her.

They both looked out on the twinkling, snow-covered city, the future unknown, but their shared hopes as bright as the scene that lay before them.

"Merry Christmas," he whispered softly.

And for Penny, for the first time in a very long time, it truly was.

MAGIC IN MANHATTAN

A CHRISTMAS SHORT STORY

CHAPTER 1

*A*lice walked through Central Park. She could feel the snow on the end of her tongue, and for the first time in weeks believed that things were beginning to get easier.

It was about time.

Harry had died in October. It had been six weeks from the diagnosis to the funeral. The apartment that they had spent two years setting up on the Upper East Side had not even been lived in.

She had stayed there last night for the first time in the master bedroom, the one that Harry had painted a pretty tortoiseshell green.

She could remember each and every one of the items in that bedroom, and the discussions and arguments they had had about them all.

She felt closer to him there, but the pain lay in her chest like a physical lump.

It hurt so, so bad.

The snow in the park was getting heavier, but instead of heading home she sat on a bench near the tree - their tree: the one where Harry had spontaneously kissed her during a walk here in the fall.

"I love you, Alice," was all he had said, but it had been enough.

The park was empty at this time of day and apart for a few kids building a snowman, no one had passed by.

Last night in the bedroom, she'd found the tickets for a concert in his best coat pocket.

It was to have been a surprise for her this Christmas. The Beatles were to play Carnegie Hall the following spring and Harry had been involved in setting up their tour.

"You've got to hear this group, they are the tops," he'd told her and he was right, the up and coming English band were indeed wonderful.

Just then a squirrel jumped through the snow and bounded up the tree to her left.

Alice looked up at it and realised she'd never really appreciated how beautiful the tree was. From the top, a squirrel might be able to see all the way to Staten Island. Assuming the squirrel was interested in looking.

She smiled to herself as she walked over to it.

The snow was falling harder and clinging to the bark. Alice pressed both hands into the snow, just like she and Harry had done up in the Catskill Mountains last winter.

She hugged the tree. It was nice to hug something.

As she did she noticed a small hole in the bark, one that was just large enough to fit a hand into. Alice had no idea why she did it, but she placed her hand in the hole, almost expecting to get bitten.

But instead she felt something else entirely. She pulled out a crumpled piece of paper which she quickly realised was not just a random piece of trash, but a letter.

She went back to the bench, cleared some snow and sat down to read it.

H,

I waited for you, but once again you didn't turn up. I know I said some hurtful things for which I am sorry. I was just so scared of losing you. I don't understand why you won't leave him. If you tell him about us, we could be in London soon. This was why I wanted to see you, to tell you that the company have agreed that I should spend two years in the UK office. I said yes, because it would mean that we could be together and he would be out of our lives for good.

My heart is your heart. S xxx

ALICE WAS PLEASED to see that there was still some love out there in the world. She sometimes felt that all love and hope had died with Harry.

The world went on, life moved on.

She decided to immediately put the letter back where she had found it.

There was some lucky, (if unhappily attached) person out there waiting on it.

lice didn't return to the park for a few days.

This was going to be her first Christmas without Harry and she didn't want to spend it with her family.

So early Christmas week, she took the train to Poughkeepsie to visit her sister and then after a couple of days of trying not to argue, continued on to Albany to see her mother.

By the time she got back to the city and the park, just two days before Christmas, the snow was still lying on the ground.

Alice embraced the solitude. She loved her mother but a few days had been more than enough.

She dared to visit the tree again and after looking around to make sure she wasn't being watched, she placed her hand in the hole.

This time she pulled out two pieces of paper, one was the original letter and the other was something new.

You are beginning to worry me. It has now been three weeks since we last spoke and I don't think I can go on without a word from you. I think about you all day, I even dream about you. Please, please, get in touch.

S. x

THAT NIGHT when Alice got back to her apartment some of Harry's work friends came round for a visit. It was good to have company and it even better to be able to talk about Harry properly, not the skating around the subject that her mother and sister seemed to indulge in.

However as the night wore on, her mind began to drift back to the letters.

She wondered who the couple were, how old they might be and why were they leaving notes for each other in a tree in Central Park?

Perhaps this was just a quick distraction for one of them but it seemed the other had invested significantly more in the relationship.

"More coffee?" asked Harry's oldest friend, Jim.

Alice shook her head.

"You seem to be somewhere else tonight, though I guess that's understandable," he added gently.

"I'm sorry," apologized Alice. "I've been to see my mother and traveling has taken a toll...."

"No need to say anything. I'll round up the rest of the guys and we'll let you be."

Jim was always her favourite of all Harry's pals. He understood, and was sensitive.

When the apartment was all hers once more, she went to the study, the one that Harry had intended to use at weekends.

Then, not entirely sure what she was doing or why, Alice started to write a note.

I am so sorry that I have taken so long to reply. He has started to get suspicious and follows me around. I know I must tell him but please give me a few more days.

She had no idea why she was doing this. Perhaps she didn't want to let 'S' down?

Or maybe she had done it for herself

CHAPTER 3

She could only hazard a guess as to when that second letter had been placed in the tree.

It might have been early morning or late at night - perhaps on the way to or from work.

So Alice took the safe option and went to the park in the early afternoon. Again, there was far fewer people around, so she removed the two letters from before and replaced it with her note.

She had to be honest and admit she was getting a thrill from all of this.

She felt excited as she crossed Columbus Circle, and as she passed several men entering the park, she wondered if any of them were 'S' on his way to the tree.

Later, Alice thought she would go back to check to see if there had been a response. She pulled out the note but she was disappointed to find it was just the one she had left.

She sat on the bench for a while, scolding herself for being so stupid, for being so childish. Then out of the corner of her eye, a figure stopped at the tree then moved on.

Alice didn't get to see the person properly but she was sure it was a man. And sure enough, when she went back to the tree her note was gone.

THE FOLLOWING MORNING the snow was beginning to melt a little so she thought she might take an early morning walk around the park.

If 'S' wasn't going to come until the afternoon, her journey would probably be fruitless.

But to her delight, there was another letter already there.

You have made me the happiest man in the world! To know you care about me and are still thinking of us being together has suddenly made me look forward to Christmas. Please tell him soon, so that we can put all of this behind us.

I love you more than I have, or will, anyone in the world. S xxxxxxx

Alice knew the letter was meant for someone else but it had been written to the author of the last letter and that was her.

She sat on the bench and tears began to flow.

This girl 'H' was far luckier and richer than she possibly realised.

She decided to head back to the apartment and write a reply.

Of course I care about you.

That was all the words she felt were necessary.

Though Alice grew worried after her note had been collected but there was no response the next day or the day after that.

In fact, there was nothing for a whole week.

CHAPTER 4

*T*hen on a bright snowy afternoon, when she had decided to stop being so stupid and give up this silliness altogether, she found another message.

I put your note in my wallet and took it with me to London. I have found an apartment or a flat as they call it over there, one that would be ideal for the two of us. I have to start work on January 7 but it means we could have Christmas and New Year together. Would you like that?

S. xxxxxxxxx

Alice's heart sank. Was this all wrong? She was leading this poor man into believing, that the love of his life was going elope across the Atlantic with him.

What if the real 'H' decided she had made a mistake? What if the real 'H placed another letter in the tree?

What then?

Alice told herself that she should just stop this whole charade now and come clean. But first, just one more note, one final message so that she could arrange to meet S and try to explain the truth about her actions.

I would love to talk with you soon so we can discuss everything. They say it is going to snow tonight so could we meet here in the park tomorrow,

Christmas Eve, by this tree? There is so much I want to say to you, to explain.

SHE WENT down at the crack of dawn to place the letter in the tree to make sure S had time to reply. When she passed by later in the day, there was another note.

What a romantic idea! Of course I'll meet you by the tree. Say 1pm and then we can go for a walk. There is so much I want to tell you as well. I will be working in London for a PR company; the same company who represent that new British group, The Beatles? There is talk that I may be working with the group directly. How exciting is that? I can't wait to see you. Until tomorrow.

*A*lice sat most of the night looking out of her apartment window at the most exciting city in the world, her mind turning over the options.

The Manhattan skyline had never looked brighter and full of promise.

What should she do? Go to the tree? Sit on the bench and wait for the man to arrive as arranged?

S was sure to be disappointed and indeed annoyed that Alice had taken it upon herself to intercept the notes, but she'd been so taken by the romance and adventure of it all that she hadn't thought this through.

She just hoped that when she explained all this to him that he'd understand.

And perhaps the universe had meant for her to find the letter, and bring two lovelorn people together?

Clearly H, whoever she was, had no interest in being with S given that she hadn't responded to any of his notes.

Although on second thoughts, what if he became really angry? Then she'd end up feeling even worse and on Christmas Eve too.

Suddenly she wondered whether going to this meeting was a good idea after all.

She sighed. Once again she wished Harry was here; he'd give her advice on the best course of action, would know whether or not she should just let this lie or follow her instincts.

But Harry wasn't here was he?

Alice was just getting ready to go to bed when she noticed something sitting on the bedside locker. It was the tickets to The Beatles concert that he had bought.

She smiled, realising the significance and the odd coincidence that the man she planned to meet was also connected to the group in some way.

And there and then Alice knew that her beloved was indeed pointing her in the right direction, and that whatever happened at the park tomorrow was meant to be.

In fact, it didn't even matter what happened.

She was moving on - just as her husband would have wanted.

Merry Christmas, Harry.

THE HOLIDAY SWITCH

A CHRISTMAS NOVELLA

CHAPTER 1

$\mathcal{I}$t was unbelievable how a couple of snow flurries could make everyone in Boston suddenly forget how to drive, Ally Walker mused, frustrated as she sat in the back of the taxi winging its way to the airport.

Granted, it wasn't often they made it all the way till December without any significant accumulations. But none of that especially mattered right now. All she could think about was making her flight.

"Outta the way!" her cab driver remonstrated as the car in front stopped suddenly at the airport terminal's no stopping zone.

Ally scooted towards the edge of the back seat in an attempt to see out of the windshield. "You know what ... this is good. I can walk the rest of the way."

The driver pulled up to the curb, and tapping her phone to pay him, (adding a nice holiday tip) she exited the car quickly and hopped round back to grab her stuff from the trunk. Extending the pull handle of her carry-on suitcase, she was off and running into the terminal building, not even letting her three inch pumps slow her down.

Using her free hand to pull her trench coat tighter around her body and her wool sheath dress, Ally attempted to create a barrier against the bitter cold. And questioned what she could have been thinking this morning not wearing pantyhose while bitter snow flurries pelted her bare legs.

Inside, she made it to the security line in quick time. After years of practice, Ally could do this in her sleep. Which was fortunate because after a non-stop work day that began at 5am this morning, she *felt* half asleep.

"Come on, come on," she muttered impatiently as she waited for the airline app to load so she could pull up her digital boarding pass.

But with 'no reservation found' displaying onscreen, Ally reluctantly gave up her place in the line to call her assistant.

"Walters Tech," Mel answered, in her most professional and chipper voice.

"It's me," Ally greeted, trying not to make herself sound too demanding, but time was of the essence. "Why can't I check in for my flight?"

"You know you're not with your usual, right? They don't fly into your friend's location. I thought I'd mentioned that. "

Ally winced. She hated changes of plan.

"I didn't know that. Text me the info? Maybe if I run to the gate I can still make it."

"Yeah you're cutting it kinda close, considering…"

"I had to make a stop by my apartment on the way," Ally explained, glancing at the garment bag laid carefully on top of her luggage, sequins sparkling brightly through the plastic covering.

She'd fallen instantly in love with the dress nearly four years ago when she happened to pass by it in a department store window and threw caution to the wind, purchasing it without any particular occasion in mind.

Since then the gown had been sitting in her closet, just waiting for the right moment to shine. And in her suitcase was a gorgeous pair of silver heels with jewelled straps she'd purchased a week later to match.

Just in case an opportunity presented itself, which it seemed would happen this weekend, courtesy of Ally's best friend Lara's invite to the Snow Ball, a gala event being held in her Maine hometown.

A girl couldn't just wear any old shoes with *that* dress.

Ally hadn't put much else thought into packing for this particular visit though, since her friend had more clothes than Saks and she and Lara were pretty much the same size.

Lara's was by all accounts a *very* small town, so she figured most other outings while there would call for a pretty casual dress code.

Besides, the visit was just a short festive diversion from her final destination; Florida, which called for shorts, bikinis and not a whole lot else.

Ally always preferred to travel light.

"You wouldn't *believe* how crowded the airport is today," she muttered to Mel now.

Ally had flown over 100,000 miles that year, and never had to fight her way through this many people. All of them just taking their time, walking in large groups, talking, laughing, carrying huge wrapped gifts.

Didn't they know about gift cards? Or online shopping? Granted she had a couple of small things in her luggage for Lara's kids, but they barely took up any room.

Ally prided herself on travelling light.

"Two days before Christmas and you didn't expect it to be crowded?" her assistant laughed.

"Well, Christmas Eve and Day are usually quiet; that's why they're usually my favourite days to fly," she said, scowling at a man who'd almost rolled his suitcase right over her toes.

"Because most people spend those days with family, not travelling on vacation," Mel said. "Which reminds me, you're all set for your usual Clearwater Beach hotel. As soon as Christmas is done, you'll be en route to palm trees and sunshine."

Which to Ally right about now, sounded like heaven.

CHAPTER 2

*S*he certainly wouldn't be getting any sunshine and palm trees in upstate Maine.

Looking around again at the crammed airport, Ally started to doubt whether she'd in fact made the right decision visiting Lara and her family for the holidays, rather than going straight to Florida.

But time spent with her old friend was long overdue and since she hadn't yet visited her friend's house, and rarely took time off from her tech consulting business, this time of year was a good opportunity as any.

"Thanks Mel," she said to her assistant now. "Enjoy your time off, and Merry Christmas."

Out of breath a little from running in heels, Ally scrambled to check in at the other airline's digital kiosk with only minutes to spare.

As her boarding pass printed, a sudden horror filled her when she saw the seat number printed next to her name. Not only was this the first time in recent memory she hadn't been upgraded, but to add insult to injury, they had the nerve to ask her to board in the *final* group.

Ally had been pretty much royalty on the biggest airline in the country for the last four years in a row thanks to her weekly travel schedule and copious airmiles.

SkyAir rewarded her for her loyalty by treating her like gold. She was usually the first one on the aircraft, whereupon she almost always enjoyed a complimentary upgrade to first or business class.

What would it be like to fly as a regular person again?

She barely had time to think about what lay ahead as she hurried onwards to her gate.

"Last call, boarding group #5," someone called over the loudspeaker just as she arrived. Looking around the gate, Ally saw only four other people waiting to board.

She quickly scanned her pass and wheeled her bag through, only to find the line at a standstill on the jet bridge.

No doubt the passengers already onboard were searching for overhead space or playing musical chairs with their fellow seat mates trying to secure seats next to the family members they were traveling with.

As if it would be so difficult to spend a two hour flight apart.

"Ma'am," a flight attendant approached her then. "I'm afraid we are going to have to check your luggage today."

"Excuse me?" Ally asked, in the hope she'd misheard. Her bag was TSA approved. It fit perfectly in the overhead storage compartment and was just the right size to hold her clothing, her work computer and toiletries. This lady had to be mistaken.

"Overhead storage is limited on these smaller puddle hoppers," she explained pleasantly. "Don't worry, we'll just store it beneath the hold and it will be waiting for you at the carousel on the other side."

Worry wasn't the right word. Annoyed was more like it. Though not wanting to prolong the boarding process any further, Ally reluctantly handed over her case, first grabbing her garment bag off the top.

"OK, well is there somewhere on board I could hang this maybe?" she asked.

"We only have a small area for the crew's items. We're not supposed to, but that dress is gorgeous. It would be a real shame if it got wrinkled."

"Thank you," Ally smiled gratefully, as the attendant took the garment bag and headed back out the gate.

A little bit of separation anxiety kicked in and she felt compelled to watch as her trusty suitcase and favourite dress were spirited away somewhere.

It occurred to Ally then she hadn't arranged for a bag tag, but before she had time to get the flight attendant's attention, the line started moving again and she needed to keep up.

Ally attempted one final peek behind, when the line once again stopped abruptly and she collided into a taller man in front. His plaid sports coat felt soft again her cheek and she was close enough to see the slight wear in the leather patches at the elbows.

Assuming he was older based on his style of clothing, when he turned around she was surprised to find that he was in fact, much younger - likely in his early thirties, just like her.

And cute.

"Pardon me," he apologised gently, his blue eyes laser- focused on hers and normally, the intensity of such a gaze would make Ally uncomfortable.

But this gave her time to study his face. She could see that his eyes also had specks of green, his nose was straight and his square jaw line was covered with light stubble. He looked like the kind of guy who would normally be clean shaven, but for some reason had skipped his morning shave for a day or two.

"No, my fault," she mumbled. "I wasn't paying attention."

Ally was almost sorry when he broke their eye contact as the line began to move again, leaving her to stare at the back of his head once more.

Maybe boarding last wasn't so bad after all.

CHAPTER 3

A few more minutes passed before Ally was finally able to board the aircraft and locate her seat.

The sight of the narrow, cramped coach class seat after traveling primarily in the comforts of first class was a rude awakening, and deflated her spirits yet again.

The seat appeared to be only about two feet wide, the armrests were narrow and metal and it clearly didn't have a footrest.

Even at only 5' 3" she still had to crouch down and scoot her legs sideways to fit into it. Though at least she was seated in the aisle and could possibly stretch out her legs a bit that way.

She spent the final minutes before take off on her phone trying to get through all unread work emails that had come in since she'd exited the taxi.

One was from a client confirming a conference call for the 23rd and Ally updated her calendar. She would be in Maine for that one. Lara surely had to have a spare room or some private space she could take the call from, so this shouldn't be a problem.

She made it through another seven or so emails before she heard the dreaded announcement.

"Ladies and gentleman, please switch all cellphones to flight mode, power down computers and other electronics equipment and safely stow them."

Ally harrumphed. How much more pleasant the flying experience would be if someone could figure out a way for passengers to use their phones while in flight?

Not that airlines seemed at all concerned these days with their customer's comfort. The small seat and lack of overhead storage space on this one were alone a testament to that.

Loss of productivity was certainly an inconvenience, but on the bright side at least she could use this time to unwind and read. About the only time she got the opportunity to indulge in reading just for pleasure. So at least there was that to look forward to.

A couple of minutes after take-off, the drinks cart pulled up along side Ally's seat before she even had a chance to unfasten her seat belt.

She brought her elbow in towards her body to prevent it from inadvertently being bumped with the sharp edges of the metal cart. The arm rest was way too narrow for even her elbow to comfortably rest.

"Can I get you a drink ma'am?"

Ally smiled, thinking how a chilled glass of wine would be just the thing to help her relax for the almost two hour flight. "I'll have a glass of chardonnay if you have it."

"Sure. That will be $8. Cash only."

It has been such a long time since she had flown coach that Ally had completely forgotten that drinks were extra! She reached for her purse, but already knew she didn't have any cash on her. Carrying paper these days was like lugging around a stone and chisel, outdated to say the least.

Was this airline the final frontier of the digital revolution?

"Actually, maybe just some water."

"Sure. That will be $2."

Water was no longer free either?

Frustrated, Ally leaned back into the headrest of her seat, wishing she had stopped for something before she boarded.

"You know what, I'll pass - I don't have any cash on me right now."

She swallowed, her throat already beginning to feel dry at the thought of two hours without anything to drink.

"Here, I've got it."

Ally looked up as she heard a man's voice pipe up from somewhere nearby. Across the aisle, one row behind and diagonal to her own seat was the guy with the plaid sports coat she'd bumped into while boarding.

And much to her embarrassment, he was extending a couple of dollars towards the flight attendant.

"Thank you, that's very kind," she said. "But I'm fine really."

The flight attendant hesitated a little at the guy's outstretched hand, unsure what to do.

"Please - I insist." He nodded and the attendant duly accepted on her behalf.

"Thank you," Ally smiled and took a sip from the plastic cup once it was set on her tray table, while trying to think of how to properly thank the generous stranger.

"Not a problem," he said, as the cart moved on.

"Here, let me pay you back." She tapped her phone screen, and began to pull up her mobile banking app. "If you just tell me your email address, I can Revolut it to you now."

"It's only two dollars, I think I'll survive. In fact, I have more if you really want that wine."

She chuckled. "If we hit any turbulence I may take you up on that." The man reached for his wallet once again, not seeming to pick up on her lighthearted tone. "Hey, I was just joking, honestly."

"Well, the offer is there."

"Thanks." Ally moved her gaze to the back of the seat in front, avoiding more eye contact. The feeling of being indebted to this stranger for his kind act was foreign to her.

It had been a long time since she'd wanted anything that she'd been unable to provide for herself. Even long before her mother died really.

Even during her last relationship, Ally was more often than not the one footing the bill when they went out for dinner.

"I take it you don't fly this airline often?" The helpful stranger spoke again.

"First time."

He offered a knowing smile and Ally found herself unsure of what to do next. For some reason, she didn't want their conversation to end.

"What are you reading?" she asked, noticing the book he had resting on his lap.

When he held it up, she recognised the name of a bestselling author.

"Oh, snap. I've actually just started his series; I'm almost done with the first book. I was hoping to finish it … aw, damn." Just then she remembered her device was in her carry-on bag. The one the flight attendant had whisked away earlier.

When the stranger looked puzzled, she explained this to him.

"I just realised my e-reader is in my luggage. They made me check it."

"They took mine too. The flight's so busy I guess," he shrugged, while Ally wondered what she'd do now to pass the time.

The guy turned back to his book, but then stopped. "I can read aloud if you like. I've been told I have a voice for radio. Or is that a face."

She couldn't help but giggle at his cheesy joke. It reminded her of what Mel referred to as a 'dad joke'.

The kind of joke that would embarrass a teenager if it had been their father making it. Having grown up without a dad, Ally was never able to fully relate to the expression. The thought of a little embarrassment seemed like a small price to pay.

"Henry looks over the horizon in search of …" He read from his book in a dramatic tone, while the passenger seated next to him shot a stern look, clearly not amused.

"Guess he's not a radio fan," Ally leaned across and whispered. "But don't worry - I'll be fine. Enjoy yours in peace. And thanks again for the water."

"No problem." He winked. "But maybe next time you should rethink your reliance on digital."

Ally smiled. She didn't have the heart to tell him that digital was not only her job, but pretty much her life.

She didn't know what she'd do without tech. As it was, missing her iPad on this flight was like missing an arm.

Instead, she turned back and closed her eyes, suddenly exhausted by her hectic day.

And before Ally knew it, she'd relaxed into a deep and peaceful slumber.

CHAPTER 4

*T*he next thing Ally felt was someone patting her arm. Startled, she sat up in her seat and looked wildly around, trying to remember where she was.

"Must've been a nice dream," the flight attendant who'd just woken her teased, "flight's landed."

Ally scrambled to get up, only to find her neck stiff and her legs heavy. Further adding to her confusion was the fact that she seemed to be the very last person on board.

She looked around, wondering how the passenger sitting next to her in the window seat had made it past without her waking. And then instinctively she glanced at the seat across the aisle where the helpful guy had been sitting, and found herself wishing it weren't empty.

It would have been nice to thank him again before they parted ways.

Then her cheeks felt hot at the thought of him seeing her fast asleep while making his way off the plane. What if her mouth had been wide open with a line of drool down the side of her mouth? What if the altitude made her snore?

She shook her head in an attempt to rid her mind of these embarrassing thoughts.

Hopping up, she automatically opened the overhead bin out of habit to retrieve her case, forgetting that it wasn't in there. It was only when the flight attendant returned with her garment bag that she remembered she would have to wait for it at the carousel.

As she exited through to the terminal, Ally was greeted by the sound of tinny Christmas tunes in the background.

She couldn't understand for the life of her why an airport would play background music so loudly, let alone the old festive favourite that was currently blaring. A shame no one could come up with any new original holiday tunes anymore. Hearing the same songs year after year was a bit depressing.

As she approached the quiet carousel, she realised that at least one advantage to being the last person off the plane was everyone else had already picked up their stuff and she wouldn't need to fight for her spot.

Her case was the only one left on the carousel, and cut a lonely sight, wandering round and round the circuit.

Ally grabbed it by the handle and hoisted it up, noticing that it felt a little heftier than she remembered.

She really was exhausted.

As she set off to exit the terminal, she quickly powered her phone back on to figure out where she was meeting Lara, frowning a little when she realised how little battery it had left.

Her best friend answered after one ring, and she strained to hear over the background music. "Hey, I've just landed, you here?" She heard a baby crying on the other end of the line.

"Almost there sweetie," she cooed, in a tone Ally had never heard before. "Be right there!" she yelled back into the phone then, sounding much more like the Lara she knew.

Outside the building, almost as soon as the phone disconnected, Ally spied a mini van pull forward to the curb.

One hand was still on the wheel, but as soon as she spotted the messy heap of dark blonde hair pilled on top of the driver's head, she knew it was Lara.

Her friend's hair had been the first thing Ally noticed about her when they first met back in college.

She was sitting behind Lara n an art history class, and while the professor was showing slides of Hagia Sophia, she was memorised by the way her soft curls bounced each time she moved her head.

Ally had always wanted to be able to do her own hair the same way, but hers was poker straight. Her mom had been the only one who was able to get it to cooperate in any way.

One day during class, she finally decided to ask the girl how she did it. Lara was only too happy to show her, and they were pretty much inseparable the rest of college.

Ally always felt such a sense of nostalgia and joy when she remembered her carefree years as college student.

She had initially selected History as her major, since it was something she was endlessly interested in. Luckily enough, by the time she was a sophomore, her college advisor was kind enough to show her the starting salaries of various majors.

Ally's mother's declining health meant she would be on her own soon enough and she immediately switched to Computer Science, the top-paying field at the time.

Now, one hand on her luggage, the other raised in greeting, she walked towards the mini van that was stopped in the designated pick-up area.

"Riley, pick that up for your sister and she'll stop crying," she heard as she approached the van. Even with the windows rolled up, her best friend's voice was still audible.

She waited a few seconds before tapping lightly on the widow with her knuckles, hoping the noise didn't startle everyone.

"Thank you honey," Ally heard, before Lara turned around and looked out her window. She beamed and hurriedly undid her seat belt as she reached for the door handle. "Hey big city girl!" her friend exclaimed jumping from the car and throwing her arms around her. "Let me help you with your bags."

"No, don't worry, I've just got one. Pop the trunk and I'll throw it in."

Ally went to the rear of the car, peeking inside the widows at her adorable five year old godson and brand new goddaughter.

This would be her first time meeting Charlotte since she was born six months earlier. Another reason for this visit since she would get to do so while she was still a baby. Something her schedule hadn't allowed five years ago when Riley was born.

When Lara and her husband eventually did make a trip with Riley to Boston he was already walking by the time Ally got to meet him.

Opening the trunk, Ally hesitated when she saw the mountain of toys, fresh diapers and what appeared to be trash, piled almost as high as the back of the seat.

"Just throw it anywhere, don't worry - nothing back there is important," Lara called back and Ally followed her friend's instructions and hoisted the suitcase up and onto the shortest pile of the debris, once again laying her dress neatly over the top of it.

"Aunt Ally!" Riley squealed once she'd settled in to the passenger seat. It took her a few minutes to situate her feet since the floor was also littered with food wrappers.

"There you are honey. Riley you are even more handsome than the last time I saw you."

"Can I play some games on your phone?"

Lara swiped her outstretched hand past her neck, the universal gesture for 'do that and I'll kill you.'

"Sorry bud, my phone's almost dead. I need to charge it." That was actually the truth though. Ally glanced down at screen and saw she was now at 10%. Bummer.

Another downside of the different airline - there were usually charging stations in the armrests of her usual. But this one had been basic and without frills - to say the least.

"We are having a tech free Christmas," Lara supplied.

"Sounds like fun," Ally said, with as much sarcasm as possible.

"We want to spend the holidays connecting as a family without all these distractions. And it's not good for developing young brains to be so overly stimulated."

"Poor kids. My mom certainly never limited mine, and look how I turned out."

"Exactly, a cautionary tale."

Ally laughed and moved aside empty juice boxes on the car's console in an attempt to locate a phone charger.

"Lara you have got to be kidding me…" she said, holding up the end of the adapter.

"What?"

"Your phone must be at least two years old if you still use this to charge it."

"Like I have time to keep track of how old my phone is. It still works, so why would I buy a new one?"

Ally shook her head in amazement, realising she'd need to wait until she could unpack her own.

"Oh I can't believe you're finally here!" her friend enthused. "Especially on Christmas. I thought for sure you'd have made plans with Gary. How is that going?"

Ally made a face. "It's not - going I mean. According to him we were never actually dating in the first place. Really fooled me."

"Unbelieveable. Men these days."

"So what are the plans for tonight?" she asked, changing the subject. "We heading out somewhere? I checked the OpenTable app but couldn't find anything … "

"Like for dinner?" Lara bit her lip. "With these two, restaurants are more trouble than they're worth these days."

"I can imagine. What time do they go to bed? We could head out then."

"Ha! By the time I get them both down I'm almost ready to pass out myself."

"Oh, sorry." Ally did her best to hide her disappointment. She had been looking forward to a night out with her best friend forever. Although she supposed it was foolish to think they'd be able to recreate the kind of fun they used to have in college.

"Don't be sorry, I'm sure not. I used to think bar hopping was so fun. Now it just seems empty compared to what I have now."

Lara looked into her rearview mirror at her smiling baby and fidgeting toddler in the backseat. "I've some pizza back at the house. We'll show you what real fun is."

"Great, I like pizza." As Ally looked over at her friend in her oversized sweatshirt, a Christmas elf on the front and her fuzzy black sweatpants, it was hard to remember what Lara was like before she become a mother.

How was this the same woman who used to complain at 2am when the bars would close because she didn't want to go home?

"Anyway, better to save our energies for the Snow Ball," Lara added then. "I've hired a sitter so we can go all out, hair, false eyelashes, the works. So I really hope you packed a knockout dress."

"Sure did."

"Oh we're going to have so much fun! Tomorrow is the ice maze, and then the tree lighting. You'll really like that one."

Ally swallowed hard. A bunch of people standing around in the freezing cold waiting for someone to flip the switch on a few lights didn't exactly sound like a rip-roaring time.

And the ice maze sounded very much like a kids thing.

Oh well, she'd get into the spirit of all this stuff, for Lara's sake at least.

It was a couple of days, tops. After that Ally would be chilling beneath the palm trees, pina colada in hand, Christmas a distant memory.

Heaven.

CHAPTER 5

*A*fter a forty-five minute drive through mostly woodlands, Lara turned onto a dimly lit road.

"Country living at it's finest," her friend declared.

Out of the darkness, a massive house appeared and Ally made no attempt to hide her surprise.

"Uh you didn't think to tell me you lived in a mansion?"

She was shocked enough when six years ago Lara broke the news that she was leaving Boston with her new husband Mark. The two women had done everything together, it was hard for Ally to imagine them living in different states.

Mark's grandmother had just passed and left them a house in his home town. He was also apparently the family heir to a small business, a restaurant and a few other things in the place.

Funny how Lara, the one who'd stuck with Art as her major in college, knowing she'd likely never make a lot of money and didn't care, ended up living in a house like this.

Wealth and material things never mattered to her best friend though, which is probably why Lara never told her about this place.

All these years, Ally had felt sorry for her friend living in

Hicksville. But now, she felt a bit sorry for herself thinking how her entire apartment could probably fit into her friend's foyer!

Lara proceeded to pull into the wraparound driveway with trees surrounding either side, all lit by beautiful white fairy lights. A coating of fresh white snow sat on top of each tree as if it had been hand-placed by a professional decorator.

Columns surrounding the porch were decorated with alternating red and green festive garland.

It all looked like something out of a Christmas card.

"Nice isn't it? It belonged to Mark's grandmother. Way too much space for us, but it means a lot to him raising his family here."

"I'll say. It's like the McAllister's place in *Home Alone*."

Ally grabbed her bag and helped Riley out of his car seat while Lara picked up the baby carrier and headed inside.

A massive Christmas tree took up over half the entryway, and every branch had beautiful, distinctive ornaments dangling. The angel on top was pretty much level with a grand second-story staircase.

The whole effect was magnificent, truly like something out of a movie and Ally almost thought of asking Lara for a map of the place, just in case she got lost.

"Mommy, I'm hungry," Riley declared, as he threw off his coat.

"Alright, let's get the pizza in. Will you show Aunt Ally where the guest room is? I'm sure she's dying to get out of those work clothes."

Ally glanced down at her dress and pumps. She had never really thought of her outfit as 'work clothes' before. But perhaps something casual would indeed be more appropriate for pizza and playing with the kids.

She headed upstairs, struggling a little as she hefted her case up the grand, seemingly never-ending stair case.

Inside the guest room, she threw it onto the bed and undid the zipper. Then throwing the lid back, she stopped and frowned.

A beige sweater lay on top, a fancy expensive looking cashmere one that Ally couldn't recall packing.

Or *owning* for that matter.

Moving it aside, her frown deepened with what she found underneath; a bunch of books and notebooks.

Three had the same cover, with mountains in the background - proper books. Ally didn't even own four hardcopy books, much less three of the same.

She continued to dig, hoping that whomever put these relics in her suitcase on top of her stuff, wasn't also a thief that would have taken her phone charger.

But came up empty handed, as she pushed aside a tuxedo, a pair of slippers, until finally realization dawned.

This was *not* her bag!

Yes, it was the same type and model as the one she'd taken on every trip since she founded her tech consultant business six years ago, but it definitely wasn't the one she'd boarded the plane with.

She must have grabbed it by mistake. But no, this was the only one left on the carousel, which was why she'd taken it in the first place.

Which meant that someone else had picked up hers.

They were the one who had made the mistake.

What on earth was she going to do?

CHAPTER 6

*A*lly fell backwards onto the bed as the realisation sunk in even further.

She had no laptop, no VPN, no phone charger. Let alone personal belongings, like a toothbrush or makeup or underwear even!

How was this possible? And what should she do? Once the phone on her battery died, she'd be completely cut off from the outside world.

Ally struggled to keep her breathing even, as she went to find her friend.

"Lara!" she called helplessly down the hallway. "All of my stuff is gone."

Her friend came out of the master bedroom with baby Charlotte on her hip. "What do you mean - gone?"

"I grabbed the wrong bag at the airport. Well, I mean I didn't - someone else did and I got this one instead which obviously isn't mine, so I don't have any stuff and ..."

"OK calm down. I can lend you anything you need for the moment - I've got spare toiletries and we can grab the basics in town ..."

"No, my stuff, work stuff. My laptop was in here and my charger and iPad … I have important calls and a couple of Zoom meetings coming up - I can't miss them."

"You'll get it all back in no time, I'm sure. Just relax. First things first, let's get you some clothes and then we can call the airline. With your status they'll probably hire a limo to hand-deliver it all back to you."

If only it had happened on my airline, Ally thought, unable to share her friend's optimism. Taking a deep breath, she followed Lara into her bedroom, doing her best to focus on the clothing options she was offering, but all she could think about was a finding a way to get her bag back.

"I know - I'll get my assistant on it. She'll be able to figure it out with the airline."

"Great idea."

Though Ally wasn't sure exactly how, since the bag she had didn't have an airline identification tag. And neither did hers. Which meant like hers, it must also have been stowed unexpectedly.

Then she groaned, remembering that Mel had officially logged off for the holidays.

Still, she was sure she wouldn't mind, and pinged her a quick text, before her phone ran out and she was *seriously* stuck.

"If you could just lend me something to wear tonight to sleep in? And maybe something for tomorrow morning at that ice maze thing just in case."

With the arm that wasn't holding her baby, Lara reached for a pair of pants draped over the arm of a rocking chair. "These are thermals. You can wear them under these jeans tomorrow. And I'll find you a sweater and some boots."

"Thanks." Ally examined the pants trying to determine if they'd fit her.

"And for tonight, take this." Lara threw her two large flannel items, a pair of decidedly unfeminine pyjamas, the kind a grandfather might wear.

Ally returned to the guest room to try on the nightclothes her friend had been kind enough to lend her. It felt strange to be wearing pyjamas when she hadn't yet eaten dinner, but the feeling of the warm flannel against her skin was too good to pass up.

She caught a glimpse of herself in the floor length mirror on the back of the door before heading down the stairs.

Despite her worries, the festive red and green and poinsettia flowered pattern made her smile at her own reflection.

Never in a million years could Ally have imagined herself wearing Christmas pjs, but something about it had almost magically made her feel better already.

CHAPTER 7

"$\mathcal{M}$erry Christmas," Jake Turner called to the driver as he exited the cab in front of the chateau his family rented every year in this Maine small town for the holidays.

As a kid, having to spend Christmas so far from his friends in Boston was a total drag, but as an adult, he anticipated this break from hectic city life.

"Jakey!" his younger sister Meghan squealed and ran towards him from the doorway. She had her arms wrapped around him before he could even set his luggage down.

"Hello to you too. Did I miss anything good?"

He hated the fact that he wasn't able to join the rest of the family when they'd arrived a couple of days ago. But the holiday shopping season was a busy time for his profession.

His publisher had somehow landed a book signing at Barnes & Noble and being in desperate need of exposure (and sales), Jake was only too happy to agree.

"Just the same ole, same ole," said Meghan. "I'd much rather hear about your book signing."

He let out a big sigh.

"That bad?"

"Just wasn't quite the turnout we'd hoped."

"I'm sorry. But hey, don't worry about it. Your job is to write, theirs is to take care of sales. Your new book is amazing. If that publisher can't sell it, maybe you should just find someone else."

Even in adulthood his baby sister thought he could do no wrong.

"The business is changing now, though. According to my agent, I need to connect more with my readers. She keeps trying to get me on social media." He wrinkled his nose.

"Well, I actually agree with her on that one. You are *way* behind the times. A real techno dinosaur."

"Not behind, I just prefer my privacy. I know that kind of makes me an anomaly in our generation," he laughed.

"Hey, enough about work, hurry up and get changed out of that old man history professor vibe you've got going on," Melanie urged, her nose wrinkling at the sight of his jacket. "Everyone's here and we're just about to eat."

"Great, I'm starving. Let me just drop my stuff up and get settled in."

The chateau was rustic in the most literal sense of the word, and all of the ceilings were made of exposed dark wooden beams. Though the open fire and twinkling lights of the Christmas tree in the living area made it wonderfully welcoming and festive, especially for family gatherings.

Jake took off upstairs to his usual room, the same one he stayed in every year.

Putting his suitcase on the bench along the end of the bed, he hurried to unzip it and retrieve his slippers for starters, so he could get out of these constricting leather shoes.

But upon opening the case, Jake knew immediately that something wasn't right. He most certainly didn't pack a pair of sparkly, four inch heels. Nor a pearl-studded clutch. Or an entire department stores-worth of colourful bikinis…

What the…?

'You've got to be kidding me…"

He'd picked up the wrong bag at the airport. At the realisation, a panic ignited with such force that his heart began to beat rapidly.

Jake tried to calm himself so he could think. He quickly zipped the bag back up, almost as if he was doing something illegal, and raced back downstairs, signalling his sister out to the hallway.

"My bag - I grabbed the wrong bag at the airport," he whispered loudly to Meghan, trying her utmost to stay out of earshot of any others.

She gave him a curious look. "OK, I'm sure we can call the airline. They probably still have yours. Calm down."

"I can't calm down! Is Heidi in there?" Jake indicated the living room as he paced back and forth, his mind racing.

"No, she's in town with Mom - why? Oh, no!" Meghan suddenly realised the seriousness of the situation. "You don't mean to tell me *that* was in the…"

"It was." Jake looked around wildly. "Which is why I have to get that bag back. Now."

A little later Ally was greeted by the most wonderful cooking smell as she entered Lara's kitchen downstairs.

Her friend stood by the quartz island in the middle of her massive gourmet kitchen, looking all the world like a culinary professional.

Besides the jaunty elf hat she was sporting, and Ally had to giggle at the sight.

Lara pulled a steaming hot flatbread pizza from the oven and set it in the middle of an impressive spread of delicious-looking salads and dips. She then drizzled olive oil out of a very fancy green bottle over the mushroom and goat cheese pizza toppings.

"Hope you're hungry..." she sang as Ally got closer.

"Starving. Though I wish you hadn't gone to so much trouble. When you said pizza in the car, I just assumed..."

"That I'd be serving you junk? Like I would do such a thing." Lara grabbed half a lemon and squeezed it over a large bowl of baby arugula, topped with freshly shaved parmesan.

"Boys dinner!"she yelled and as if on cue, her husband Mark and little Riley came racing into the kitchen and each grabbed a plate from the pile on the counter.

"Riley eats arugula? And mushrooms?" Ally asked in surprise.

"Oh yes, he's very adventurous. Grab a plate and dig in."

She tried to remember the last time she'd eaten a meal that someone else had prepared for her, and sadly couldn't.

Once everyone had a full plate, they all gathered around the kitchen table to eat together. The lights were low and soft festive tunes played in the background.

It was unbelievable warm and cosy and Ally got a sense of why her friend loved her little family so much.

This was … wonderful.

"Aunt Ally, want to see my trains?" Riley asked when they'd finished eating.

"Sure, I'd love to."

He grabbed her by the hand and almost yanked her out of her seat in his excitement, leading her to the corner of the living area where there were almost 50 pieces of wooden train tracks on the floor, and dozens magnetic trains.

The warm glow of the fireplace lit up the family room and made it magical. Five stockings hung from the mantel, each awaiting a visit from Santa. Ally could only imagine the excitement the kids would experience on Christmas morning.

Riley sat on the floor and immediately went to work connecting the pieces of the tracks. His eyebrows furrowed as he concentrated on his design.

"Ally would you like some more wine?" Lara, ever the gracious hostess, called out from the kitchen.

"Sure - if you are."

"Ha! If I drink this late at night I'll be asleep before anyone else. But don't let that stop you."

"No no, I'm busy over here. But thank you."

In no time, Riley had built a massive circular train track, complete with a bridge and two junctures. He slid his six engine train around the corners, making whistling sounds.

Ally stood a few feet in front straddling the tracks with one leg on each side. "Tunnel!" she teased playfully, causing Riley to look up with a huge smile.

He expertly steered his cars past, ducking to fit under and screamed in delight as he passed.

"Again!" he shouted, still laughing.

This time, Ally got down with her hands and knees on either side of the tracks and just as he cleared her tunnel, she grabbed him from behind in a giant bear hug. "You forgot to pay the toll."

He erupted with laughter as she lifted him into the air and Charlotte began to giggle too, in the way only a small baby can.

She continued to play with Riley, coming up with at least twenty different tunnel challenges, until Mark announced it was time for bed.

"But Dad ..." he whined, not happy the fun was over and Ally had to stop herself from objecting also, not wanting their game to end. She was enjoying herself a lot more than she'd expected.

"Will you be here tomorrow?" Riley asked before heading upstairs.

"I sure will, and we're going to have so much fun. Tomorrow is the ice maze, right?"

"Yay!"

After, Ally insisted on cleaning up so Lara could rock Charlotte. She couldn't help but stare at the baby's sweet face as she nestled close to her mother and closed her eyes.

Lara caressed her baby's head, and Ally wondered if her wispy blonde hair felt as soft as it looked.

"I'm so glad you decided to come and spend Christmas with us," her friend said in a soft whisper.

Ally nodded, almost afraid to answer.

"It's OK, she is a very sound sleeper. Has to be, with a five year old brother."

"I know. And I can't believe this is only our second Christmas together. Remember that year, the big snow storm when I was marooned at your place?"

They'd dressed up in two of the ugliest holiday sweaters and thrown together some food from whatever was in Lara's fridge, then spent the rest of the evening talking until the early hours.

The next morning, Ally awoke to a present under the small tabletop tree in her friend's place. The tag read 'from Santa'.

She still had the fuzzy socks that were inside the perfectly wrapped package.

Her friend had always been Christmas crazy but it was only now that Ally was beginning to appreciate it.

"I promise, *this* will be a Christmas to remember," Lara said. "This town goes all out with the holiday cheer and decorations - and the ice maze. Plus the big Christmas Eve Snow Ball. Honestly, by the time I'm finished with you, you won't have time to think, much less work."

At the mention of work, Ally felt her heart deflate afresh at the realisation she was without any of her conferencing equipment.

And her phone battery was now running perilously low.

"Do you have an office I could maybe use for my meetings tomorrow?" she asked Lara.

"Yeah, we have a den, next room over. Very quiet and private. But why do you have meetings set up anyway? Who wants to work on the holidays?"

But Ally had already gone to check out the den, making a mental checklist of what she would need; phone, computer, an extra monitor, decent internet.

She sat in the large leather desk chair, powering up the desktop and ran a quick diagnostic test to determine Lara's wifi speed. Much to her surprise, it wasn't fast enough to run her mobile conferencing software, even if she did have it. It wasn't even fast enough to stream a movie.

How on earth did Lara and Mark survive?

Going back to the family room, she made a mental note to see about getting their internet speed upgraded.

It would be her gift to them for being such gracious hosts.

Ally was tempted to take out her phone and create a reminder for herself, but until she secured a charger, she had to maintain what little battery life was left.

The thought of being completely without her phone too was enough to make her panic. It was her lifeline; she'd be completely lost without it.

There was still no reply from Mel about her missing luggage, and she hoped against hope that her assistant hadn't well and truly logged off for the Christmas break.

But why wouldn't she? The last time they'd spoken, as far as Mel was concerned, Ally was all set.

Just as she was about to express these worries to Lara, she noticed her friend's eyes were closed while Charlotte curled up against her chest.

Ally stopped, in awe of the cosy maternal scene.

Then Lara's eyes flickered open. "Oops, sorry about that. she's been teething, so I'm a little behind on my sleep."

"Sounds rough. You should get to bed."

"I feel terrible though. Here you are on your first night and I'm falling asleep on you." Lara stood up, gingerly carrying a still dozing Charlotte. "Look, try to get some sleep yourself and try not to worry about the luggage thing. It'll be returned in no time. In fact, I'm sure whoever took yours is already figuring out a way to get it back."

"Hope so." Ally nodded and quietly followed upstairs in her friend's wake.

Still fuelled by the trauma of losing her suitcase and the nap she took earlier on the airplane, she wasn't ready for sleep though.

She ran through any potential options for entertainment in her mind. No iPad, laptop, just an almost-dead phone - and no TV in the guest room either.

It wasn't looking very promising.

Wandering around the bed, her gaze drifted to the suitcase and the books she had discovered earlier.

She picked up a hardback and rang a finger across the embossed author name on the front: J.T. Walker.

Never heard of him.

She flipped the book to its back cover, whereupon reviewers sang their praises for this apparent fictional masterpiece.

Huh.

Ally moved the suitcase onto the floor and crawled into bed with the book.

Perhaps a few chapters of this would be just what she needed to drift off.

*A*lly awoke the following morning to the sound of footsteps. Having lived alone the last fifteen years, it was enough to rouse her from a deep sleep.

Her body begged her to close her eyes again, but the realisation of what had happened the day before awakened her quick-smart.

She had a mission to accomplish.

"Morning!" Lara greeted her over a mug of coffee.

"Please tell me you have lots more of that," Ally groaned, walking into the kitchen mid-yawn.

"A whole pot. Help yourself."

She duly grabbed a mug from the cupboard that Lara gestured towards, and filled it to the brim.

"I hope Charlotte didn't wake you last night."

"Not at all, I was just late up reading. I got stuck into a really great book."

Lara's stared at her, surprised.

Ally shrugged. "I found it in that other person's suitcase. And as crazy as it sounds, I think the owner of the suitcase might be the writer of the book."

Lara frowned. "I don't follow. Why would you think that?" she asked, while whisking pancake batter.

"It had three copies of the same book in it, plus a notebook with handwritten outlines of what I think is going to be a sequel. And he's got some nice clothes. Rich guy's clothes."

"You looked through a stranger's stuff? What else did you do, try on his clothes?"

"No, I wasn't trying to be nosy. I just thought maybe there'd be a name or a phone number in there, some way of contacting the guy."

"Good idea. Was there?"

"No. Though he must travel quite a bit, he had all of his toiletries in travel size and they had been used before." It took Ally ages to realise what a time saver it was to have a special set of travel toiletries always ready to go.

"You're like a detective. What else did you find?"

"A few really nice cashmere sweaters, a pair of slippers, some socks and a carefully folded tux even. The quality of everything was top notch too."

Lara made a face. "Sounds like what my grandpa packs when he travels."

"But if I'm right, and he is the author of the books, then I also know his name - well kinda. J.T. Walker."

"Great, well that's a good start isn't it?"

"You'd think. I googled him to see if there was maybe a social media profile, or author website I could reach him at, but there were little to no personal details at all online, just book stockists and reviews. If his clothes are that nice he must be pretty successful. So strange."

Ally wrapped her hands around her warm coffee cup and savoured a few sips, waiting for the caffeine to activate the rest of her brain so she could think of a way to contact JT Walker.

Bad wifi or not though, she'd need to use Lara's desktop computer, because thanks to that little spate of online research in the early hours to find out more about the author, her phone battery had finally given up the ghost.

Though at least she'd be able to secure a charger today. While Ally was confident her assistant would surely come up with the goods in the meantime, she was feeling a lot brighter about the prospect of getting her bag back.

Of all the things she did on a daily basis as a tech consultant, locating this J.T. Walker guy should be a piece of cake.

CHAPTER 10

*J*ake opened his eyes and was relieved to see the sun was finally up.

That meant he no longer had to force himself to try and sleep like he'd been doing for the last eight hours, while his mind continued to bombard him with different ways of potentially getting his bag back.

Usually, when he found himself unable to sleep, he'd use the time to write, so not having his notebook was adding injury to insult. Especially when he had a plot to outline - preferably by the end of holidays.

He'd make a stop at the general store in town for a new one though; one thing at least, that was easy to replace.

The evening before he and Meghan had racked their brains till the early hours to see if there was anything they could do to locate his bag, but to no avail.

He'd been waiting on the line for almost an hour to speak to somebody from the airline, and in the end they'd told him to lodge a lost property query and they'd get back to him.

The representative seemed bored and patently uninterested in his plight, but Jake thought, she had no real idea what was at stake here.

And it wasn't as though he could tell her either - just in case it made things worse.

Though at least there had been one spark of hope.

"Maybe the person who owns the case you took by mistake, picked up yours?" Meghan had suggested much later, after a family dinner during which Jake spent much of the time fretting. "Did you check it out - see if there's maybe any contact details in there?"

"Good idea."

Telling the others he needed an early night after the day's travel, Jake was finally able to examine the bag properly.

And mercifully, attached to the top handle, he spied that there was indeed one of those plastic inserts with a business card and - thank goodness - office phone number inside.

But having little choice but to call it a day given the late hour, he planned to call the number first thing, and with luck he'd have his bag (and it's precious contents) back in no time.

Maybe the other person hadn't even realised the mix-up yet?

But when earlier that morning he'd phoned the number for Walters Technology, the line rang out. Not especially surprising given it was so close to Christmas, but what was he going to do now?

"Morning," he greeted Meghan dully, as he entered the kitchen, looking for coffee.

He was relieved she was the only one awake at this early hour. Unlike last night, when he'd no choice but to share the news about the business card in a hush, now they could strategise freely without being overheard.

"You look well rested," she teased, raising an eyebrow.

"Yeah, a bit too much on my mind to sleep."

"Don't worry. I have a lead."

Jake almost dropped his cup.

"You do?"

"Yes, if you weren't so behind the times you could have done this yourself last night. A quick google and I found Walters Tech on social media. It took like, thirty seconds."

Meghan pulled up the page and handed her phone to her brother. From what he could make out it was a generic business page - something to do with electronics and technology, which was already pretty apparent from the company name.

"OK, this is great and all, but how is this going to help? I just tried the number, and there's no reply - presumably they're finished for the holidays."

"Yes, but the business seems like just a smaller one-man show than some big enterprise. According to this, the owner's name is Ally Walters - and *this* is Ally's personal profile," Meghan pointed out with a flourish. "She must've been travelling on the same flight, and if you have her bag, then most likely she has yours." She shrugged. "So now we just need to a way to find Ally. Makes sense actually, that a tech consultant would be carrying that weird-looking charger."

Unfamiliar electronics aside, Jake did his best to be patient, still not understanding how a social media page was going to help him get his bag back - today.

Unless they could send this ... Ally a message somehow?

Though Meghan seemed to have it all figured out. "Now, look at this," she told him, trying to remain patient with him. "See that, at the top of her page?"

Jake looked again at the screen and read a post from someone called Lara Clark which read; *Excited to be setting my high-achieving bestie a* real *challenge today! Knowing Ally she'll be out by midday.*

He frowned at his sister. "I still don't get it."

"Ally - the woman whose bag you have - is tagged in that post, linking to the ice maze."

He looked blank.

Meghan rolled her eyes. This person, Lara Clark tagged her

'bestie' Ally Walters, who it seems happens to be headed to the ice maze - right here in this town - *today*."

Jake eyes widened. "Oh wow! Good detective work."

That was surprisingly easy actually. He'd go to the ice maze this morning, find this Ally, who by now surely must have also realised the mistake, and would be only too happy to make the switch.

Out by midday...

Finally Jake's heart lifted. He'd have everything back before he knew it.

CHAPTER 11

*A*fter breakfast, Ally spent most of the morning on Lara's phone to the airline, being directed from pillar to post.

But none of the four representatives she spoke with, nor indeed anyone at the airport, could shine a light on the location of her bag.

Nothing had been handed in at the terminal, and with no trackable luggage tag for the airline to trace, by the end of multiple conversations and hours on hold, she was still no closer to being reunited with her bag.

She'd also tried in vain to contact Mel, but her assistant clearly wasn't picking up email or her phone since logging off for the holidays - and certainly not from an unfamiliar landline.

While Lara was adamant Ally could borrow whatever she needed for the duration of the stay, there was still the pressing matter of the upcoming work calls, and indeed the subsequent Florida trip.

She needed to get her stuff back pronto and if it meant chasing down this J.T. person to see if he'd been to one to accidentally take her bag, so be it.

By now she was willing to try *anything*.

But first and foremost, she needed to get her phone back up and running so that she wasn't completely cut off and dependent on Lara for everything.

It was a weird feeling for Ally, being so helpless and out of control like this. But the return of her beloved phone would soon set her back on track.

Now, as she entered the town's general store, she was taken aback at the wide array of items the tiny retailer carried. Everything from hardware items, gifts, home decor, plus books and magazines. Impressive though probably necessary, given it was one of only three stores in the little town.

If you needed something, your choices were here, the grocery store, or the clothing boutique Ally hoped stocked bikinis in winter. Just in case.

But there was one category of items she wasn't seeing in this place yet, and that was electronics.

"Can I help you ma'am?" an older man greeted from behind the counter and Ally knew from Lara's description that he was the owner of the shop. A true town fixture.

"Yes, I'm in desperate need of a phone charger. Do you have one for this particular model?" she asked, showing him her device.

"Well, I haven't come across that one before, but I have a few that might work, I think." The man proceeded to pull out a large box from under the counter.

It contained six different types of chargers, sadly none of which would work, Ally realised, her spirits dropping. Hers was a brand new model and had only been on the market for a couple of weeks. Clearly the price of early adoption was steep.

She thanked the man for his time, and was just about to leave when she noticed some distinctive looking spiral-bound notebooks near the counter. They reminded her of the one in the suitcase and immediately, she thought of something.

"Hey did anyone come in to buy one of these today by any chance?" she asked, figuring it was a long shot, but what the hell…

He stopped to think. "Come to think of it, yes a little while ago actually. A couple - on their way to the ice maze apparently. He needed gloves too."

Now *this* news was music to Ally's ears. Maybe small town living wasn't as bad as she thought. And she congratulated herself on her good ole fashioned detective skills.

"Did you catch a name by any chance?"

"No didn't get that much - like I said, they were in a hurry. Definitely from out of town though, much like yourself I'd wager."

That made sense too. "Yes, I'm here to visit my friend - she recommended I come here, Lara Clark?"

The man beamed. "Of course I know Lara, and Mark too. Great couple, pillars of this community."

Ally smiled. "They are a great couple. Well, she's actually waiting for me in the car, and we're on our way to the ice maze too, so I'd better get going, but thank you so much for your help."

"No problem. Tell Lara I said hi. And little Riley too."

"I will. But I might need to pop back before tomorrow - besides a charger, I'm also in need of some Christmas gifts for Lara and her family." She sighed, reminding herself again of her current predicament. "You see, I lost my luggage en route here, and if I don't get it back soon I'm out of luck until after Christmas. My gifts, along with my clothes were in there too. About all I have left is a sparkly dress and that's not much use in this weather."

The man smiled. "Coming along to the Snow Ball then? It's a great evening, the holiday highlight of the year in this town."

Ally gulped, not having anticipated the event as that big of a deal. With luck by then she'd be reunited with her shoes too. Otherwise she was going to cut a very sorry sight tomorrow night in her sparkly dress with no accessories, or even decent underwear.

"Well, maybe I'll see you there," the shop owner continued smiling, and Ally nodded politely.

Then, before turning again to leave she thought of something. "That couple ... who bought the notebooks earlier - can you tell me what either of them looked like?"

The man thought for a bit. "Well, she was maybe early thirties with long, curly hair, green jacket and grey bobble hat and very friendly like you. He was tall - lighter hair maybe? Wearing corduroy trousers. And a red knit sweater. Typical out of towner stuff." He chuckled.

"Wonderful, thank you so much." Ally headed back to the car to tell Lara what she had learned.

"Guess who could also be on the way to the ice maze?" she said, answering her own question before she even gave her friend a chance to guess. "J.T. must be in town too."

"Well, I hate to sound negative, but we do get a lot of out of towners coming to the ice maze at this time of year. Could be a needle in a haystack."

"I do know whoever bought the notebook is wearing corduroy pants, and a red sweater," Ally said, proudly filling her in on the couple's description.

Lara wrinkled her nose. "Old guy clothes. Well, at least *that* should narrow it down."

CHAPTER 12

"OK, if this is Lara, how do I find Ally at the ice maze? Or even know what she looks like?" Jake was asking, as he continued to scroll on his sister's phone.

Meghan showed him where to click for Walters Technology, and they both looked for a photo or more pertinent info about Ally, as he scrolled through various pictures of office space, computer equipment, and a few business articles.

They continued to search, hoping to find at least one picture of their mystery woman.

And while her friend had lots of personal photographs on her social media profile, there seemed none at all of Ally.

"This is obviously more of a business page," Meghan pointed out. "All her posts seem to be tagged reviews from clients. And very satisfied ones at that."

Jake began reading some of the rave reviews. Clearly this Ally was very good at what she did. Not that he understood any of the technological lingo.

All these years he had been reluctant to get involved in social media. The idea of posting pictures of his private life for all to see was enough to make his skin crawl.

But if he could make a page like this one, just about his work and perhaps interact with people at arm's length? That might not be so bad.

"Can we send her a message or anything?" he asked Meghan then. "Ask her to meet with us at the maze and maybe bring the bag?"

"We'd have to find out if she has it first. I'll send a friend request and add a little message."

'You're a genius." Jake grinned as she typed away.

He knew he should probably try to relax and just wait to see if this Ally would reply, but again it was so close to Christmas - would she even be checking business messages?

No, the idea of sitting around and not doing anything was impossible - especially considering what was at stake.

He needed to explore all options, including the ice maze.

"I'm going to head down there anyway, see if I can maybe even spot the friend there. She said out by midday right? "

"Ice Maze? Sounds like fun," another voice approaching the kitchen piped up and Jake froze, knowing who it was, but almost afraid to look and confirm his fears.

"Morning Heidi," Meghan greeted in a high voice, as an attractive blonde approached and kissed Jake on the cheek.

"What time were you thinking of heading out?" Heidi asked.

"In about like fifteen minutes or so actually, before it gets too crowded," Jake replied, in the hopes she wouldn't want to tag along. Then he'd have a lot of explaining to do.

"OK, I'll go jump in the shower first."

Before Jake could think of another excuse, his sister beat him to it.

"But I thought Mom needed you for food shopping today. You know, to help with Christmas dinner"

Jake did his best to act calm, as Heidi frowned considering. Then much to his luck, she smiled. "I'd forgotten all about that. You're right, maybe I'll just catch up with you guys later."

And as he and Meghan grabbed their coats and hurried outside to the car, Jake let out the breath he didn't realise he'd been holding.

*A*lly spent the entire car ride to the ice maze thinking of the best way to try and identify the guy who'd bought the notebook, assuming it was the same guy whose case she had.

If he did indeed happen to be J.T. Turner, it was a real shame that there was no author photo on those books.

A needle in a haystack for sure.

Still, as soon as Lara's minivan pulled into the parking lot, she began scanning every person they passed, looking for guy in a red sweater and corduroy trousers and a dark haired woman in a green coat.

"Ally?" Lara's mournful voice pulled her back to the present, as her friend lifted the baby out of her car seat.

"What's up?"

"I can't believe this, but Charlotte's just had an accident - a messy one, by the looks of it. I think I'm going to have to either take her home or a to a restroom somewhere to change her."

Ally looked at the baby, still smiling despite the fact that she was indeed a mess, and then back at the very long line already formed at the ice maze entrance.

"Maybe we should all go - looks pretty busy here."

But the look of disappointment in Riley's eyes nearly broke her heart.

"You go on ahead, and maybe just meet us after?" Ally suggested then, grabbing Riley's hand. She was sure they'd be in and out of here in no time.

And anyway she wanted to keep an eye out for red sweater and corduroy pants guy - just in case.

"You sure you don't mind? We'll be back soon."

"Course not. They take virtual pay right?"

Lara chuckled. "This isn't DisneyWorld." She rummaged in her purse and gave Ally a couple of twenties before heading back to the car with Charlotte.

But her friend was only a few feet away when she turned back. "Look!" she urged.

Ally looked to the man her friend was pointing towards, heading their way, and immediately scrunched up her nose. He was indeed wearing the right colour combo, but he looked to be about eighty years old.

Still …

"Excuse me, are you J.T Turner?" Ally asked, when the guy neared the back of the line, feeling a bit ridiculous.

He was far too old to be the owner of the suitcase. And his pants were more olive, not green.

"What did you say?" He leaned closer, obviously a little hard of hearing.

"I'm looking for a man named J.T? Maybe an author?" she repeated, a little louder.

The man smiled, and Ally felt her heart lift a little until he spoke again. "I wish I could help you. The only J.T. I know is long gone. But if you're ever in need of a Malcom, that I could help you with," he added, with a wink.

"Thanks anyway." She grabbed Riley's hand and shuffled back up her place in the line, feeling a little stupid now.

When finally, they entered the ice maze, she glanced dubiously at the ten foot walls of ice and did a rough calculation in her head of the approximate square footage.

It had to be at least five thousand square feet.

Once they were inside, it would be almost impossible to continue her hunt for her mystery notebook guy - unless he happened to be directly in front of her in the maze.

As she and Riley headed off down the first corridor, they had two choices; right or left.

Ally peered down each of the options, trying to gauge which was correct and which would lead into a dead end. There was no way to tell. And she didn't like the odds.

"Let's go this way, Aunt Ally," Riley chose the left without any thought.

But Ally was frustrated. If she had her phone, she could've grabbed an aerial view of their current location, focused in on the ice structure, downloaded the data into a GPS and then programmed it to find the quickest route possible to the exit.

They'd be in and out in no time.

But without GPS, this was going to take forever. And if they got lost, there was no way to call for help either!

She broke out in palpitations a little at the thought of being without her trusty phone, until Riley tugged on her jacket. "Come on! It's this way."

Ally forced herself to smile through her panic; this little guy was depending on her.

He took off running and Ally caught him at the next fork, just as he was turning left. She figured this was taking them backwards though, and he was most certainly heading in the wrong direction.

"Riley? I think we went the wrong way."

Laugher filled the ice passage, as he once again turned left, causing Ally to lose all sense of direction.

"Think we're lost?" he teased.

"I know we are." This made Riley laugh even harder as he took off once again, taunting her to catch him.

And despite herself, and for the first time since she'd got here, Ally began to forget about her missing suitcase, and actually have some fun.

CHAPTER 14

$\mathscr{J}$ ake sat in the car with his sister, feeling like a couple of detectives on a stakeout as they watched everyone enter and exit the ice maze from the parking lot.

At least they knew what Ally's friend Lara looked like, given she had so many pictures on her social media profile.

But most importantly they'd garnered from her post that she'd be here this morning with her businesswoman friend, who presumably had Jake's case.

Despite this very promising lead, he still couldn't relax - at least not until they'd successfully located the woman and gotten his luggage back.

"You know, I still can't take you seriously, dressed like that," Meghan commented, with a snicker.

Jake looked down at the outfit he'd borrowed from his father. The clothes, while old-fashioned were warm and perfectly suited for the circumstances. Ice mazes by their nature were ... icy cold.

And why his sister was focused on something so irrelevant when there was so much at stake here, was beyond him.

As they approached the entrance to the maze, the line was already stretching halfway to the parking lot.

Jake watched a small boy, patiently waiting in line holding his mother's hand. It reminded him of the very first time he'd come to this place as a child.

He could feel the kid's excitement as he marvelled at the ten foot walls made entirely of ice. Probably wondering how anyone could create such a thing, just like Jake had.

For the next few minute, he and Meghan continued to scan through everyone entering and exiting, hoping they'd be able to spot Ally's friend.

As they did so, Jake's gaze suddenly stopped on a woman with sleek mid-length brown hair.

He studied her profile, trying to figure out why she looked so familiar. Then he realised - it was the woman on the flight here, the one who didn't have any cash on her.

"Jake," his sister's voice brought him back to the present. "Why are you staring? That woman looks nothing like Lara."

"Uh I know." He looked back to where the woman from the flight was standing, to see her grab a young boy by the hand and smile down at him.

Oh she was a mom. For some reason he hadn't pictured her that way on the plane. At all.

"Look, look, I think that could be her!" Meghan exclaimed then, grabbing her brother by the arm.

He turned quickly as his sister pointed out a blond woman fitting Lara Clark's description, pushing a stroller back through the crowds at a very fast pace, only about a couple of feet away.

As he tried to follow, he did his best to avoid bumping into all the people who were headed in the opposite direction.

"Sorry," he apologised, colliding with someone, then turned once the man assured him he was fine, only to come inches from running right into someone else.

Jake felt like a complete jerk; this wasn't him. He stopped, took a deep breath and looked once again to see how far away he was from reaching Ally Walker's friend.

But she was now at the door of her mini van, effortlessly lifting her baby's car seat in, folding down the stroller and speeding away.

Clearly this Lara had somewhere to be other than the ice maze. Was there some emergency with the baby that she had to leave?

And where was her friend? Was Ally already inside? Should he maybe go inside and search?

But neither he or Meghan had any idea what she looked like….

Frustrated afresh, he resisted the urge to fall to his knees. He'd been so close too.

The idea that if he had just been fast enough to reach that woman, he might well be holding his bag right now was enough to make him want to kick himself.

And the fact that he, a writer, was considering such a cliche made him even more annoyed.

"I just can't believe we just missed her," he groaned to Meghan.

Now it felt like he was right back at square one.

Not to mention that in the meantime, there was still no return call from the airline and without his precious notebook, no way for him to finish plotting out his next book in time.

To say nothing of the most pressing loss of all.

Heidi…

Tomorrow was Christmas Eve, and this situation truly was going from bad to worse.

*H*aving changed Charlotte and taken the opportunity to grab a peaceful gingerbread latte while her son and Ally were in the maze, Lara returned to the parking lot, deciding to wait for them at the exit.

There was no point in dragging the baby in there now, not when she was already ornery after her diaper accident.

And knowing Ally, they would surely have made it out by now.

Sure enough, within a few minutes, the two came running through the exit.

"We made it!" Ally cried with some relief, when Lara drove over to meet them.

"See I told you!" Riley said proudly. "Mommy, you should have seen it in there. It was so hard, but I found the way. It was so much fun."

"So glad you guys enjoyed it."

"I never would have made it without you," Ally laughed and the two high-fived each other as they got back into the car.

"So, any sign of green trousers guy?" Lara asked her then.

"Nope. The man you pointed out wasn't him and I didn't see anyone else fitting that description inside. It was a long shot but ..."

"Well, we can keep an eye out at the tree-lighting ceremony later. And … wait!" Lara added, her eyes widening suddenly. The gala. You said there was a tux in there?"

The tux - of *course!* The guy surely wouldn't have packed a tuxedo unless he was going to The Snow Ball.

Ally felt her spirits lift, as she realised that if all else failed, maybe, just maybe, she had a real shot at finding J.T. Turner.

CHAPTER 16

hat afternoon Lara baked peppermint fudge in the kitchen while Ally and Reilly made paper snowflakes by warmth of the fireplace, soft carols playing in the living room.

Through spending time with them all, Ally was beginning to finally understand why people traveled such great distances to enjoy the holidays with their families for the holidays.

It was so cosy and festive, it was almost enough to make her forget all about her conference calls scheduled for later that evening.

Almost.

She managed to get through them on Lara's rickety old wifi, but must to her friend's regret, the timing meant that she had to miss the tree-lighting ceremony.

While normally Ally would've jumped at the chance to forgo such a cheesy outing, she was now kinda sorry she'd scheduled any work stuff at all, she was enjoying herself so much.

Maybe now she could also understand why Mel had gone AWOL - clearly her assistant, unlike Ally, was able to leave the office behind.

But it meant that with Lara's family partaking in more festivities, she had the cosy house all to herself, and feeling a little stuffed after all the hot chocolate and peppermint fudge, from earlier, went upstairs to read more of the book, while awaiting the others' return.

In truth, the story had really grabbed her now, and she'd fallen a little bit in love with J.T. Turner's writing, especially the way he seemed so emotionally intuitive and interested in his characters.

Author or not, it kind of made her want to meet the owner of the suitcase all the more, and when Ally eventually reached the final page, she instinctively went to the case and idly looked through it again.

Weirdly drawn to feeling some way closer to the man who'd also been reading the same heartfelt words.

Then, suddenly conscious of how stalkerish it was, she deftly began zipping back up all the pockets, as if to hide evidence of her snooping.

But on one of the outside pockets (the one where she usually kept her phone charger) the zipper seemed strained.

Ally reached into the pocket to see if she could push the bulky object blocking it out of the way. Rummaging further inside, her fingers brushed up against something hard, yet velvety to the touch and curious afresh, she pulled it out.

To discover that it was a small navy blue box - a jewelry box.

Eyes widening, she tentatively opened the lid and sure enough, inside was a stunningly beautiful diamond ring.

An engagement ring...

For reasons that she couldn't quite explain, Ally's heart sank to the pit of her stomach.

The guy was obviously planning to propose to someone this Christmas.

And the realisation struck Ally then, that she really needed to get this bag back to its owner - for more reasons than one.

CHAPTER 17

*A*s he sat with his family over dinner after the tree lighting ceremony, Jake had a fresh spring in his step.

Finally, he had a lead - a proper lead!

Despite multiple calls to the airline subsequently, he'd heard nothing at all, and after missing Ally Walker's friend at the ice maze, was seriously beginning to give up all hope of getting his bag back.

Until on the way back from the maze, he'd popped in the general store, before joining Meghan for a hot chocolate at the cafe next door.

He knew he'd go out of his mind between now and Christmas trying to figure out a way to locate his bag - and the ring - and needed to distract himself.

What better way to do that than bury himself in his writing? To say nothing of the fact that he needed to finish plotting out the new book.

So, deciding to pick up a replacement notebook from the collection he knew they carried at the general store, he chatted briefly to the friendly owner.

"Must be something in the air today, Jake," Harry the owner

commented, when he placed his purchase on the countertop to pay. "That's the second one I sold today, and your usually my best customer for these."

"You mean, only customer." He nodded distractedly, not exactly in the mood for small talk until Harry said something else. "And there was a woman in earlier too, asking if anyone had bought one."

At this Jake's ears picked up, his author brain whirring instinctively. "Seems like an odd query."

"I thought the same. You know these out of towners though, strange as they come."

Jake smiled and was about to put his wallet away when Harry's next words stopped him in his tracks.

"Wanted a charger for some futuristic phone she had - vever seen anything like it."

The phone charger... the unusual one from Ally Walter's bag that even Meghan didn't recognise.

"Did she say anything about losing a charger along with her luggage?" he asked, and Harry looked up at him, surprised.

"Yes, as it happens. Some problem with the airline. Said all she had left was a dress for the Snow Ball tomorrow night."

The shoes .... suddenly all the pieces were clicking into place.

"What else did she say?" Jake pressed, thanking the heavens for small-town gossip, as Harry told him everything he could glean about the woman he was trying to find.

But most important of all, Ally Walters was heading to tomorrow night's gala.

So all Jake had to do now was arrange to connect with her at the Snow Ball, swap the bags back, and be reunited with his luggage - and the ring.

Now, as he looked across the dinner table at Heidi's pretty face shining in the candlelight, he finally allowed himself to relax.

Just in time.

CHAPTER 18

On Christmas Eve, once the kids were asleep, Ally and Lara went upstairs to the master bedroom to get ready for the gala ball.

The size of the bathroom was about the same as her entire Boston apartment.

She watched as Lara looped large strands of her hair around the barrel of her curling iron. As she let them go, they fell into perfect rings.

"So are you excited about tonight?" her friend asked.

Earlier that day, Lara had gotten a call from the general store owner, passing on a message from the owner of the bag, who'd somehow managed to track her down.

They'd made arrangements to switch the bags back at tonight's event, and while Ally knew she should be thrilled about getting her stuff back, for some reason she felt … flat.

It meant that J.T. would be reunited the ring and get to propose to some lucky woman this Christmas as planned, while she, Ally would be reunited with … her phone charger.

"Ally, do you have a crush on this guy?" Lara's questions automatically made her cheeks redden. She looked down at the hairbrush in her hands, afraid her expression would invite more questioning.

"What? No. Nothing like that. At all. I think maybe I've just built up a picture of him from his stuff and his writing. He just seems so … intuitive."

As soon as the words were out of her mouth, she realised how foolish they sounded.

"I knew it! Oh this could really be the start of something you know. Maybe he's done the same with your stuff and tonight, will take one look at you and think losing his suitcase was the best thing that ever happened to him. So let's finish getting ready and get you to your Prince Charming."

Ally didn't have the heart to tell her about the ring, to say nothing of the fact that she didn't want to admit she'd been prying in the bag to that extent.

Better to let her idealistic friend enjoy her fantasy, nice and all as it was.

Lara put down the curling iron and Ally shook her head, and watched her shiny curls bounce. It was exactly how her mother used to do her hair each Christmas Eve when she was a child.

She went back to her room and lifted the sparkling dress off of the hanger. Then held her breath as she slipped it on, hoping it still fit after four years waiting.

After struggling with the zipper a little, Ally went to the mirror and barely recognised her own reflection.

"Here we come! Get your cameras ready," Lara called to her husband, as Ally stood at the top of their huge staircase.

"Wow! You look … incredible. Doesn't she look great Mark?" Lara said proudly.

"She sure does - you both do."

Lara and husband looked like proud parents standing at the bottom of the staircase as Ally descended past the twinkling Christmas tree, feeling almost like a fairy princess.

She smiled doing her best to join in the excitement and despite herself, couldn't help but wonder what J.T. might say when they finally met and he caught sight of her in this dress.

Then she kicked herself for thinking the guy would say anything other than, 'thanks for my suitcase.'

Lara and her silly, romantic notions were well and truly starting to get to her.

CHAPTER 19

When her friend had told Ally that Mark's family ran the town inn, she'd pictured a small bed and break-fast, maybe converted from a large older home with a few guest rooms.

She couldn't have imagined they in fact owned a full scale hotel, with eighteen rooms, a fine dining restaurant, plus a ballroom big enough to hold the entire town's population.

"This is … incredible," Ally gushed, as she climbed the massive centre staircase that lead from the lobby to the ballroom, fully bedecked in sparkling holiday finest.

Holding the hem of her dress with one hand to prevent herself from tripping, she took a quick peek to see if the shoes she had borrowed were visible as she walked.

It was kind of Lara to lend her some heels since her own were still in her bag. Though these were a bit big for her and she could already feel blisters forming on the backs of her heels.

The three made their way through the crowd at a snail's pace, stopping to talk with a few of Mark and Lara's friends.

Everyone was very cordial and polite to her, an out of towner, but once they had asked Ally an appropriate number of questions about her career and Boston, the conversation would once again turn to community or children.

And once again Ally felt herself at a loss, beginning to realise that her life was totally defined by work.

J.T had requested to meet at the top of the staircase at 9pm.

Which was only a few minutes from now.

Ally was eager and nervous all at the same time. Though once the exchange was final, at least she'd be free to head home and put herself out of her misery.

She didn't belong here, and the realisation made her sad.

"Hey, it's almost 9pm," Lara said, touching her arm gently. "Are you sure you don't want Mark to just meet the guy and switch back the bags?"

"Thanks but no, I'm fine." Ally couldn't quite put her finger on it.

But for some reason this felt personal.

SHE MADE her way back out front, where the there was a small table and friendly volunteers that checked everyone's tickets.

They had been kind enough to watch the suitcase and Ally did her best to smile as she grabbed the bag, and headed back up the staircase to the meeting spot.

Feeling unaccountably alone, she just hoped he would be punctual so they could get this over and done with.

And instinctively reached into her purse to check the exact time on her phone, feeling silly yet again for relying on it when it was long dead.

She looked around and spotted a grandfather clock at the top of the stairs whereupon a loud chime announced 9pm exactly.

"Ally?" The voice from the bottom of the stairs made her breath catch in her throat a little.

And as her gaze moved down the stairs to the marble tile of the lobby floor, the first thing she spotted was her case.

The slightly worn wheels, the wonky top zipper ... how had she not noticed at the time that the other one was far too pristine to be hers?

The man holding hers picked it up in one hand and began climbing the stairs. As he climbed higher, Ally noticed first what a nice tux he had on. Obviously must've found a replacement somewhere.

And then next, that Lara was wrong about J.T. being an old man.

In fact he seemed to be about the same age as she.

It was only in that moment that it finally registered; he'd called her by name. How on earth did he know her name?

Ally finally looked up at his face, and the instant she looked into his blue-green eyes, she couldn't believe it.

The guy from the flight ... The plaid sports coat, the water, him jokingly reading his book - all the memories of the brief encounter suddenly came rushing back.

"It's ... you," she gasped.

CHAPTER 20

*B*ut still, how on earth did he know her name?

Then Ally felt silly, realising that she'd forgotten her business card was attached to the handle.

Which meant that it should've been easy for him to reach her.

But of course, she remembered then, her phone was long dead and Mel had since disappeared into the festive ether.

So how *did* he find her?

"Jake," he greeted, extending his hand. "Nice to meet you - again."

"I can't... believe it was you all along." For some reason she felt completely tongue-tied.

"I'm so sorry I picked up your stuff by mistake. I'm sure you've missed this." He gestured towards her bag.

"I have. And same with you." She went to hand the other case to him then, then hesitated. "Actually I not a hundred percent sure this is yours. I think it belongs to a writer named J.T."

He laughed, and she wondered what he could possibly find funny about all this.

"J.T. is my author name. I take it you found my books ... and my notebook? At least I hope that's still there." He grimaced.

OK, maybe that made sense.

"It is. And don't worry; all your stuff is still inside. Although I should admit I did read a book. Sorry about that."

"Don't be. In fact, if you want to keep it, I have plenty."

Jake took his suitcase and lightly patted the outer pocket while Ally did her best to not feel a little offended.

Or deflated.

"Don't worry, the ring is still there, too."

He exhaled. "Man, you have no idea what a relief that is! My brother would've killed me."

Brother … Her mind froze as she stopped to think what this meant. The ring belonged to his brother?

"He's planning on proposing to his girlfriend, Heidi tomorrow morning. I offered to pick up the ring at the family jeweler in Boston on the way here. To be honest, I didn't even tell him my bag was missing, but I was beginning to really worry I wouldn't find you in time."

"How did you find me?" she asked, genuinely curious.

"Well, my sister found your social media profile and we went to seek you out with your friend at the ice maze yesterday. And believe it or not, I even saw you standing in line - with a little kid."

"You saw me with Riley? But why didn't you come up and talk to us? He's Lara's son." She couldn't believe it. "Especially when I was looking for you there too. The guy at the store said…"

"Exactly. I couldn't believe it when he told me that a woman had been in looking for a charger and asking if anyone had bought a notebook. I knew it had to be you. Well, not that I knew that it was actually *you*, in that you are Ally. But I'm really glad it is."

Her eyes flickered upward, and her heart began to speed up. "You are?"

He smiled, eyes twinkling. "Yes. And I'm not sure if you've realised this yet, but this is pretty much a tech-free town. Cash only. So if you need someone to buy you a drink …"

Ally winced a little.

"Aw I'm sorry, I guess I shouldn't have assumed," Jake said quickly, colouring.

"No, I just need to change my shoes," she admitted, reddening too. "My feet are *killing* me. I had to borrow these from my friend and they're way too small."

She shifted from one foot to the other, trying to minimize her discomfort, while also trying to figure out what exactly was going on here.

The guy from the plane was J.T.

Jake.

"I'm sorry it took me so long to find you," he was saying, while Ally did her best to squat down low enough in her dress to unzip her suitcase.

She tottered a little and almost fell backwards toward the stairs, but Jake put a hand out to steady her.

"Let me."

He unzipped her bag for her, knowing the shoes were right on top.

Ally happily kicked off Lara's torturous heels, and awkwardly tried to balance on one foot as Jake set hers on the floor in front of her.

Then incredibly, he crouched down and steadied her with one hand, while using the other to hold up a shoe for her to place her foot inside.

Ally felt dizzy.

"Better?" he grinned once both sparkly sandals were duly fastened on her feet.

"So much."

Then Jake gallantly extended his elbow and Ally smiled, feeling a little like Cinderella as she placed her arm inside it.

And with the ring now safely in his inside pocket, Jake and Ally stowed their cases, and together set off back to the ballroom.

CHAPTER 21

*J*ust as they were halfway across the dance floor and heading for the bar, the lights turned low.

"Time to find that special someone and make your way onto the floor," the singer of the band announced as the opening bars of *A Lot Like Christmas* began to play.

Ally stood frozen with awkwardness, while all around men took their partners and wives by the hand.

Turning to Jake, she was certain he felt the same discomfort, but when her gaze met his, she saw him smile.

"Talk about timing. Shall we?" He gently took Ally's right hand and placed it on top of his shoulder, then took the other and placed it on his side, before wrapping his own around her waist.

Her arms felt rigid as wooden boards. What must everyone be thinking?

She looked around the room, feeling reassured then that absolutely no one else was even looking in their direction. They were all too busy with their own dance partners. So she began to relax a little and enjoy the moment.

Ally and Jake began to move slowly to the music, their bodies finding a natural pace within seconds.

Then over her shoulder she spotted Lara, whose eyes were out on stalks. She grinned and gave Ally a big thumbs up before placing her head back onto Mark's shoulder.

Copying her example, Ally did the same.

As soon as her head found a comfortable position on Jake's shoulder, a sense of almost surreal calm descended upon her. Following his lead felt so natural that she was able to completely lose herself in the moment.

And in his arms.

They continued to dance for what seemed like hours, until eventually Lara tapped her on the shoulder.

"So sorry to interrupt you two, but we really should get going. I promised the sitter."

"Oh! I totally lost track of time."

Jake stood back and still smiling he grabbed her hand and kissed it.

"See you the day after tomorrow? I'll text you the address - now that you've got your charger back. And Merry Christmas."

Ally nodded, and once she'd collected her case and they headed back to the car, Lara could hardly wait to hear all the details.

"The day after tomorrow?" she urged. "Tell me everything!"

"Yes, Jake - J.T. - invited me to dinner with his family. And his brother's engagement celebrations."

"Amazing!" Her friend hugged her. "You guys look so perfect together. And he seems wonderful. But I thought you were leaving for Florida the day after tomorrow?"

"I think I might stay on a while longer if that's OK with you?"

"Of course - as long as you like!"

Ally smiled as gently falling snowflakes cooled her rosy cheeks. This truly was turning out to be the best Christmas yet.

So much for travelling light…

THE CHRISTMAS ESCAPE

A HOLIDAY NOVELLA

CHAPTER 1

*L*ibby Pearson woke with a smile on her face.

It was a couple of weeks to Christmas and already she could feel magic in the air. She leapt out of bed and hurried into the shower to get ready for work.

She was one of the few people she knew who actually liked getting up to go to the office every day - adored her job and the certain thrill that came with walking into Jefferson & Jacobs Marketing.

Her hair was dark and damp as she slipped her arms in the sleeves of her new red jacket, which matched the pencil skirt she was wearing. Her blouse was white with an oversized collar and cuffs that folded over the ends of the jacket, and she wore black and white polka dot heels to match her bag.

"Morning Mom and Dad," she said with a smile as in the living room she passed photos of her parents on the mantle over the fireplace.

Libby always went the long way to the kitchen just to say good morning to them each day. Her parents passed away six years ago. Her father had a heart attack and just one day after he died, her mother went to sleep and didn't wake up.

In the kitchen, the smell of freshly brewed coffee filled her senses and made her feel even happier. She loved coffee in the morning. Food was a second thought, usually something she didn't feel like until lunchtime, but coffee was an absolute must to start the day.

Jingle must've heard her because seconds after she walked into the kitchen, the dog door opened and her friendly, fearless pooch came trotting in. Jingle was a Weimaraner and his stubby tall wagged eagerly at the sight of her.

"Hey boy," she said with a smile as he followed her around the room. "How's it going this morning?"

She poured the coffee into her festive thermal mug, grabbed her lunch from the fridge and packed it into her bag. Libby was trying her best to improve on what she ate, especially so close to the holidays.

She left food for Jingle. He could eat it all and even the bowl too, so she liked to leave a little something extra for him during the day before she gave him his dinner when she got home.

Her parents' house, and forever the Pearson family home was decorated from top to bottom for the season, just like every other house on Clayton Drive.

Nearly every building in the neighbourhood was decorated in hundreds of lights, and those who didn't have hundreds had thousands.

It had taken Libby three days to finish decorating theirs inside and out, but she adored every second of it. Christmas was her favourite time of year and she couldn't imagine it without all the trimmings and festive cheer.

She was barely behind the seat of her little beat-up Fiat 500 when her phone rang. She pressed her Bluetooth button and a second later her brother's voice filled her ears.

"Hey Andy," she greeted as the garage door opened and she began to reverse.

"Sis, don't forget to pick up the turkey," her older brother reminded her. "And you need to make sure to get the cranberries. That canned stuff made Molly itch all night last year."

Her brother's wife was allergic to a great many things, mostly preservatives, so everything had to be made from scratch as Libby had painfully learned last year.

"I remember. I got them up yesterday."

"What about pumpkins? You know how everyone loves your pumpkin and pecan pie," her brother continued.

"I haven't gotten to that yet," she informed him, as she pulled onto the main road and started the journey toward the city. Her office lay at the heart of Rochester's business hub and usually took her about twenty minutes to reach.

"What're you waiting for? You know what the markets will be like the closer to Christmas you get. You risk not getting the good stuff," he brother insisted.

Libby sighed and rolled her eyes. What did Andrew know about markets during the holidays?

In the six years since her parents' passing, Christmas dinner had fallen solely on her shoulders to prepare. She was the one who stood in line at the store to make sure they had all the traditional stuff their mother used to give them.

Though at least her mom had help with the preparations and shopping. Libby had none.

Her phone beeped again and now her sister's name appeared on the screen. "Andy, can you hold? Emma is on the other line."

"OK," her brother replied. "Tell her hi for me and remind her that Kelsey and Brittany are supposed to come over next weekend for their Brownie campout thing."

"I'll remind her," Libby replied before switching the call. "Hi, Ems."

"Libby, did you get the turkey yet?" her sister asked in a rush.

Why was everyone calling her to ask about a dead bird?

"I got it yesterday," she informed her.

"And the cranberries. Andrew was such a mess last year …"

"Yes, I know. He's actually on the other line and was just telling me the same thing. He also wanted me to remind you about Brit and Kelsey's Brownie camp thing this weekend."

"Right, I almost forgot. Tell him he can drop them at my house for eight. I can give them breakfast before they have to go meet the rest of the troupe."

"Em, why don't you just call and tell him that yourself?" Libby questioned. "You don't need me as an intermediary."

"You're already on the phone with him though," her older sister remarked. "Just tell him what I said OK?"

"Fine." She waited for her sister to continue.

"Well? Aren't you going to tell him?" Emma replied after a moment of silence.

"You meant *now*?" Libby asked incredulously.

"Yes, I want to know what he says."

Libby *really* hated it when her family made her the go-between. Why they didn't just call each other and leave her out of it was beyond her.

She spent the next several minutes playing phone tag with her siblings and listening to them remind Libby of all the things she needed to get done before Christmas.

Story of her life.

CHAPTER 2

W hen Libby arrived at the office, the cheer had all but left her.

It was one thing for Andy and Emma to call, but then her other sister Megan plus Emma's twin Eden had also phoned to tell her the same things.

It would be nice if instead of ordering me around, even one of them would maybe help me for once.

"Not all, but just one would be *very* much appreciated," she muttered to herself as she got out of the car and walked into the building.

Was it her fault she was the only one who was still single and didn't have a spouse or children? Was it her fault she didn't have in-laws coming for a visit?

She wanted to be married and have a family like the next person, but husbands didn't just drop out of the air like snowflakes nor children sprout up from cabbage patches.

Libby walked into the office and was greeted by another example of her yuletide efforts. She'd spent all weekend decorating to make sure the staff had something bright and keeping with the season when they arrived on Monday morning.

"Libby, great work - I can't believe you did this all on your own!" Janice the head accountant said as they passed in the hall. "Let me know next time, I'd love to help."

Colleagues were willing to help her when it came to the office, so why wasn't her own family willing to when it came to a family tradition that had been established long before she was even *born*?

They had enjoyed forty-five years of Pearson Christmases in that house; the first five was just her parents before Andrew joined them.

So why was it that her, with only twenty-six years under her belt with their parents and six without, was charged with carrying on the tradition for the entire family? It didn't seem fair, but then again, whoever said life was when it came to family...

Libby loved this time of year but her siblings were taking it too far. They acted as if she had nothing better to do than prepare everything.

Thank goodness for work. If there was one sure thing that could take her mind off of her worries it was that.

As if on cue, the phone rang and her boss's extension appeared on the display.

"Libby, could you come into my office for a few minutes?"

"Sure thing, Steven, I'll be right there."

That was odd. What did he want that she needed to come into his office? Her mind immediately began to conjure up every conceivable scenario to explain it.

Steven Jefferson was a marketing genius, and one of the main reasons Libby had applied to the company right out of college.

She walked the long corridor to the door on the right.

"Come in," Steven said and Libby quickly turned the handle and entered.

"Morning," she greeted with a smile as she walked over to one of the chairs facing his desk and took a seat.

He smiled at her. "You did a really great job with the office decorating, Libby. I needed to commend you."

He's called her in there to congratulate her on her festive decorating skills? There she was, getting nervous over nothing.

"And since as you did such a great job with the office, I thought you would be the perfect person to pitch Hershell Chocolate's new Christmas campaign."

Libby's eyes almost jumped out of her head. Hershell Chocolate was one of their biggest clients.

"What about Amanda?" Libby asked, referring to the executive who usually handled Hershell.

Steven sighed. "Sadly, Amanda has decided to leave us," he informed. "That means we're in need of another senior marketing exec."

Libby's heart began to leap in her chest. Did this mean he was considering *her* for the job?

"I hadn't heard," she replied as she tried to remain calm.

"We were keeping it under wraps until the time came that we could announce her departure and the new appointment," Steven explained. "So we've asked you and Mark Clarke to come up with a presentation. The one Hershell likes best will be the one who takes over the account and the rest of Amanda's portfolio. Are you up for it?"

"Yes!" Libby answered a little too eagerly.

Steven laughed. "I like your gusto. You have ten days to prepare for the presentation," he continued as he explained what they were looking for in the new plan, and who would be present for the meeting.

This was quite possibly the biggest thing to happen in Libby's career since the day she was hired.

If she landed this account it could make her at the company. Ten days wasn't a lot of time, but she was sure she could make it happen.

"Thank you for considering me," she said as she got to her feet.

"You're a great worker Libby. We notice that here and we

reward the effort we see," Steven replied as he got to his feet to show her out. "I look forward to seeing your pitch."

"I won't let you down," she replied determinedly.

CHAPTER 3

*L*ibby could hardly contain her excitement as she walked back to her office.

She kept looking around to see if anyone was noticing the ridiculously large grin on her face, but they were all busy being productive.

She sat her desk and stifled a squeal of glee at how the morning had turned around. Then her phone disturbed her joy.

"Hey Megan," she said immediately, recognising the number from the display.

"Libby, can you pick up Justin and Julia from school for me today? Ron's parents are arriving later and his car just broke down on the highway so I have to go get them."

"Meg …" she tried to interrupt, but her sister's focus was so honed to her own desires she didn't even hear her.

"They need to be picked up at three and then Justin needs to go to soccer and Julia to dance class."

"Megan, I just got a big project at work. I can't leave the office early today," she protested.

"What? But you're the only person who's close enough to do it. What do you want me to do?"

"Maybe call one of their classmate's parents and see if they can?"

"You want to just pass your niece and nephew onto a stranger?" Megan argued.

Libby sighed. Why did they never understand? "Fine. I'll pick them up. I'll just skip lunch and leave early."

"Thanks sis, you're a gem," her sister replied quickly hanging up.

Libby sighed as she held the dead receiver. "So why don't I feel like one …"

CHAPTER 4

$\mathcal{C}$hristmas music was playing softly in the background as Libby hummed along.

This truly was the cheeriest time of year, and if all went well, it was going to be even more so for another reason – her promotion.

Her entire career was riding on this one presentation and Libby was determined to nail it.

She'd stayed up late for nights on end trying to come up with a concept, when suddenly it struck her while she was watching *A Muppet Christmas Carol* for the millionth time.

"The Hershell Company is going to be blown away," she mused as she worked.

Since then, her design boards were coming along brilliantly. A few more and she'd have everything ready to print and present. She'd called the Henson company regarding the potential use of muppets, and they agreed to discussing a deal if the client came onboard.

Everything was working out perfectly, all she had to do was complete and execute it, and the job of new senior marketing executive was all hers.

"Hey Miss Christmas, we were thinking of having a little

holiday party on Christmas Eve. What do you say?" her colleague Sharon said as she poked her head around the door to Libby's office.

"I thought we were already having an office party?"

Had something changed and Libby wasn't informed?

"Not here. At my place. Brian and Russel from accounting are down for it. Rob and Joan from printing said they'd join too. And Bobby, Stuart, Leslie and Hailey."

"So I'm the last to know?" Libby mused and Sharon grinned.

"No. I'm just going floor by floor."

"What time?" she asked. Sharon was always looking for a reason to party. She was single, thirty and gorgeous. She had no desire to marry or have a family. She was a career woman with a plan to open her own company in a few years. Libby had no doubt she could do it if only she would get her head out of fun and into some serious work. She spent more time planning events than she did getting her work done.

"Count me in," Libby said with a smile. "I could use some holiday cheer."

Just then her phone rang. It was her sister. Again.

"Hey, Eden."

"Look, I know I said I would pitch in to help you get things ready for Christmas, but I just can't. I am completely swamped. You're going to have to get it done yourself this year, sorry."

"Like every year you mean? Aw, you promised to help this time. It's a lot to do for one person. At least setting up and making dessert would make things easier. I cook the entire meal and clean and set up the house..."

"I know, but I really can't. Also, I don't think I'll be able to make dessert either. Adam surprised me with an early Christmas gift and he's taking me to Las Vegas for a few days. We won't be back until Christmas Eve and there's no way after a jaunt like that I'd be able to function."

Libby sighed. There was always a reason more important than

helping her. Eden had one, Andy did ... all of her siblings. It was as if they believed their lives were more important than hers.

Still, Libby did it every year because it wouldn't be Christmas otherwise. A Christmas with no turkey, cranberry sauce, yule log and all the other trimmings, plus her family, just wasn't Christmas.

It was an important time for them as a family.

"I guess I'll have to figure it out on my own again," she sighed.

"Forgive me?"

"Don't I always?" she answered as the weight of the additional preparations she had to make began to weigh on her. She could feel a headache coming on.

"That's because you're great. Love you. See you when I get back."

The call ended and Libby was left wondering how this had happened to her yet again. Sharon was still staring at her when she finally came back to her senses.

"Sorry Sharon, but..."

"But you have stuff to do for Christmas. I know. It's always the same with you. Let me guess, one of your sisters flaked on you again?" her friend said as she entered the room and shut the door.

She crossed the floor to the chair on the opposite side of Libby's desk and sat. She crossed her legs at the knees and began to strum her perfectly manicured nails on the corner of her desk.

"Why don't you ever just tell them to take a hike and that you're doing something for yourself for a change?" Sharon questioned.

"Because I can't," Libby replied as she picked up some loose papers and moved them from one corner of her desk to the other.

"Why not? You are a thirty-two-year-old puppet. They pull your strings and you do whatever."

"That's not fair," Libby retorted. "It isn't like that."

"Really? What about Thanksgiving?"

Why had she ever told Sharon about that?

It was the day before Thanksgiving. Megan had offered to take on the challenge this year. Everything had been going great until

Libby had got a panicked call from her sister telling her how she'd forgotten to defrost the turkey.

She'd burned up the sweet potato mash she'd prepared before time to save her the effort on the day. Everything was going up in flames and she needed Libby's help.

She was always the one to answer the call. She couldn't help it. She was the baby of the family. The one who was always called on to do things whenever her siblings wanted something. It was what she was used to and unfortunately, that hadn't changed in their minds even with the passing of twenty years.

So that day, Libby had left work early. Got into one of the mile-long lines at the butcher shop near her to get a fresh turkey for them to cook. She then went to the market to get the things her sister had wasted before going over to her house to take over the ship.

Megan wasn't used to cooking for so many and she underestimated what it took to prepare for such a big crowd.

Libby also gave up her dinner plans with Todd, the handsome partner from the law firm that occupied the floor below. He'd broken things off with her the day after Thanksgiving. He said she lived her life too much for her family and didn't have time for him.

"I know they're family and you love them, but Libby, there comes a time when you have to tell them 'no'," Sharon was saying now. "One word. Two letters."

"I know how it's spelled," Libby answered.

"I know you know 'I can't' and 'Maybe next time' but honestly, I don't think I've ever heard you say no - at least not to them. Everything is always 'yes'."

"I understand what you're saying," Libby sighed. "I just don't know how to do that. How do you disappoint your family at such a special time of year?"

"I don't know. Why don't you ask yours? They do it to you every year."

Sharon's words hurt. Mostly because they were true and Libby knew it.

"Libby, I hate to be the Grinch to your Cindy Lou Hoo, but maybe it's time for you to take a break from all the Christmas is for other people stuff, and look at having a holiday that *you'd* enjoy for a change. Tell me the truth. When the food is gone and it's time to go home, who's the one *also* left with the cleaning up and rearranging the furniture?"

Libby sat back in her seat and thought about it. The more she thought about it, the more unhappy she became.

She couldn't think of a single time since her parents' death that any of her siblings had stayed back after to help either.

"Me," she finally answered.

"Let me guess. They always have children to get to bed, or a long drive, or some other reason why they can't give you a helping hand." Sharon got to her feet and looked at Libby sadly. "I'm sorry to say it hon, but your siblings don't appreciate you. Maybe it's time you look at doing something for yourself. Take a vacation maybe. Go someplace warm or exotic to get away from this cold, and take a break from the crazy shopping lines and big family Christmas dinners. Just my suggestion."

Libby watched as Sharon left. She was gone but the words she'd spoken remained.

She swiveled in her chair and looked out the window at the falling snow outside.

A vacation from Christmas? It sounded lovely. More than lovely, it sounded like a dream, but there was no way she could do it.

Christmas was about family and togetherness. Libby couldn't just up and leave hers.

Could she?

CHAPTER 5

$\mathcal{T}$he phone rang agains as she sat thinking.

She hesitated to answer it when she saw that it was Megan on the line again. Still, she just couldn't resist picking up.

Hi Libs. It's me. I need a favor."

"What is it? I'm pretty busy here."

"Nothing too urgent. I just need you to pick up some groceries for me at the market. My in-laws are here as you know and I didn't get to the store yet. They won't have anything for dinner."

"Why can't you pick something up on your way home?"

"You know Laurel doesn't eat takeout. Besides, I have to work late tonight. By the time I get in it will be very late."

"And what about Ron? They're his parents," Libby pointed out.

"He was called out of town unexpectedly. It's just me and them at home for the next two days. You know how Laurel and I are. She tries everything she can think of to find fault. She's upset that I haven't made her a grandmother yet. You know what she says. ..."

"'A woman isn't a woman unless she has children.' Yes, I remember," Libby groaned. She knew what was coming. She was going to have to leave work early and skip lunch again in order to help her sister.

"Libs, please?"

"Alright, alright," she conceded huffily.

"Excellent! Thank you. Oh, could you possibly pick up my dry-cleaning from too? It's on your way. And if you could possibly make something quick for dinner I'd be eternally grateful. If Laurel has to cook there'll be no end of complaining…."

Libby was speechless. Her sister had gone from her collecting groceries, to picking up laundry and cooking for in-laws that weren't even her own!

"Megan, I'm working on a really big project right now. I'm up for a promotion."

"That's great. I'm sure you'll get it."

"But I really need to work on my presentation."

"You can still do that when you get home can't you? How long do you have?

"Just a few days."

"See, plenty of time to complete the task successfully. But today I really need you. Please, little sister?"

Libby sighed. She couldn't very well leave Megan in a bind. Her mother-in-law was the she-beast from hell.

If she didn't help now, she'd hear about it forever when Megan called to complain of the torment she was under.

"I'll leave work early, but you owe me," Libby replied tersely.

"I will treat you to dinner. Order anything you like."

"You owe me five dinners already."

"And you'll get them. As soon as I can, you'll get them." There was a pause. "Libs, I really have to go now. Do you have everything? Groceries, dry-cleaning, and dinner for my in-laws?"

"I have it, Megan."

"Great. Call you later."

The phone hung up immediately and Libby set the receiver down with a sigh. "No, you won't."

. . .

SHE GOT HOME AROUND NINE. The grocery store lines were longer than expected and it took a while to get to Megan's. Once there, she prepared the meal and chatted with her sister's in-laws. She'd stayed as long as she could to be polite, but Megan had yet to arrive by the time she left.

Libby strolled into the house and was met by a delighted Jingle. "Hey boy."

The little dog barked and began to circle, sniffing for any hidden treats.

"I didn't bring you anything, sorry. You're smelling the dinner I made for Megan," she said to him as she shuffled to the kitchen, kicking her heels off in the living room and walking barefoot.

When she passed the phone in the living room she was shocked to find there was a message from Megan. She pressed the button.

"Libs, you forgot the shirt I wanted to wear tomorrow –"

She stopped the message midway. Well, at least her sister had been honest.

She *did* call her later.

CHAPTER 6

The next day Libby found herself sitting on the couch in her living room looking over old photos.

Their father had been a constant photographer since before any of them were born. He had every traditional photo one could take during the holidays.

There were some of their mother putting the turkey in the oven. Some of Megan and Andy as children fighting over the last piece of stuffing. There was even a baby picture of Libby with fat cheeks and her face covered in chocolate frosting from the yule log.

"Such good times ..." she said with a sad smile. She missed her parents. There were hardly any holiday photos since they had left them.

Libby had tried to step into her father's shoes but it was impossible when she was doing everything else. Still, she managed to take a few shots from time to time.

One year she had enlisted her eight-year-old nephew to do pictures and he'd taken plenty but there were far more out of focus than in.

Then she found a picture of her mother surrounded by all of

her children. They were all grinning and her mom's cheeks were rosy and her smile bright.

"I miss you, Mom," Libby said softly. "Christmas isn't the same without you and Dad. Things have changed and I don't know if you'd be happy about it. Andy and the others are hardly here anymore. It's almost Christmas and again I am again doing everything on my own. When you were here this would never have happened."

She chuckled lightly. "Do you remember? You and I would team up and tackle every task. The others would come to help once the smell of the food started to fill the house." She laughed. "There's no one here now to do that though. I buy the groceries. Clean and decorate the house. Cook the food and clean it up after."

The phone rang. It always rang more often during the holidays.

"Hey big brother," Libby said as she slid down in the couch and put her feet up on the arm of it.

Andy sounded as if he was driving. She could hear the sound of the traffic blowing past the window and sound of horns honking.

"I need to borrow your laptop if I could."

"What's the matter with yours?"

"It died this morning and I need it to finish a document for work that's due tomorrow. Can I borrow yours?"

"OK, but you'll have it drop it back to me straight after. I need it for an important presentation that's in two days."

"I'll have it back. No worries."

"I mean it Andy. I need it back tomorrow so that I can finish the project in time. It might land me a promotion."

"It's about time you got one. You're the best they have."

"Thanks. It's for the Hershell Chocolate account."

"Hershell? That's a big deal. Are you sure you're ready?"

Her eyes widened. Didn't he just say she was the best they had? Libby did her best not to express her disappointment.

"Where are you?" she asked him.

"On my way to you."

"You mean you already knew that I'd let you borrow it?" she asked, a little taken aback.

"Sorry. But you never let us down, Sis. It's something we can always be sure of."

CHAPTER 7

"*A*ndy, it's me again. Why haven't you called me back? I need the laptop. Call me back."

Days had passed since she'd leant him the laptop but Libby couldn't reach Andy on the phone.

She paced her office again, as nettles covered her skin.

The client would be here today and her stupid brother had done a disappearing act. Which she wouldn't have minded it if it weren't for the fact that he still had her laptop.

Her phone rang minutes later and a wave of relief washed over her as she saw her brother's name appear on screen.

"Andy, where on earth are you? I've been calling and calling."

"I had to fly out to New York."

"*What?* New York, New York? But what about my laptop? I told you I needed it."

"I'm sorry. I had to take it with me, but I'm back now and I have it."

Libby's heart dropped into her stomach. "Oh my God. Where are you now?"

"At the airport. I just landed. I'm headed to you as soon as I get through arrivals."

Libby ran her fingers through her hair in dismay.

"The *airport*? Andy, that's too far. You won't get here in time. I told you I needed it back before the presentation!"

"I'm sorry. The work thing totally slipped my mind."

"The biggest day of my life and it slipped your mind?" Libby cried in disbelief.

She hung up. Her phone rang several times afterward but she wouldn't look at it.

Everything was ruined. Her PowerPoint was on that laptop and there was no way for her to access it otherwise. "I should have saved what I had to a memory stick ... why didn't I do that?" she winced, as tears filled her eyes.

The client would be arriving soon and she had nothing to show them.

Libby walked toward Steven's office. She had to tell him the bad news. She had no idea how he would take it, but she was disappointed enough for both of them.

She passed Mark Clarke in the hall on the way there. There would be no end to his arrogance once he got the promotion. The entire marketing team would live to regret her foolishness.

Libby's pace slowed as she approached Steven's office. She looked at his nameplate outside, written in gold, and trembled. She couldn't believe this was happening. Her boss had given her a chance and now she was here to beg for another.

She took a deep breath, raised her hand, and knocked.

"Come in."

Steven greeted her with a smile that Libby tried to return but failed.

Just as she'd failed at the task he'd given her.

"Libby, all ready for later?" he asked with a smile.

She hesitated. "Actually no. There was a problem with my laptop and I don't have the PowerPoint file to hand."

The words left her lips like molasses from a bottle on a cold day.

Steven's gaze leveled at her.

"What do you mean? Can't you just upload it to a PC here?"

She shook her head. She swallowed the lump in her throat.

"I didn't save and download it because it wasn't quite finished. Tomorrow - I can have it completed tomorrow. Is there any chance the client might be persuaded to delay until then?"

Libby was internally crossing her fingers and her toes.

She just needed another chance. She could have everything ready by tomorrow. She just needed time.

"There is nothing I can do for you Libby. The client's only free window was today. Plus the board wants to make the announcement as soon as possible regarding the new senior marketing executive." Steven stood and walked toward her. He laid a comforting hand on her arm. "I'm sorry."

That was it. One mistake and she'd lost the biggest opportunity of her life.

She should never have allowed her brother to borrow her laptop. It was the company's, so she really should've known better, but he needed her help.

Now she was paying for it.

"Steven," Libby pleaded. "Isn't there any way? I know this is really good."

"I'm sorry Libby. This was a one-time chance."

Libby stood dumbfounded as Steven turned his back on her and walked back to his seat. He sat with both hands on the armrests and looked at her. "If Mark successfully completes the presentation, I will announce his appointment at the Christmas party."

Libby stared at him for several seconds as she tried to internalize what he'd said.

She'd blown it. It was over. Really and truly over.

"Thank you for the opportunity. I'm so sorry I let you down," Libby said softly as she lowered her eyes from him.

"Not more than me. I was sure you were the best person for this position, but I had to prove it to the board," Steven said bitterly. "It'll be a hard pill to swallow when I have to go back to them."

"Steven, just twenty-four hours?" Libby pleaded again. "That's all I need. I know my presentation will blow them away. I'm sure of it. If you could just postpone it for a day? A few hours, even. I can get it all together for you. I can make this happen."

"I wish I could Libby. I really wish I could. But there is nothing I can do. Hershell set the timing because it worked with their schedule. There is no tomorrow or a few hours. It's now or never."

CHAPTER 8

*L*ibby could barely process anything as she trudged slowly back to her office.

People passed her on the way to wish her good luck with the presentation, but nothing reached her.

She returned to her office, closed and locked the door and then sat at her desk and wept.

Her eyes were puffy and sore by the time the knocking on her door got her attention.

She forced herself to wipe her face and got a tissue to blow her nose before she dared open it. Unlocking the door, she took a deep breath.

Sharon was standing there with the saddest look on her face. "I heard."

Libby let her in and then quickly closed the door behind her. People in the hall were staring. She couldn't deal with them right now.

"What happened?" her friend asked.

Libby walked around her desk and flopped into her chair.

"You had this. What went wrong?" Sharon persisted.

"Me. That's what went wrong. Me."

"You? What did you do?"

"I loaned my brother the laptop when he had an emergency with work. I told him I needed it back the next day. He forgot and took it with him to New York."

Sharon's eyes looked as if they were about to explode from her skull. "Are … you … *kidding* me?" she bellowed

"Shhh…keep your voice down."

"How can *you* keep your voice down? Your brother shafts you over the biggest opportunity of your life, and you're this calm about it?"

"It was my fault. I should never have lent it to him in the first place. It was company property, not mine. I was the idiot here."

"Libby, are you for real? You're blaming yourself for this? Your brother is the absolute worst! Yes, you were wrong to give him the laptop, but he was worse for not bringing it back when he knew you needed it. He really took it to New York?" Sharon's head was shaking as she sighed deeply.

"It doesn't matter now," Libby stated. "It's over."

"Libby, for goodness sake, get angry. Do something. This can't go on. You can't spend the rest of your life being your siblings' scapegoat for everything. You need to think of having a life of your own. I know you want to hold on to traditions, but for your own sake, you need to create new ones."

Sharon was on her feet a moment later and striding to the door.

She left Libby alone and confused.

She thought about everything that had happened over the last few days and weeks - the endless demands, and requests for 'favors'.

And Andy's words as he casually drove to borrow the laptop he already knew she'd lend him.

You never let us down, Sis. It's something we can always be sure of.

CHAPTER 9

The following afternoon, Libby dropped her stuff at the door, stomped into the living room and flopped down on the couch with a groan.

Andrew had since apologised about the incident with the laptop by saying there would be other promotions and not to sweat the small stuff. Small stuff. He saw the biggest opportunity of her career as 'small stuff.'!

It was getting beyond ridiculous.

Today she'd received another call from Eden informing her that *her* in-laws had come in early to surprise them, and could Libby take her children and their friends Christmas shopping.

She'd spent three hours with eight children between the ages of six and ten, as she tried to help them manage their money and pick up the toys they were searching for.

It was a test of anyone's nerves and Libby's were fried.

Jingle trotted into the room and flopped on the rug by her feet. "Hey little guy," she said with a frustrated sigh. He looked at her with his big dark eyes and snorted. "That's exactly how I feel," she replied as she stretched out a hand to scratch behind his ears.

She lay on the couch for several minutes as she decided whether she wanted to move or not. Her feet hurt, her back hurt and she was hungry. She had taken the children shopping but she wasn't about to manage all of them at one table with food.

She rolled onto her side and noticed the light blinking on the phone. She had another message from Andy. Maybe he'd had second thoughts and was calling to properly apologise?

"Hi, Libs. Meet me at the mall tomorrow? I need some help finding a present for Molly. I'll be there around five. Meet you at the west entrance. Bye!"

She couldn't speak. Tears were stinging the backs of her eyes.

"He didn't even ask," she said to herself as a tear rolled down her cheek. *None* of theme ever asked, or if they did, they took it for granted that the answer would be yes and if it wasn't they made a fuss until it did.

"OK, that's *it*," she announced, so loud that it made Jingle jump up from his nap. The dog gave a started yelp as he tried to figure out what was going on. "Enough."

She got to her feet and hurried upstairs, Jingle scurrying after her. She could hear his large paws as he came up the stairs behind her.

"Someplace warm," she muttered to herself as she began rummaging in her closet. She pulled out her suitcase and tossed it on the bed.

Libby wasn't thinking, she was just packing. She found her bathing suit, some shorts, a few dresses, and shoes. Anything that would work.

"If they think I'm sticking around to be their Christmas Girl Friday this year, they're mistaken," she said angrily. Jingle was completely bewildered and stuck his nose in her stuff to see what was going on.

When the suitcase was packed she opened her laptop and began searching for flights. Her favorite discount site had tons of offers but nothing was grabbing her.

That is until she saw a special and her eyes widened. *Hawaii?*

Perfect.

Libby didn't hesitate; she booked the flight and used her discount coupon to get a further $25 off her ticket.

"Now where to stay…" she asked as she began another search. Jingle barked beside her. "I know. You're hungry," she commented as her fingers nimbly skated over the keys. Her eyes flicked through pictures of potential accommodations, but it was taking longer than expected and Jingle was getting increasingly agitated.

While Libby was starting to feel increasingly better, as the prospect of a quieter, more relaxing Christmas materialized.

She hummed a festive tune as she danced around the kitchen pulling together something for herself for dinner. She grabbed kibble from the cupboard and a can of canned dog food. She mixed them together and put them in Jingle's bowl. He was already eating before she got it to the floor, and so she returned to her laptop.

There were so many options to choose from, but she didn't want to stay anywhere too commercial or crazy.

So the Marriott and the like were definitely out.

Then Libby came across an option for a guesthouse just a few minutes drive from the airport, and right on the beach.

"Kalea Inn," she mused out loud, as she began to skim the reviews. They were all overwhelmingly positive. The place rated four and a half stars which was excellent, and the price was perfect.

Finally, her decision was made. She pressed the 'Book' button and it was done.

Libby smiled to herself as she leaned against the kitchen counter.

This year, she was getting out of town and heading for somewhere a million miles from small town Christmas central.

She needed an escape.

CHAPTER 10

*F*our days later Libby was standing outside Kona Airport waiting for her ride.

The guesthouse owner had sent her an email about her booking at the Kalea Inn later that same night and they'd been corresponding over the past few days to ensure that everything was ready for her arrival.

The second she stepped off the plane Libby found herself with a beautiful purple lei around her neck and she smiled.

Outside, the sun was blissfully bright and warm, and the air tropical. It was just what she was hoping for.

A warm breeze blew across her face as she waited for someone from the inn to pick her up. She got her phone out and called home.

"Hey Sharon how's Jingle?"

Her friend was dog-sitting for the week she'd be gone.

Before leaving she'd called Andy to let him and the others know she was going away and wasn't going to be back until after Christmas.

That didn't go over well but Libby hadn't listened long enough to hear his surprise or remonstration.

She'd made up her mind and she wasn't letting anyone change it.

A jeep pulled up and a man got out.

The vehicle was like something she'd seen on safari videos on Discovery Channel, but the side of it read Kalea Inn.

Libby's eyes grew large at the sight of the man walking toward her. He was over six feet tall and the roots of his hair were dark but the ends were lighter from the sun.

His skin was golden tan and his short-sleeved cotton shirt clung to his muscles. On his left arm, the ends of a black tattoo peeked out from beneath the sleeve. His chin was covered in a short, neatly cropped beard beneath a mustache.

The guy should be on the cover of a romance novel.

The man strode toward her, a folded sign in his hands which he opened as he looked around.

It took Libby a few seconds to notice the name on the card was her own.

She walked toward him and dragged her bag behind her.

"I'm Libby," she said brightly as she flashed him a smile. He looked at her and gave a polite smile so quick that if she blinked she would've missed it.

"Rob," he nodded. "Welcome to Kohala."

"Thanks. Nice to meet you. It's good to have a face to go with the name," she replied amiably. She was smiling more than she should but she couldn't help it. She was in a tropical paradise for the holidays, and her driver looked like someone from a movie.

"Sure," he replied as he took Libby's luggage and started for the jeep.

She looked around as she followed him. "Isn't there anyone else?"

"You're it today," Rob said as he hoisted her bag into the back. "You can sit up front with me," he added as he walked to the driver's side and got in.

Libby walked around the front of the vehicle. He opened the door for her from the inside and she climbed in.

The cabin of the car was neat. She couldn't help the surreptitious inspection as she got in. His car was much cleaner than hers. She always had an extra pair of shoes or three on the passenger side.

Rob started the engine and they began the journey to the inn. Lava fields spread before her in red and black earth splendor, amidst verdant palm trees.

Libby could hardly believe she was really in Hawaii.

"It's so beautiful," she commented to herself as she stared out at the landscape.

"You said it was your first time to the island?" Rob questioned. He was driving with one hand and leaning on the window with the other.

"Very first," Libby answered. "And you? You've been here long?"

"Seven years," he answered shortly.

"I guess this beauty is normal to you, then."

Rob didn't answer. He just looked out the window.

"So how far is it?" she asked eventually.

"Just over twenty minutes. The inn is just up past Waialea Beach."

Libby smiled at the way the strange names rolled off his tongue. He looked like he belonged on an ad for lumberjacks or something. She could definitely see him in one of her ad campaigns. He'd be perfect.

"What?" he asked shortly. She was so lost in her own head she hadn't realized she was staring.

"Sorry," she laughed. "I was just thinking."

"Your mother never teach you that you don't stare?"

Now Libby was a bit taken back by his abruptness. "Actually she did. Sorry," she replied shortly.

So much for an Aloha welcome.

. . .

233

THE DRIVE TOOK LESS time than she imagined. Twenty minutes went by very quickly when everything around was so spectacular.

The next thing Libby knew they were stopped outside a simple two-storey building, painted in cream with a brown roof and trim.

What stood out to her was that there wasn't a single Christmas decoration apparent. She glanced around a little more while Rob unloaded her bag.

Nope, nothing.

"You guys don't decorate for the holidays?" she asked in surprise. The rest of the Big Island she'd seen on the way had some signs of festive cheer, but not the Kalea Inn.

"I don't do Christmas," Rob answered gruffly. "This way to check-in."

Libby's forehead wrinkled as she followed him into the building.

What did he mean that he didn't *do* Christmas? Who didn't do Christmas?

But there wasn't a smile on his face and she knew instinctively that he wasn't joking.

They were met at reception by a pretty dark-haired woman who had a brilliant smile.

"Apikalia, could you see that Ms. Pearson gets checked in. She's in room nine," Rob informed her as he left Libby's bag at the desk and then disappeared into a room behind it.

"Mele Kalikimaka," the receptionist said brightly. "Welcome to the Kalea Inn."

Libby swallowed, realising that if she truly wanted to escape Christmas, she'd very definitely picked the right place.

CHAPTER 11

$\mathcal{T}$he next couple of days passed by in a blur and Libby was loving every second of it. She'd *definitely* made the right choice to embark on a last minute adventure.

Her room was on the top floor overlooking the ocean. The guesthouse had its own private beach, a secluded cove up the coast from Waialea.

In fact, there was nothing else nearby as far as the eye could see; the absolute perfect getaway.

It was also nice to have people taking care of her instead of the other way round. Libby usually didn't mind, but after a while, it began to weigh on you, especially when the people you were doing it for didn't seem to care just how much it was taking out of you.

Today she wore a red sundress with a white tropical flower print along the skirt. It was sleeveless and showed off her slightly toned arms.

She'd worked very hard for that little bit of tone. Libby tended to be softer; she wasn't overweight, but she had gentle curves and a propensity to gain even more of those if she didn't pay attention.

Mint green sandals were on her feet. She had a matching bag too, but she didn't have plans to leave the inn that day. She just wanted to spend it on the beach enjoying the warm breezes and golden sunshine.

She walked down to the breakfast area and found it relatively full, but there were still a few tables available.

The inn had twelve rooms and they were all occupied for the festive season.

Libby had briefly encountered several of her fellow guests over the past few days, but none touched her heart like Naomi - a seventy-three-year-old woman who reminded her so much of her mother.

Now she walked over to where the older woman was sitting. "Good morning."

"Nice to see you, dear. Join me?"

Libby didn't need to be asked twice. She pulled out the chair beside Naomi and took a seat. "Thanks for letting me sit with you. How're you doing today?"

"I'm very well thank you. How are you?"

"Great. Have you ordered already?" She skimmed over the menu. There weren't many choices, but what they had was fresh and always wonderful.

"I was just waiting for the waitress," Naomi informed her. "What are your plans today?"

"Nothing," Libby sighed happily. "Just enjoying the sunshine. What about you?" she asked as the waitress poured water when they'd placed their orders.

"Well, I'm on a mission today actually," the older woman said intriguingly. She then turned to the vacant seat beside her and picked up a silver urn.

"I'm going to see my Charlie off," she added with a gentle smile.

"Oh Naomi ..." Libby began but she wasn't sure what she wanted to say.

The older woman had mentioned her husband had died but she didn't realize it was so recently.

Naomi smiled as she patted the top of the urn lovingly. "He

always wanted to come back here," she said. "He proposed to me on this island fifty years ago. We planned to come back this Christmas to commemorate it, but poor Charlie didn't make it."

Libby swallowed the lump that had formed in her throat. She couldn't help it, hearing Naomi's heartbreaking words made her want to cry.

"Don't get upset," the other woman said brightly. "Charlie wouldn't want anyone crying over him. He always lived his life a second at a time, and he enjoyed every minute of it. That's why I'm here. He wanted me to come, even though he wasn't going to be with me in body, but promised he'd be with me in spirit." Naomi hugged the urn to her before setting it back on its seat.

"Where on the island are you going?" Libby asked as the waitress returned with their coffee and juice.

"To Pu'u Ku'ili," she replied, referring to the famed old cinder cone, a popular sightseeing spot on the island.

"How are you getting there?"

"I've arranged a ride," the woman answered.

Libby looked aghast. "You're going to do this alone?"

"It's fine. I promised Charlie. The sooner the better to get it over with."

Libby was resolute. There was no way she was going to allow that. "If you don't mind the company ...may I come with you?"

A small smile spread across Naomi's face. "Are you sure?"

"I'd really love it if you'd allow me," Libby replied. "I'd feel a whole lot better knowing you weren't alone."

"I'd like that."

The pair continued to sit and talk while they waited for breakfast to arrive. Once it did they took turns sampling from the other's choice and laughing about having made the wrong decision for themselves.

It felt good to just enjoy a meal with someone and actually make plans with them, instead of hearing their demands.

Libby truly wanted to be there for Naomi. She couldn't imagine saying goodbye forever to the one you loved would be easy.

She'd never been married, not even close, but she remembered the interactions of her parents. Theirs was the ideal that she based all her relationships on.

Her parents had a love that transcended most norms. They genuinely loved one another and sacrificed for the other.

It seemed Naomi and Charlie's marriage had been the same.

*a*fter breakfast, Libby excused herself momentarily to get her bag from her room and rushed back, unwilling to keep Naomi waiting long.

On the way, she ran into Rob – literally. Their shoulders collided as she was going up the stairs and he was coming down.

"Sorry," she apologized in a rush as she continued on her journey up. She felt his questioning gaze follow her but she didn't turn around.

Minutes later she was rushing through the reception area outside to where she'd told Naomi she'd meet her.

The older woman was already standing beside the inn's jeep.

"All set?" Libby asked.

"We were waiting for you," Naomi replied.

"We?"

A second later Rob stepped out from the other side of the jeep. He looked at her silently and Libby felt the hairs on the back of her neck stand on end.

He had an intense expression on his face that even though not unpleasant, formed knots in her stomach.

"Rob said he'd take us," Naomi informed her.

"Let's get you ladies boarded so we can get going," he stated as he stepped forward to help Naomi into the jeep. He turned to Libby after and gave her a hand into the back.

She sat on the bench that lined the back of the jeep's flatbed and watched as the lava fields once again came into view.

Once or twice she thought she caught Rob's eyes looking back at her in the rearview mirror. It was nice of him to offer to take Naomi here today.

And a little perplexing how he could be so cold one minute, then do something kind and courteous the next.

It wasn't long before they arrived at Pu'u Ku'ili.

Rob drove them as far as he could along the trail, but they still had to walk a short distance to get to the top.

He held Naomi's hand while Libby carried the urn.

When they reached the summit Libby stood on the cone and looked around her.

The view was unforgettable. Inland, the earth was charred and the dirt either black or a dark red. There was hardly any vegetation nearby, but in the distance, she could see sprigs of grass and the green of a few shrubs.

Towards the ocean, she could see buildings standing uniformly together, their roofs various shades of brown and more greenery to be found nearby. The ocean was the most beautiful blue she'd ever seen. Paler near the shore, it deepened from azure to a rich cerulean.

It was breath-taking.

"Give Charlie to me," Naomi asked then, as Libby stood staring. She nodded quickly and handed the urn over.

Then she stepped back a little to where Rob stood a few feet away, to allow Naomi the privacy needed for her last farewell to her husband.

Libby watched as it unfolded. She wanted to make sure Naomi was all right, but she also couldn't help but admire how unaffected and unflinching she was to so something she herself was sure would have her in tears.

She wondered where the woman got the strength from.

"It must be such a horrible thing to lose the one you love," she mumbled to Rob as they watched. "To have to say goodbye after so many wonderful years together. Knowing that you will never see them again."

He exhaled. "Hurts no matter how long you were together," he muttered, much to her surprise.

Libby turned to face him but found he wasn't looking at her at all, but at Naomi.

Her gaze shifted to where the older woman stood. Was that it? The reason he always seemed so cagey and distant? Had he lost someone too?

She turned back to Rob and this time their eyes met. "Why did you come?" he asked. "You don't even know her."

"You don't have to know someone well to want to be there for them through something difficult," she answered, then turned back to Naomi. "I just didn't want to let her do this alone."

"Neither did I," he said and Libby's eyes moved back to him. "Like you said, it isn't something you should do alone, especially at her age."

Maybe he wasn't as boorish as she'd first believed him to be. Maybe he was just a man who was dealing with something she could never understand. Something that Naomi could though.

Did Rob truly identify with the older woman's loss? Was that why he couldn't let her say goodbye alone?

Libby had more questions now than when she'd first met him. Who exactly was Rob and why was he in Kohala?

He obviously wasn't a native Hawaiian. So what had brought him to the islands to run the inn?

The faint sound of a song wafted toward Libby's ears then and both she and Rob again focused their attention back on Naomi. She was singing.

It was an old song, something from the forties or fifties Libby guessed. She was swaying in place as she turned the urn over and allowed her late husband's ashes to spill into the breeze to every note.

"Goodbye Charlie …" Libby whispered to herself as she watched the scene.

Now the older woman walked toward them, the empty urn hugged to her chest. She smiled. "He's gone now," she said. "He'd be happy."

Libby couldn't help it; she had to give Naomi a hug. The older woman accepted her embrace and patted her back soothingly. "Thank you for being here - both of you," she said.

"You're welcome," Rob answered quietly. "It was an honor."

CHAPTER 13

*L*ater, Libby couldn't sleep, still affected by the events of the day. She kept thinking of her family and wondering how they were doing.

Her siblings had been calling her incessantly since her arrival, and while she was happy to send the odd text, she still refused to take any calls.

This trip was all about escape, some time for herself, away from them.

She stood on the balcony outside her room and looked out over the dark water. The sky and sea seemed to meet like ink on the horizon. Only the stars differentiated one from the other.

She leaned against the rail, the silk nightgown she wore danced around her calves as she watched the white peaks of waves appear and disappear in the distance.

Half an hour passed and she was still unable to sleep. So she changed into a sundress and went downstairs for a walk.

Voices coming from the dining room caught her attention as she headed for the front door.

She followed the sound to find Rob and two other men sitting talking around a small table.

"Seems we aren't the only night owls," the first man commented when he saw her in the doorway. She recognised him as another guest.

He was cleanly shaven with a bald head and a slender face.

"I'm sorry. I didn't mean to intrude. I just heard voices …" Libby explained hesitantly.

"No intrusion. Come on in," the man said with a friendly wave of his hand beckoning her to join them.

Another man sat beside him. He looked similar, though his hair was dark and closely cropped, and his face fuller and more tanned.

"I'm Nate," the other guest said as he extended her hand to her. "This is my twin brother Greg."

Now Libby saw the resemblance. It was in the eyes. They both had bright blue eyes.

"Libby," she answered as she shook each man's hand in turn. She looked at their host. "Rob."

He nodded but said nothing. He was reclined in his seat with his foot folded over the other casually and his arms crossed over his stomach.

"So what brings you to the island?" Greg asked with a smile.

She smiled. "Escaping Christmas," she admitted truthfully. "Family mostly."

"They giving you a hard time?"

"More like they don't see me as anything more than their go-fetch-it girl," she chuckled but there was no mirth to it. "My favorite time of the year, and all I hear from them is what they need from me. No one ever seems to realize that I need things too."

"Material stuff you mean?" Nate questioned.

"No. More for them to be there for me the way I'm always there for them. It gets pretty tiring being the one whom everyone depends on, yet there is no one there when you need the same."

"Well, my poor brother knows all about that," Nate laughed and Libby looked at him and Greg curiously. "I have cancer," he blurted out then and she was taken completely by surprise.

She fumbled for something to say and found herself tongue-tied.

"You don't have to say anything. You were on the subject of dependency and I just wanted to make things clear from the start," Nate continued.

"I'm so sorry," she muttered.

"I told you that you didn't have to say anything," he smiled. "People always say they're sorry. It's nice but unnecessary. I'm alright. I've made peace with everything."

"So Kohala is part of your adventure?" Libby asked.

"It's the seventh thing on my bucket list."

Libby was completely astounded at Nate's positivity. She had never met anyone who knew they were dying.

She couldn't imagine what that must feel like to know that your end was imminent. The thought gave her a slight chill.

"Rob was telling us that you helped Naomi scatter her husband's ashes the other day," Nate continued while his brother sat quietly and Libby could immediately see that while he had accepted his fate, Greg had not.

They chatted on for a while before eventually Nate yawned. "I think it's time for me to go. I'm getting tired."

"Goodnight guys," Greg said as he helped his brother to his feet.

"Goodnight to you both," Libby replied. "See you guys in the morning."

"Maybe we can do breakfast?" Nate suggested. "I'd love to hear more about your work for the chocolate company."

"See you here."

Libby watched the brothers as they went.

It was odd, but meeting them only made her think of her own family even more. Nate and Greg depended on each other and there was no animosity between them. One was dying and the other was doing everything he could to be there for him.

It made her feel like her problems with her siblings were silly really.

Now, she turned to look at Rob. He'd remained quiet for most of the conversation, only choosing to say something if a question was directed to him.

She shifted uncomfortably in her seat. Maybe she should go now too? It wasn't as if Rob was going to stay on and chat. He hardly ever spoke to her.

"How's Naomi?" he asked then.

"Great. I had dinner with her earlier."

"Good," Rob replied. "The other day must've brought up a lot of memories. Good and bad."

Libby watched him carefully. The visit to Pu'u Ku'ili had affected more than just Naomi.

"Who did you lose?" she asked softly. She watched him as she spoke and his face was impassive as he turned to her.

"What makes you think I lost someone?"

She smiled weakly. "I recognize it. When I lost my parents I looked like that whenever someone started talking about them," Libby explained.

Rob stared at her for a long time and she could see the hesitation in his eyes. "My wife."

"Your wife? I'm ... so sorry."

"Her name was Kalea. I named this place after her. She was born on the island and wanted to come back to start a business and give back to the community. We poured everything we had into getting this place. Then she died, so I was left to run it alone."

Libby couldn't imagine how he felt losing his wife. "I truly am sorry Rob. May I ask what happened to her?"

"A brain tumor. We were married for just over a year when it got her," he continued. "On Christmas Eve."

Which explained why there were no decorations and why Rob didn't do Christmas. He was still missing his wife.

"She loved this time of year. It was what she lived for really. The holidays and decorations, and family get togethers. Kalea always wanted to make people happy."

Libby felt a tear roll down her cheek as Rob talked about his late wife. There was still so much love in his voice.

"I'm sorry. This is hard for you. I shouldn't have asked," Libby apologised as she wiped her cheek.

"I don't know why I'm telling you actually," he continued. "I never talk about her to anyone. It must be everything with Naomi … and now Nate that has me thinking about her." He turned to her. "Sorry for getting you down."

"Don't apologize. I asked."

"When did you lose your parents?" He had turned in his seat to face her better. It was the first time Libby noticed how bright his eyes were, even in sadness.

"Six years ago. They died days apart, and it was pretty much left to me to take over everything they cared about," she admitted. "All our family's stuff. The house. Traditions. It all became my responsibility."

"Why you? Didn't you say you had siblings?"

"Four of them," Libby answered. "They all have families of their own. Children and in-laws. They don't have much time for anything else."

"Including you, I take it?"

Her cheeks warmed at the inquiry. "Sometimes I feel like I'm a servant instead of their sister. Running around to pick up their children. Collect their dry-cleaning and deal with upholding our family stuff all on my own. It's been hard. Honestly, this year I was so tired of having to do everything for the holidays that I decided that I wasn't - going to do it, I mean. That's why I came here."

"Do you hate them?"

Her eyes grew wide. "No. Of course not. I love them a lot. That's why it hurts so much to be treated like I don't matter to them. That what's important to me, means nothing to them at all."

"I understand," Rob said as he got to his feet. "It isn't easy to bear the weight of a legacy on your shoulders. Or someone else dream."

Libby stood too, feeling tired all of a sudden, and realising that she and Rob kind of understood each other in some strange way.

He was doing all of this in the name of a wife who could no longer fulfil her dream, while she was doing all she could to keep her parent's traditions alive.

"Walk you back to your room?" he stated as he started for the door.

"How do you do it?" she asked, following as he left the dining room and up the stairs.

"Do what?"

"Continue on every day on your own with no one here who understands?"

"I surf," Rob said with a smile. "When I'm out on the waves there isn't anything for me to worry about. It's just me and the waves. It makes me think of her. She loved the water. We met at a surf competition in California. It was love on the waves," he said with a smile. "I knew the first time I saw her cruise through that curl that I'd found the perfect woman for me."

Libby smiled. "It sounds wonderful."

"It was wonderful." He looked around him. "I know she would've done more with this place, especially now, but I just can't seem to get my mind there."

"I'll be honest with you. I was wondering about it when I arrived. I was surprised that there were no Christmas decorations, or anything remotely festive."

He sighed. "I don't know why I should bother really. No one's complaining. Except for you," he added lightly.

Libby considered what he'd said as they walked the corridor to her room.

There were quite a few people here escaping the holidays for their own, mostly sad reasons. Even the owner had a tale of woe.

Maybe, despite what Rob thought, Kalea Inn *did* need a dash of Christmas spirit to brighten the mood and hearts of everyone staying there.

CHAPTER 14

*S*lowly but surely, Libby was falling in love with Hawaii.

She was used to the fast pace of the marketing world, but here, they did things differently.

It was the most relaxed Christmas she'd ever had. No running to the grocery store a thousand times to stand in mile-long lines. No excessive list of gifts to buy, because Christmas wasn't Christmas if you didn't break your credit card with buying toys and presents.

Then there was the absurd pressure she put on herself to make sure everything was just as her mother and father would have made it when they were alive. They way her siblings expected it.

No, life didn't have to be that way.

Today, the sand was cool as she walked along the beach in her brand new swimsuit. She was still a bit bashful so she'd bought a cute floral print, halter neck tankini her second day on the island. It fit her perfectly and made her feel confident about her body without making her feel exposed.

The wind skated off the ocean sending a cool breeze over her skin. Libby couldn't help but smile at how wonderful it was to feel sand between her toes and smell the salty freshness of the ocean.

She looked out onto the water. Whitecaps peaked the waves,

and a lone surfer occupied the water beyond the reef. She stopped to watch.

The waters near the inn weren't the type that called international surfers to try their luck, these were calm and could easily be maneuvered by a novice.

Beyond the reef, however, the waves were larger, forming into curls, and the surfer was making the most of them. Lowering beneath the barrelling edge of a wave he was a master on the board.

Libby never pretended to be brave. Climbing on a surfboard and going out into water she couldn't stand in and probably couldn't even *swim* in, was not her cup of tea.

However, it didn't mean she didn't appreciate watching those who could. She stood and watched as the surfer tamed the waves and rode the final one into shore not far from where she stood. She stared as he carried his board in, dragging his long dark hair back with a hand before jogging in her direction.

It was only as he got closer that she realized who it was.

Rob smiled at her. "I see you're out early," he commented.

"It's such a beautiful day I thought a walk on the beach would do me good," she answered.

"Just on the beach? The water's perfect."

Libby looked at the ocean. He was right, it did look inviting. "I haven't done much swimming since I got here …"

"How much have you done?"

"None actually," she laughed. "I've been spending my days wandering or sunbathing or just meeting people. I've met so many nice people since I arrived here. You wouldn't believe some of the stories I've heard."

"I can imagine actually," Rob informed her lightly. "You'd be surprised how many broken-hearted and lonely people end up here."

Libby thought about what he was saying. She'd already encountered a number of people with stories like those of Naomi, Nate, and Greg.

Even a few like her who felt unappreciated and were seeking a change.

However, she also saw another element. She saw what they were truly after – a getaway from Christmas commercialism to somewhere more laidback and easygoing, where they could find their own kind of peace and joy away from the noise of traditional festivity.

"Rob, have you ever thought of doing something different for Christmas?" Libby asked.

His forehead wrinkled. "Like what?"

"Not traditional Christmas obviously, but different to what other places offer at this time of year. I'm talking about something beyond the surface. Something that touches the heart."

"I never really thought about it," he admitted as he studied her carefully.

"Well, I have."

Libby took a deep breath.

What she was about to suggest was insane and completely none of her business, but it was something that had been nagging her since the other night.

"I work in marketing for a living. I'm used to figuring out what people want and giving it to them. It's how you sell. You give people what they want, or make them believe they want something they never know they did."

"You think this place needs better marketing?" Rob questioned with some skepticism.

"Not marketing per se. I'm talking about doing something for the people here who are trying to get back to what Christmas is truly about."

The moment the words left her mouth Rob's expression changed. The lines in his forehead smoothed out and he sort of squinted at her.

Then he laughed softly. "That sounds like something Kalea would've said."

Libby wasn't sure if resembling something his late wife would've thought of was good or bad, but it didn't stop her from presenting her case.

"Your wife wanted this place to mean something. You said so yourself. It was her dream. So this year, why don't you make it the dream of all the staff and guests too?"

Rob stuck his board in the sand. "What exactly do you have in mind?"

She smiled. "A day of honoring what Christmas is really all about. No gifts, or spending money on each other, but instead time and sharing."

Rob's small laugh grew to a chuckle as she continued. "You sound more and more like her the more I listen to you."

"Then your wife was a very wise woman," Libby grinned.

Rob's eyes met hers. "She was."

She felt her stomach knot as he looked at her.

"Do you surf?" he asked unexpectedly.

"No," Libby laughed. "I've never even tried."

"I can teach you."

She shook her head. "I don't know about that…"

"I'll make you a deal," he countered. "If you let me teach you the basics about surfing, I'll allow you to execute this … plan of yours."

Libby's eyes grew wide. Did he just say he'd let her run with her idea? She couldn't describe the feeling in her stomach. It was like getting another shot at the promotion she'd missed out on.

"Great. So where do we start?"

"First things first," Rob chuckled. "Hold your board with two hands when you're carrying it out. You can tuck it under your arm like this when you're on the beach," he said as he showed her what to do, then handed the board to her for her to try.

Libby tucked the board under her arm.

"This is going to be too long for you given your height and weight," he informed. "You'd need one more than a foot shorter.

But I can still show you a few things with it before we hit the water"

Libby nodded until she realized. "Hit the water?"

"Yes," Rob smiled. "You can't surf if you aren't comfortable out there," he said as he turned toward the water. "I need to see how you handle yourself."

Seems she was going to get wet that morning after all.

$\mathcal{R}$ob continued to explain the basics of surfing while Libby listened quietly, nodding and following his example when she needed to.

Before she knew it, he was telling her it was time to hit the water. She waded out into the surf as he led the way.

Her heart was beating a bit faster in her chest as the water climbed higher and higher up her body.

She was good for a few feet but soon she could no longer feel the bottom and had to begin to tread water.

"You okay?" he asked as he looked back at her. He looked so at home in the water. His limbs moved effortlessly to keep him up.

Libby felt like a failed experiment. It had been so long it felt unnatural. Still, she vaguely remembered what to do.

"Yes. I'm fine," she replied.

He smiled at her and held out his hand. "Take my hand."

Libby didn't think twice about the offer. A second later he'd pulled her to him and they were face-to-face.

"You sure you're okay?"

"Yes," she said a little breathlessly. "I just haven't been swimming in a long time. I just need to get back in the swing of things."

"Don't be scared," he said firmly, but comfortingly. "I've got you."

She nodded as he led her closer to the reef. She wasn't sure how deep the water was, but she knew it was a lot darker beneath than it had been before.

"Do you think you can hold your breath?" Rob asked.

"Why?" she asked with just a pinch of fear.

"There's something I'd like to show you, but you have to go underwater to see it," he said as the water lapped around his shoulders. He once again raked a hand through his hair to remove it from his face.

"Okay. Show me."

"Hold your breath."

Libby did as she was told, and the next second she was descending beneath the waves. She blinked several times to adjust her eyes to the salt. The moment they did so, the most spectacular sight greeted her.

Waving fans and corals of multiple colors stretched out before her. There were some that looked like fingers and others that looked like spines. More looked like purple flower clusters.

A turtle swam by and Rob turned to point it out as it approached. Above the water it was amazing but below it was incredible. The turtle was at least three feet long with a head and fins covered in dark scales.

Libby breathed deeply as her head broke the surface of the water. Rob was still beneath. He was better at holding his breath than she was.

The waves were rolling in faster now. The tide seemed to be coming in.

"What did you think?" he asked when they'd both resurfaced.

"It was spectacular."

"Maybe I can take you snorkeling some time and we can see more of it," he suggested.

"I'd love that. But right now," she said as her head bobbed above another wave. "I think we should go back. The water's getting a little higher."

Rob seemed completely unaffected, but Libby was getting nervous.

They swam back side-by-side and sat on the shore after, enjoying the sun. It warmed her skin and Libby couldn't remember having a better time in her life.

Rob turned to her. "So what do you need me to do for this Christmas plan of yours?" he asked.

Libby smiled. "Not much. I think I've got this covered."

CHAPTER 16

*I*t was quite shocking to Libby how many people were just skating through the holidays, hoping to stay above water.

Some wanted to forget. Some needed money. Others, like her, just wanted to escape Christmas.

The more people she talked to, the more Libby realized the idea was a lot bigger than she imagined.

One example was Tua, one of the waiters from the dining room. He had no family and saw the holidays as a time to distract himself from the fact that he was alone.

Ululani, one of the girls who cleaned the rooms, had a family that had fallen on hard times. Her mother and father were both out of work and she had six younger siblings to take care of. She was nineteen and the breadwinner. She was working because if she didn't they'd have nothing to even remotely resemble the Christmases they once enjoyed.

Though Libby wasn't just learning the bad but the good too.

"Every year my mother would make these amazing coconut biscuits," Ululani said with a smile. "They were like dog biscuits almost, really hard with a good crack and so much flavor. We'd help her roll them out, cut them up and then bake them."

"What about this year?" Libby questioned.

Ulalani shook her head. "Not this year."

"Why not?' she asked. "You can still hold on to the good despite everything."

"Tell that to my mother," Ululani answered. "Since she and dad lost their jobs they've sort of lost themselves as well. They worry and they try to find work. That's all they do. Now it's Christmas and nothing is the same. This is the third Christmas since it happened. The first year they tried, believing that work would come. The second, things weren't so great. This year is horrible. If it weren't for Rob letting me work here, I don't know what we'd do."

"He seems like a really good guy," Libby stated.

"The best," Ululani said as she turned the sheet over at the top and tucked it beneath the mattress. "It's a shame he's always alone."

"What do you mean?"

"You know. He doesn't have anyone. You'd think someone like him would be drowning in women, but he barely even notices them," the young woman divulged.

"Seriously?"

"Yeah. I guess he still misses his wife."

"Did you know her?"

"No. She died before I found out about this place, but Honi who works in maintenance, he was here from the very beginning. He said she was a really great woman. Kind, like Rob and that everyone was really sorry when she died." She sighed. "They said if he hadn't had this place to hold onto, they weren't sure he would've made it."

Libby considered what Ululani was saying.

It seemed that the person with the most need for a change in their perspective was Rob.

"Ululani, I'll see you later," she said as she got to her feet and headed for the door.

"Okay, see you, Libby," the young woman replied as she continued to work on her bed.

She went to the office to look for Rob but he wasn't there. She checked the rest of the inn and he wasn't there either.

"Can I help with anything?" a staff member asked as she entered the kitchen.

"I was looking for Rob."

"Oh he's at home," the woman replied. "He's got a house just up the beach."

"Thanks," Libby said in a rush as she turned and left. She stopped short. "Which direction?"

"North."

She might be overstepping calling on Rob like this, but she needed to tell him what she was thinking.

Christmas was just a few days away and if they wanted to do this properly, they had to do it now.

CHAPTER 17

The walk was longer than she thought, but soon a Tiffany blue colored beach house with white trim came into view.

Libby stood on the sand looking at it.

There was a gate that led in from the beach to a small yard area and she wondered if she should just walk in, or if she should call out to Rob first and let him know she was there.

In the end, the choice wasn't hers to make; he saw her before she had a chance to do anything.

"Libby? What are you doing here?" he asked as he looked at her over the line of fresh laundry. He was shirtless and his hair was pulled back in a low ponytail.

"I came to talk to you."

"Come on in," he said casually as he continued to hang out his laundry.

She let herself in by the gate and came to stand beside him. "Want some help?"

"Sure." He tossed a damp pillowcase at her and smiled. "You can talk while you help me hang these out."

Libby began pinning laundry to the line.

"So I think I've finalized my idea for a different kind of Christmas."

"Oh?" Rob asked as he grabbed a pair of pants from the basket and hung them next to the sheet.

"We need to remember and honor the good. Bad things happen, but good things do too. We need to focus on that. We can each do something that reminds us of the special times we had, at Christmas and otherwise."

Rob stopped what he was doing and turned to look at her. A smile began to spread across his face.

"Kalea used to do this thing ... what the Hawaiian people used to do before they celebrated Thanksgiving as we know it and it happened on the last day of December."

She smiled. "So why don't we do something like that? A day of remembering the best things about our lives. A day to forget all the bad?"

He stared at her, his eyes wandering along her face as if he were looking for something.

"You don't like the idea?" she questioned finally when he remained quiet.

"No," he said calmly. "I do. It's just ... it really is the kind of thing Kalea would've loved."

"Rob," Libby said as her hands picked up another pillowcase and held it. "I don't know anything about your wife. I don't know what it must've been like to lose someone you loved that much, but I do know that no one who loved you would ever want you to go through life hurting because of them."

The words stunned even herself as they left her lips. They sunk in as though they were a warning to her too.

She'd been trying to live up to the standards her parents had set instead of making her own. Each year for the holidays she was trying to replicate something that was her mother's and what was expected instead of doing her own thing.

He laughed softly. "That also sounds like something she'd say."

"Then listen," Libby continued. "Do something that's going to remind you that your wife really loved this time of year. That it meant something to her because of the love she could share and the lives she could touch. You may have lost her physically, but the spirit of what she believed in isn't gone. It's still in you. You kept the inn open in her name. So now run it the way she would want you to. Touch the lives she knew you could."

"What makes you think she believed I could touch lives?" Rob questioned.

"I know that every one of your employees thinks you're amazing. The people you allow to come here, all think highly of you and have good things to say, even if they do think you're a little aloof."

"Aloof? Who said I was aloof?"

"I did," Libby admitted. "I wondered why you were kind of distant. If you were just a big old grump or if there was something more. Then I got to know you and I realized you weren't grumpy. You were just lonely."

"You got that?" he asked as he took a step toward her.

"Yes, I did. The thing is, with loneliness, there's a sure-fire cure."

"What's that?"

"Surround yourself with people and things that make you forget it. That's what I want to do for you and everyone at the inn. I want this Christmas to be a day when we can all forget our troubles and embrace all the good there still is to this life."

He nodded. "Then let's do it. What do you need?"

"First, we need to include all the guests, staff and their families. We can invite them to do the things they love most. Bake their favorite pies or write down their fondest stories or memories to share. Also, why don't we decorate? Not too much, but a festive appearance might help lift the mood. We could ask everyone to pitch in and use *their* favorite decorations. Popcorn garlands, tinsel, lights, whatever reminds them of the best time of their lives even if it isn't necessarily what you might think of as Christmas."

"Libby, I hope they pay you well at your job because you have some pretty good ideas," Rob commented and she blushed.

"Actually, I lost out on a big promotion right before I came here," she admitted.

"You did mention something about that the night we were talking with Nate and Greg."

"Ah, I'm sure I'll get another chance sometime in the future," she replied as she turned from him to hang out the other pillowcase. It still burned to speak about the disappointment, but she knew that it was something she was going to have to get over.

"Libby?" Rob called as he laid a hand over hers. She stopped what she was doing. "Yes?"

"Don't you think you maybe need to take some of this advice too?" he said in a low voice.

"I know," she admitted hesitantly.

"So why don't we make another deal?" Rob suggested as he removed his hand from hers as she turned to look at him. "I'll let you turn my entire business upside down - do all you've suggested if you'll throw yourself completely into this plan. I want one hundred percent. Nothing holding you back. No memories of what might have been. If I have to do it then you do too. Agreed?"

She looked at him as a slight embarrassment colored her cheeks. "Agreed."

*R*ob walked her back to the inn afterward. The walk wasn't nearly as long as it was when she'd set out to reach him.

In fact, it seemed to go by far too quickly as they talked.

The first person they met was Naomi. She was walking on the beach collecting shells. It was a pastime she and her husband had enjoyed together.

"Hello, you two? Taking a stroll?" she called out as she spotted them approaching.

"Just heading back," Libby said with a smile.

"We were planning something we think you'd enjoy, Naomi," Rob commented. "A day to celebrate."

"Instead of just Christmas, we want to look at the things that make it really special for each of us and share those things with others," Libby explained. "A day to embrace all the good and forget all the bad."

Naomi looked at her thoughtfully, then a smile began to spread across her face. "I think that's a wonderful idea. In this world we spend far too much time worrying about the negative. My Charlie never did. He always looked at the grass being greener."

"Then you'll participate?" Libby asked enthusiastically. She was eager to see this idea through in reality and if they could get everyone to jump on board the better it would be.

"I will definitely," Naomi asserted. "I'll see if I can't get some of the others to join us."

"Do that," Rob answered. "We want staff and guests to come. I plan to make an announcement about it tonight at dinner."

"You should probably get some fliers printed ..." Naomi suggested.

"I can do that in my office, but I need someone to design them," Rob said.

"I can design them if you have Adobe or some other software," Libby suggested.

"I'm sure I've got something you can use."

"Then you figure out what to say and I'll work on getting the fliers made." Libby could feel the excitement building. It almost felt like the day of the Hershell presentation, but far less stress and a lot more fun.

"You two sound like a good team," Naomi commented, silencing them both.

"Libby's very talented," Rob said. "She makes things easier."

"Don't mind Rob," Libby said with a chuckle. "He just likes to make his guests feel good about themselves."

"I'd say he's speaking the truth," Naomi agreed.

She could feel her cheeks getting hot. Praise wasn't something Libby was used to nor something she hardly considered, but the sincerity with which Rob was speaking also made her feel something more.

CHAPTER 19

Christmas Eve came faster than Libby expected and the atmosphere around the inn had completely changed.

The staff were smiling and so were the guests as they helped in the decorating project. Everyone contributed something, whether it was a garland, a dish or a story.

Every guest also had something to do and Libby was completely submerged in this lovely new alternative approach to Christmas.

Garlands and wreaths hung around the building.

Naomi was spearheading activities in the kitchen, along with the cook. Two other guests were there making some of their family Christmas favorites, while Ululani was making the dough for her mother's cookies.

Her entire family was invited as well as several other family members of the staff.

"Naomi, everything smells fantastic," Libby commented as she entered the kitchen to see how things were rounding out. The event was starting in an hour and she wanted everything to be perfect.

"Thank you," she said with a smile, "but it isn't all me. The girls have worked so well together."

The cook laughed as did the other women. "We make a good team," the cook replied.

Most of the food was being made by her, but a lot of the dishes were suggested by the guests who knew what they wanted but weren't as skilled at cooking like others.

Everyone was finding their place in this crazy plan and Libby believed it was going to turn out fantastic.

Once she'd checked in with the kitchen and made sure that the music and everything else was ready, she headed to her room to get dressed.

Rob had been a surprise too. He'd really come around to her idea and had ended up being the one leading the decorating.

He was climbing on top of the building with a Santa and Mrs. Claus in shorts and floral print shirts and reindeer with leis around their necks. It was spectacular.

Libby's dress was bright red and she'd bought a pair of kitten heels for the evening. Her brown hair was swept up in a messy twist and she'd even bothered to do her makeup.

If she was honest, it was the most excited she'd felt about Christmas in years.

SHE MET Rob on the stairs as she was making her way down to the dining room. She smiled and gave him a small wave as she ascended.

"You look great," he said as he assessed her outfit. He was wearing dark blue jeans and a white ribbed shirt. His hair was down and slicked back.

"So do you," she replied as he held out his arm for her to take it. "Shall we head to the dining room?"

"We shall," Libby answered with a grin and the pair began to walk together.

"How are you feeling about this evening?" he asked as they slowly walked through the lobby.

Libby wasn't sure but it almost felt as if Rob was prolonging their arrival.

"Honestly, I'm a bit nervous," she admitted. "I really want this to work and for everyone to have a good time."

"Don't worry. They will," he assured her. "It was a great idea."

"Thanks. I couldn't have done if you hadn't consented to my hare-brained scheme."

"And I wouldn't be feeling this good if I hadn't."

Libby's face stilled and her heart quickened. "Do you mean that?

He nodded. "I'd forgotten how great this time of year used to be. You reminded me of that. I don't think I can thank you enough."

She blushed. 'Don't mention it. It was my pleasure. And you know, I think I needed this too."

CHAPTER 20

They walked into the dining room to find everyone already gathered together.

Rob left Libby near the front of the room to take his place as MC. He took the microphone set up with the sound system, and got the festivities started.

"Good evening ladies and gentlemen. Guests, staff and family, I'd like to welcome you to the Kalea Inn's holiday celebration. This evening is a time to remember all the good things we've experienced in our lives, and for one day put aside the unpleasant stuff. I know you must be thinking, 'why?' and the answer is simple really. Why not?"

A soft murmur of laughter rippled across the room.

"Many of us tend to get so caught up in the commercial aspects of Christmas we overlook the true meaning of the holidays. My late wife used to so love this time of year," he admitted as the room fell silent. "I lost her on Christmas Eve six years ago. I didn't think I'd ever have a happy Christmas again - until now."

Libby stood listening to Rob pour his heart out.

She marvelled at the way he was able to open up when he'd seemed so closed off when she arrived.

"Then someone reminded me that we need to remember the good. We need to think about the things we tend to forget once we allow the bad stuff to overwhelm us. The bad memories. The misfortunes. The losses. Today, they don't exist. Today we are celebrating only the good."

Libby smiled again as Rob turned to look at her. "Now I'd like to thank the person who came up with this idea. The person who helped me remember what this time of year truly means. You all know her. She's the one who's been running around making sure you all took part today," he mused. "Libby, thank you for being you. Thank you for being the kind of person who cares about others and who cared enough about all of us here to bring this idea to life. You brought the festive back to this place, and to all of us. Thank you."

Libby's face was red, she knew it. She hadn't expected him to single her out. Applause filled the room and several encouraging hands touched her shoulder to confirm their agreement with Rob's comments. She didn't know what to say.

She would need to soon however, as he passed the mic to the person to his right, and the chorus of thanks and remembrance began.

Everyone sat listening once things got started. People shared their best childhood memories. Some were of Christmas, others of the people they loved.

Naomi shared her best loved memories with her husband and the funny thing he'd do every Christmas Day. Charlie sounded like an incredible man, and Naomi was smiling with every word she spoke. That was what Libby wanted. She wanted people to remember only the good.

Greg stood when it was his turn. He looked at his older brother. "The great things I remember most about my life, other than Mom, is my brother, right here," he said as he held out his hand to Nate. "Typically, we honor people when it's too late to tell them how we felt about them. I don't want to do that. I want my brother to know how much he means to me now, while he's here, and why I'm glad that he's my brother. I couldn't ask for a better sibling. You have always been there to guide me and help me and I'm glad that I can be there for you now. I love you."

Everyone smiled and applauded as the two brothers embraced. Libby dabbed the corner of her eyes as she listened. This was more than she'd expected, but everything she'd hoped for too.

"Finally, the last person to share something this evening. Libby," Rob said, as he handed her the mic.

She was trembling as she took it.

"Thank you," she replied and the mic made a piercing noise. She squinted her eyes as it stung her ears. A moment later the problem was settled. "Thank you," she repeated. "The best times I ever had was with my parents. They were two of the most loving and committed people I've ever met. They were the glue that held our family together and I wanted to be just like my mother when I got older. She was the one who made it all work. She was the one who could read us all like a book and solve our problems even before we asked."

"She must've been related to mine," Nate commented and everyone chuckled.

"Maybe," Libby answered. "She seemed to be related to everyone," she mused. "Everyone certainly loved her like she was an aunt or a sister."

Libby was standing in the room, but her mind was somewhere else as she continued. "Theirs was the love that inspired the kind of love I wanted to have in my life. They set the standard I've held ever since. If it wasn't going to be a love like theirs then I didn't want it. I didn't want to settle for second best or second place. I wanted a love that made you want to be with that person no matter where they went. While I still might be waiting for that," Libby continued with a chuckle. "I know that it's out there. Real love, the kind that lasts, does exist and it waits for the right time to make an appearance, but when it does, you'll never forget it."

Applause once again filled the room as she finished her little speech. Her heart was racing in her chest but at least she'd gotten through it. It was amazing. She did presentations for a living but the nervousness never went away no matter how many times before she stood before a crowd to speak.

Once the more personal element was over it was time for the music and the food. People left their tables and lined up at the buffet to sample the best in Hawaiian food and the mishmash of other Christmas and personal favorite recipes the guests and staff had come up with.

"Libby," Rob called as he pulled her aside. "I just wanted to say thank you again."

"You don't need to," she answered. "You're making too big a deal out of this."

"I don't think so." He gestured around the room. "Look at this. Look at everyone's faces. This is thanks to you. No one else could've done it," he commented.

"She has that effect on people," a familiar voice agreed from behind her. "She always has. Ever since she was a kid."

Libby turned in surprise to find that the words had been spoken by none other than Andy.

CHAPTER 21

*S*he couldn't believe her eyes. There of all people was her brother, backpack slung over his arm and a smile on his face.

"What on earth are you doing here?" she asked in surprise.

"I came to get you," he replied jauntily.

Libby turned to Rob, who was looking from her brother to her and back again.

"It's alright," he murmured, his voice cold once again. "I'll give you two a moment."

"Wait," she called out. "You don't have to go. My brother was just leaving."

She watched as Rob's expression changed. "Your brother?"

"Yes. Andy, this is Rob."

Andy took the hand Rob offered in greeting. Libby wasn't happy to see him. This was her trip, her escape and he was ruining it by being there.

Then, to make matters worse, she saw her sister appear in the doorway. "You brought Eden too?" she asked in disbelief.

"I knew I was going to need reinforcements to get you to come home," he replied. "So brought the best."

"But how did you guys even know where I was?" Libby questioned.

"I think the three of you need to talk. You can use my office," Rob offered as he pulled the keys from his pocket and handed them to Libby. He stepped closer and whispered in her ear. "Face your problems. Don't run from them."

She looked at him pleadingly, but she knew it was no use. He was right and her siblings had come all this way after all. "Follow me."

Libby led them to Rob's office. She flicked on the light as they entered before she stood in the middle of the room, her arms folded over her chest,

"See that," Eden said as she walked in. "We're in trouble. She's doing the folded arm thing like Mom used to."

"What do you two want?"

"Libs, its Christmas. A time of family and togetherness, like Mom and Dad always wanted," Andy answered.

"It isn't the same without you," Eden added.

"Why? Because there's no one to get the house ready, to cook all the food, clean up after and do your shopping and childminding?" Libby snapped. "That's not what Mom and Dad would want, and neither do I."

"We know. We were wrong," Andy said. "We took you for granted and we're sorry for that. It's just … you always get it done. Everything always comes easier to you and I don't know, I guess we never considered that you'd need help too."

"I worked my butt off on that Hershell project and you took my laptop to New York. I lost my big shot and you acted like it was nothing. A melted candy bar to be replaced. It was my dream and you didn't even care."

"I'm a terrible brother," Andy agreed. "I know that. You disappearing like that really made me realise it."

"Made us all realise it," Eden confirmed. "We realised how much we took you for granted, and how much our lives weren't the same without you being there, and not because you do so much for us, but because you're the sunshine at this time of year, Libby. You're the one who makes it so we don't miss Mom and Dad as much, because we know you've got it all covered, just the way they'd like."

"But I can't do that anymore," she replied. "I can't do it the way they would want or what you would want. I need to do it the way I know best and not try to be anyone else. I also need for you guys to play a part. You leave me with everything like I'm a servant, and when you call you just expect me to drop what I'm doing and help you. I know it's my fault for that. I let you get away with it in the first place, but now I'm not. I've asked for help. I've begged for help. Now, I'm doing what I feel like."

"And you should," Eden said, to Libby's surprise. "You deserve to have the kind of Christmas you want, with the people you want to share it with. I see everything you've done here. When we arrived everyone was talking about this being your idea and they were so excited about it."

"If this is where you'd rather be, then we'll head back home on the first flight tomorrow without you, but if you want to come home and be with us, then we've already booked you a flight back. It's all paid for," Andy confirmed.

Libby was about to answer when something stopped her. What *did* she want? Wasn't it this, what was happening right now - for her family to appreciate her?

She might have helped bring joy to Kalea Inn, but the best thing for her right now was making things right with her family.

Greg was right. Family needed to show how much they cared for each other now, not later. It was what her parents would have wanted too, and Libby had to admit she missed her siblings. Not speaking to them wasn't natural.

She sighed. "Already paid for?"

"Yes," Andy said with a smile as he glanced at Eden. "Does that mean you'll come home?"

Libby sighed. "It isn't Christmas without you all either," she admitted. "Despite my desire to get away from you, being away only made me miss you more."

"We missed you too," Eden said as she stepped forward and hugged her tightly.

"I'm sorry little sis," said Andy, joining in. "And I promise we'll make this right. I swear."

"*Y*ou're all set," the receptionist responded when Libby checked out out the following morning.

Her flight was leaving in two hours and she, Andy and Eden were headed to the airport.

"Is Rob around?" Libby asked. She hadn't seen him since the night before when she informed him that she would be cutting her trip short in order to go home and spend Christmas with her family.

He'd seemed happy about it, but Libby sensed he was a little disappointed in her too. She'd done so much to help him out and then she was leaving just as things had gotten better.

"Sorry, he hasn't been in today," the young woman replied. "Sorry to hear you're leaving us so soon. Last night was so amazing. Everyone thought so. I wonder if the tradition continue next Christmas once you're gone?"

"I'm sure it will," Libby asserted. "I'm sure Rob will see that." She wasn't sure if she meant it or if she was trying to convince herself.

She wasn't sure how it happened, but she'd come to really care about all the people she'd met at Kalea Inn, especially its owner. She'd hate to think that Rob would allow what happened there, all the beautiful memories and companionship the guests had shared to fade, and for him to fall back into his cloud of melancholy and loneliness.

"Did you want to leave a message for him? I can pass it on when he gets in."

Libby hesitated and then asked for a piece of paper and a pen.

She folded the note and wrote Rob's name on the front.

"Libs, we need to go, the taxi is here," Eden called from the doorway.

"I'm coming," she replied as she walked toward the exit. She turned back to look at the inn.

In such a short time, it had made such a big impact on her life. She'd miss it, but maybe sometime in the future, she could return?

"Libby," Naomi's voice called out then.

"Hey," she answered as the older woman walked toward her. She reached up with her frail arms and gave Libby a hug.

"I heard you were leaving," she said. "Take care of yourself. Don't forget us."

"I could never forget you," she answered as she hugged Naomi again. "I promise, when I get back home I'll give you a call, just to see how you're doing."

Naomi smiled. "I'd like that."

"Libby," her sister called again.

"I have to go," Libby repeated as she gave Naomi one final smile. "It was really nice meeting you."

"It was really nice meeting you too. Merry Christmas."

Libby couldn't stop thinking about this trip as the taxi drove them to the airport.

Nothing had turned out the way she thought, but at the same time, it had been infinitely better.

Her only regret was she and Rob not being able to say goodbye.

CHAPTER 23

They arrived at the airport on time and Andy took care of checking-in their bags.

"Just a few more minutes and we'll be on our way back home," Eden mused. "Megan is so happy you decided to come back. She's doing her best to make sure you have a proper family welcome when you get there."

Libby's eyes widened. "I hope someone hired a caterer."

"She did actually."

They were still laughing together when a familiar voice called her name.

It was Rob.

"Hey," he said softly, as he got close.

Libby colored, despite herself. "I was hoping I'd get to see you before I left."

Her sister smiled and then duly stepped away.

"Well, I wasn't sure if I should say goodbye, but then when I got your note I knew I had to." He stepped closer and touched her arm. "I couldn't let you go without saying what's on my mind …. or in my heart."

She looked at him in surprise as her heart beat louder in her ears.

"Before you came along, I was sleep-walking through the remainder of my life hoping to never wake up, but you did. You woke me up. You made me feel again. You reminded me of all the good that life to offer if we'd just hold on to it. So that's why I'm here. I'm trying to hold on to some of the good, Libby. You."

Her eyes widened in surprise. "Rob, what are you saying?"

"I'm saying I can't lose this too. I've been dead inside for so long and you made me feel alive again. You've made me remember how to feel good about Christmas. I can't let you go back home without letting you know that I care about you. And that I want to see more of you."

"Rob…" She tried to interrupt but he was unburdening his heart and he wouldn't be stopped.

"I know it's crazy. We live so far apart and long distance relationships are tough, but if you're willing to give it a shot, I am too."

The smile turned up the corners of her mouth in an instant as his words settled in her heart. "Do you mean that?"

"Every word," he answered with a smile of his own. "I know you've decided to go home for Christmas, but if I suggested I come visit you for New Years, would you object?"

She laughed in disbelief. "I wouldn't object," she said while still laughing nervously as he stepped closer. "I'd be delighted."

"Do you know you have the best smile…." he stated. "When I see it I can't help but stare at you."

"Is that all?" she asked boldly, as she looked up at him.

"Actually, it makes me want to kiss you," he continued with a grin. "I just wonder if you'd let me."

"Is that a question?"

"More like a consideration," he said and lowered his lips to hers.

They met somewhere in between. The place between Minnesota and Hawaii and heaven and earth.

Libby certainly felt as if she were flying as Rob pulled her into his strong arms and held her there.

She was giddy by the time they parted.

An announcement rang over the loudspeaker. Her flight was being called.

"That's me," she chuckled softly.

"I'll let you know when I've got all my plans settled," he said as he forced himself to release her.

"If you change your mind, don't tell me," she said. "It'll be easier that way."

"I'll be there," Rob said confidently. "You have my word."

She stepped up and kissed him again, a quick one this time as she rushed to meet her plane.

A few minutes later Libby was seated and looking out the window of the aircraft as she waited for it to take off.

Christmas had taken on an entirely new meaning for her now. She'd discovered a new way of doing things, and found someone whose heart understood hers.

Better yet, his was leading him to Minnesota for New Years.

The engines hummed to life and Libby felt excitement build up inside her. The plane was about to take off, but her heart already had.

Her life was changing, she could feel it. And it was all for the better.

All because of her wonderful Christmas escape.

12 DOGS OF CHRISTMAS

A FESTIVE HOLIDAY TAIL

CHAPTER 1

$\mathcal{T}$he curtains were wide open when Lucy Adams woke up. She must have forgotten to close them the night before, and now she was glad for that.

Snow outlined the windowsill like a frame, and the blanketed San Juan Mountains - the sun just peeking above its summit - was the picture.

It was a beautiful sight to wake up to.

She sighed happily. Small town life was very different to what it had been like in Denver, but she should have known the city wasn't for her.

Lucy was a Whitedale native, born and bred.

Once upon a time, she thought that time in the big city would help her shyness, and allow her to live out her grandmother's dream of her becoming a success.

Gran had been so sure that Lucy becoming an investigative journalist and seeing her name on the by-line of a story would have spurred her on to even greater things, but it didn't.

Because she never got any further than being a fact-checker.

Lucy was cripplingly shy; always had been. When she was a

child her mother tried everything to help bring her out of her shell, but it was no use.

Her timidity and innate reserve around people made it difficult for her to even broach the subject of an article to her boss.

In the end, she realized that no matter how hard she tried, she'd never be as happy in Denver as she would be back home.

So home she came.

Now, she swung her legs from beneath the sheets and did a few quick stretches to loosen herself up for the day ahead. Then quickly made her bed; the wrinkled sheets and pillow depressed on only one side.

Her apartment was the best she could afford; a small upper-level two-bed on Maypole Avenue, close to all the parks and trails.

When she started renting it a couple of years ago, she'd sort of hoped that by now she'd have someone to share it with, but no such luck.

Lucy didn't know why, but she seemed to have been born without the romance gene too.

She knew she wasn't bad looking, with her shoulder-length caramel-colored hair and fair skin. Her smile was big and warm, but the problem likely was that she didn't really smile around people.

Animals yes; humans not so much.

People made her nervous, which was why having a dog-walking business was a plus. Lucy spent her days surrounded entirely by those who understood her without judgment.

Lucy was very proud of her business, 12 Dogs Walking Service. It was the premier dog-walking outfit in town, and she had dreams of making it even better.

Once she had enough money saved and found the right location, she fully intended to add other services, like doggie daycare and pet pampering.

She envisioned her little business as one day being the best animal care center in the county, if not the state.

But hey, one day at a time.

THE WOODEN FLOORS were cool beneath her feet as Lucy left her bedroom and walked into the kitchen.

She fixed herself a bowl of cereal and a cup of coffee while waiting for her computer to wake.

She loved her trusty old-model Dell PC, but Betsy was on her last legs. It used to take less than a minute for it to boot up, now it was more like seven.

Lucy hummed the lyrics to *Must Have Been the Mistletoe* as she got out her apple cinnamon granola and almond milk. She did her best to eat well, and in Whitedale that was made easier by the popularity of the farm-to-table movement.

Then she settled at her two-seater dining table by the small window overlooking the square.

The town was slowly coming to life - in a few hours, cars and people would be bustling along the streets, but for the moment it was just store owners looking for an early start, and a few joggers out for a morning run.

When the PC was fully loaded, the home screen flickered to life, and a picture of a golden-haired cocker spaniel greeted Lucy, making her smile immediately.

"So let's see what's going on today..." she mumbled as she opened her emails; a couple of subscription updates to animal magazines and journals, and a few more notifying her of pet trade shows in the area.

Then requests from her clients.

Bob St. John wanted Blunders walked on Thursday. He was a new client and Blunders, a three-year-old dachshund, was sorely in need of Lucy's services.

Bob, loving owner that he was, had been won over by Blunder's pleading looks, and now the dog was carrying a little too much weight. The extra pounds for a larger breed might've been easier to handle, but the dachshund's long body made it more easily prone to herniated discs.

The sooner Blunders got the exercise in, and if Bob stuck to the diet the vet had recommended, Lucy was sure that the little dog would be fine in no time.

"Dear Bob …" she intoned out loud, as she began to type a response confirming the date and time, and set an alert reminder for herself on her phone.

Martha Bigsby wanted Charlie walked every day that week. Charlie was a six-year-old Airedale Terrier. His coat was perfect and thankfully so was his health. He was Martha's prize-winning pooch and she loved him dearly.

Lucy loved owners who shared her appreciation for their animals. Charlie had a big show coming up before the holidays, and she wanted to be sure he was ready for it.

Dear Martha. I confirm that I'll pick up Charlie at seven each morning this week. We can return to our normal nine o'clock slot once you're back from Bakersfield.

She spent the next twenty minutes replying to her work emails before checking her personal ones, though was finished with those in less than one.

Lucy's life consisted mostly of work, and very little of the social aspects that most other people found entertaining. Socialising just wasn't her thing really.

She'd always been happier around animals than people. They, especially dogs, were easy to understand and predictable for the most part.

People weren't, and that was a difficulty for Lucy. She liked what she could rely on and she'd been disappointed far too many times by people.

Never by her furry friends.

Her phone rang then and she checked the caller display. It was Eustacia, her neighbor on the floor below; a woman who believed it was her job to marry off every singleton in their building.

"Lucy? Are you there? Of course, you're there. You're screening my calls aren't you?" Eustacia's Brooklyn accent pierced her ears.

Her new neighbor, who had moved from New York four months ago, was convinced she knew what was best for Lucy, and that she'd find her the 'perfect guy'.

"Trust me. I know all about these things. At home, they used to call me the matchmaker. I can set up anyone with anyone. You leave it to me. A young girl like you shouldn't be all alone every night. It's ain't natural."

Lucy would've appreciated the help, if it weren't for the fact that Eustacia had terrible taste in men.

"Mrs. Abernathy in 4C told me that her son Martin is back in town. And I told her you'd love to meet him. Would you give her a call? She says he'd loved to meet you too."

A perfect example of Eustacia's poor taste: Martin Abernathy was four years older than Lucy. He had a habit of snorting all the time and when she was little, he used to stick gum in her hair.

She rolled her eyes as her neighbor's shrill voice continued. She washed the dishes and put them away, and Eustacia was *still* talking.

Then, finally making her excuses, Lucy hung up the phone and got ready for work.

Her clothing and shoes were comfortable, cosy and most importantly, breathable. There was a *lot* of walking around in her line of work, and no matter what the deodorant companies claimed, she'd rather be safe than sorry.

Dogs were after all, very sensitive to smell.

CHAPTER 2

*F*irst, Lucy headed to Olympus Avenue, where one of her charges resided.

While the service was called 12 Dogs, in truth she rarely had as many pooches all at once, but could certainly handle that much.

She also didn't do favorites, and would never admit to having one. Much like people, breeds were individual, and to say you liked dog one better than the other was somewhat unfair. People couldn't help who they were and neither could animals.

However, if Lucy *truly* had to choose a favorite dog – and was absolutely pressed on the matter – she'd pick Berry Cole.

Berry was a five-year-old chocolate brown Labrador and Great Dane mix – a Labradane.

Lucy just called him a sweetie.

He was loyal and loving, and despite his humongous size, being closer in build to his Great Dane mother than his Lab father, he was very gentle.

He was also the perfect choice for his owner, Mrs Cole. Though Lucy sometimes wondered how the seventy-five-year-old woman managed to feed the colossus.

He was *always* hungry, so much so that Lucy had started carrying extra snacks soon after he'd joined her troop.

Though if she could pick a dog for herself, it couldn't be one as huge as Berry. But that was a moot point, because unfortunately, Lucy's landlord didn't allow pets in the building.

Mrs. Cole was a widow with no children, and Lucy sometimes wondered if that would be her own fate - a life alone.Though at least Mrs. Cole had a canine companion. She didn't even have that.

Now she knocked on the door.

"Morning," Mrs. Cole greeted Lucy with a smile the moment she opened the door. She looked tired today, more so than on most mornings when she called to pick up Berry.

Maybe she was feeling down.

Lucy could bring her back something from Toasties to perk up her spirits. It was the best cafe and pastry store in all of Whitedale, and Mrs. Cole had a thing for their Peppermint Chocolate Croissants.

"Hi, Mrs. Cole. Is he ready?" The words came out in a plume of white. Winter was well and truly here and Christmas now only a couple of weeks away.

They'd had their first heavy snowfall just a few days before and soon, the entirety of Whitedale would be covered in it.

The words had only just left Lucy's mouth, when the big dog came bounding to the door. He rushed past his owner and promptly jumped up and landed his big paws on her chest, knocking her back a step.

"Berry, calm down," Mrs. Cole scolded lightly.

"It's okay," Lucy laughed as Berry licked her face. "He's just happy to see me."

The older woman chuckled. "He always is. I can't contend with him like I used to with this hip. I'm so happy he still gets to go out and have fun when you're around."

"It's my pleasure, and you know I really love this big guy," Lucy

291

chuckled as she removed his paws from her chest and stooped down to scratch behind his ears.

Mrs. Cole duly handed her the leash from by the door and Lucy clipped it in place. She carried spare leashes and clean-up items in her backpack, but it was important to get Berry on the right track from the get-go.

"He's staying out for the whole day, yes?" she confirmed.

"Yes, if that's good with you."

Mrs. Cole was one of the few people Lucy could chat easily to. She supposed it was because she reminded her so much of the grandmother who had raised her.

She didn't have anyone now though. A fact she was well used to, but whenever Christmas came around, it was just that little bit harder to bear.

"Of course. You have a great day," Lucy told Mrs Cole as she began to lead Berry from the porch. "And get back inside, it's cold out. We'll see you later."

"You too," the older woman called after her, chuckling as Lucy struggled to keep pace with the dog. "And don't let the big guy wear you out too much."

CHAPTER 3

*T*he feeling of Christmas was well and truly in the air.

All the stores in town were now fully decorated for the holiday season. Garlands and wreaths were everywhere, twinkling lights in every shop window, and the local tree farm business was booming with a fine selection of firs, pines and spruces.

Lucy wasn't getting a tree though. She never did. It felt wasted when it was just her.

She stopped for a moment to look into the window of Daphne's Dreamland Toy store, smiling automatically at the holiday display. The place was every child's wonderland and had been in existence for over forty years.

Lucy could remember when her mother used to bring her there as a child. The owner, Daphne would give her candy canes whenever she came in.

She was gone now though, just like Lucy's mother.

A deep sadness filled her heart at the memory. Her mom had been a lone parent and her dad was in the military.

They married before being deployed but he never came back. He sent her mother annulment papers a few months later. He'd met someone else where he was stationed and decided that she was the better choice.

Her mother had never quite gotten over it.

A sudden jerk snapped Lucy back to the present as Berry resumed his march toward home.

It was now a little after four in the afternoon, when she usually dropped the dogs back.

Berry was her final drop-off today, and he seemed to know it was past time, because he was trotting toward Olympus so purposefully that she knew only the prospect of food could be drawing him.

"Hey, slow down there, buddy," she commanded gently. "We'll be there soon."

She'd never seen him so determined. It was strange.

"Wait. I'm coming, I'm coming," Lucy called as he rushed to the corner and made a beeline for the street. He jerked hard and she almost tripped on the curb as the leash slipped from her hand, and the big dog ran off.

He disappeared down the street and she rushed after him.

"Hey there big guy …" Lucy heard a voice call out from nearby, and rushing round to Mrs Cole's, she stopped short.

A man, over six feet tall and dressed in jeans, a red plaid shirt, brown jacket and a hardhat, was standing outside the house.

Lucy had never seen him before, but clearly, Berry had.

The dog's paws were planted solidly on the man's chest and he was licking his face eagerly, as his tail wagged behind him. The guy, whoever he was, was laughing heartily at the affection.

Lucy watched the friendly moment like an intruder.

"Hey buddy, where's your mama today, huh? Where is she?" he was asking in a sing-song tone.

It was several seconds before he noticed her and turned to meet her gaze, but when he did Lucy's breath hitched.

He was so handsome. Square jaw with a dimple in his chin. A five o'clock shadow, tanned skin and the most brilliant blue eyes she'd ever seen. He wasn't any Martin Abernathy that was for sure. She could see dark brown hair peeking out from beneath the hardhat.

"Hello," he greeted with a smile, then nodded toward the house. "You looking for Mrs. Cole, too?"

Lucy couldn't speak for several seconds. She just stared at him. This was what always happened when handsome men spoke to her; she completely lost all sense. Her shyness took over and suddenly she became an incoherent nincompoop, her mind completely muddled.

Finally, she found her tongue before she embarrassed herself any further.

"Yes, returning Berry. I'm his dog walker."

He looked at her blankly for a second, and then smiled. "Oh. Are you Lucy?"

She was shocked that he knew her name.

"Yes …" she stammered. "Who are you?"

He took several steps to close the gap between them and extended his hand with a dazzling smile.

"I'm Scott. Mrs. Cole's contractor. I just finished working on her roof."

Lucy took his hand. "I didn't know she had one," she replied.

"A roof?"

A second of anxiety struck her. "No … a contractor."

He chuckled. "I was just kidding."

Well done Lucy. Next time, try something simple like 'nice to meet you'.

"Nice to meet you," she mumbled.

"Nice to finally meet you too," he replied as he drew his hand back. He looked at the house and then back to her. "Was she expecting you back now?"

Finally? What did that mean? Did he know her from somewhere? She was certain he couldn't. She'd certainly never seen him before.

Maybe Mrs. Cole had mentioned her. But why?

"Yes. I always bring Berry back around this time. When he stays out all day," she added quickly, when she realized that she hadn't answered.

Berry himself was already at the door scratching to be let in. As always the big guy was ravenous.

"Strange," Scott stated as he turned back to her. "I've been here for a while now, and she hasn't answered. I usually check in on her when I can. I don't like that she's all alone in winter, especially given the darker nights and cold weather. So I try to stop by now and again, just to make sure she's okay."

How sweet.

"She's probably just late getting back from the store or something," he shrugged.

But that didn't make sense to Lucy. Mrs. Cole always made sure she was home when they got there.

She knew how Berry got by that hour of the day. His mind was solely on his dinner and if he didn't get it he got grumpy.

Something wasn't right.

"I have to go," Scott said then. "I've got a meeting with a client over on Hilliard. Could you tell her I stopped by and I'll pass back soon?"

Lucy nodded. "Sure." She turned and watched him walk back to his truck.

Berry attempted to follow him but Lucy grabbed a hold of his leash as he tried to gallop off. "Oh no, you don't Buster. Not this time."

Scott got into the truck and then turned back to wave in their direction as he drove off. "See you around, Lucy."

She waved back, still slightly dazed by the unexpected encounter. "See you around."

CHAPTER 4

$\mathcal{B}$ut the minute Scott was out of sight, Lucy's thoughts loosened, and a niggling discomfort began to fill her stomach.

She turned back to the quiet house. There was no sound of Christmas music coming from inside. Mrs. Cole loved this time of year and she always left festive music playing - even when she went out.

"Nope. Something's not right."

Lucy walked toward the door and took the steps two at a time. She rang the doorbell.

Nothing. She knocked. Still nothing.

"Mrs. Cole?" she called out. No answer.

She looked at Berry. He was scratching at the door and whining a little.

"Let's try the back ..." Lucy mused, as she led him from the porch and around the side of the house to check the rear kitchen window.

Inside, everything was dark and quiet.

"This isn't at all like her ...." she muttered to herself. She knocked on the back door too.

Still nothing.

"Maybe Mrs. Stillman knows where she might be?" she mumbled to Berry, as she headed back out front and next door to the neighbor's house.

Mrs. Stillman was a cat lover. The sound of mewing greeted Lucy the second she stepped onto her property. She looked up at the box window and saw a marmalade tabby looking back at her as she approached the door and knocked.

The owner answered a few seconds later. Her face looked drawn and her grey and her red hair was slightly disheveled. She looked down at Berry and her face fell.

"Hi Mrs. Stillman. I was just over at Mrs. Cole's to drop Berry back, but she doesn't seem to be home yet, which is unusual. Would you by any chance know where she is?"

The other woman's expression became more solemn by the second, and a further sense of foreboding began to slither into Lucy's heart.

The neighbor sighed. "I don't know how to tell you this Lucy, but Sonia passed away earlier today. I only just got back from the hospital."

Lucy's hearing had become hollow. The words being spoken weren't real. They didn't make sense.

Mrs. Cole couldn't be ... *dead.*

She had only left her a few hours ago, smiling and fine. Yes, the older woman had mentioned she felt tired, but she seemed in good health.

How could she be dead?

"How ...?"

"We're not sure. They suspect that it may have been an aneurysm in her sleep," Mrs. Stillman explained. "I went over earlier to drop off a pecan pie I'd made. She really loved my pecan pie," she added through tears.

Tears were filling Lucy's eyes too. She looked at Berry. His mama was gone, but of course he had no idea.

What was going to become of him?

"When I didn't hear her answer I knew something was wrong," Mrs. Stillman continued. "I called the ambulance right off. When we went in, she was in her bed in that nice floral dress she got a few weeks ago."

Lucy could only nod. If she tried to speak she'd start sobbing and she couldn't let herself do that.

It had been so long since she'd lost someone she cared about, and Mrs. Cole's death hurt almost as much as her grandmother's had.

"Thank you for telling me, Mrs. Stillman." She forced the words from her lips. "I'll be going now."

The other woman nodded her understanding as Lucy turned to leave.

She couldn't believe this was happening. She walked back to the house and took a seat on the porch steps.

Berry sat beside her and promptly lay his big head in her lap. He looked up at her pleadingly.

"I know you're hungry Big Guy, but I can't get you food just yet," she told him. She stroked the top of his head gently. "You're mama's gone, buddy. Mrs. Cole won't be able to take care of you anymore."

Berry let out a whine, as if he understood.

Lucy knew that science would say that he was just picking up on her emotions, but she guessed deep down that animals understood a great deal more than people gave them credit for.

CHAPTER 5

*L*ucy waited for over an hour for someone to come to the house, feeding Berry the remainder of the food she kept in her backpack.

The family of people who died usually came by to check on things, didn't they?

It was then she remembered that Mrs. Cole's niece, Joy, had moved to California a few months ago.

She had no family in town anymore. No one was coming.

What was she going to do with Berry?

Lucy walked back to Mrs. Stillman's.

"Me again," she said as the other woman answered the door.

"Lucy, what are you still doing here?"

"I was waiting for someone from Mrs. Cole's family to come, so I can give them Berry, but then I remembered that Joy moved."

"Months ago."

"Right, that's the problem. There's nowhere for me to take him," she explained nervously.

"I see. What are you going to do?"

Lucy forced a smile as she gave Mrs. Stillman a pleading look. "I was kind of hoping that maybe he could stay here for a bit …"

"No."

"Just for the night, even?"

"I'm sorry, but - "

"Please, Mrs. Stillman. He has nowhere to go. I'd take him home with me in a heartbeat, but animals aren't allowed in my building. He just needs someplace to spend the night. I promise tomorrow I'll find a more suitable situation. I promise." She raised three fingers in the air. "Brownie promise."

It was the best she could offer.

The other woman looked at her and then at Berry and then at the cat that was curling round her ankles.

"Fine, but just for the night. He can stay out back and I'll get some food from next door."

Lucy gave a huge internal sigh of relief. "Thank you."

"Just overnight," the woman insisted. "I don't like dogs, Lucy. They're too much trouble. Cats, they're independent. A lot easier to handle."

Lucy nodded. She didn't care what Mrs. Stillman preferred as long as Berry had someplace to sleep tonight.

"I'll be back tomorrow morning, I swear."

"What time?"

"Is seven good for you?" she asked handing over Berry's leash, and giving him a reassuring rub around the ears.

"Seven sharp."

"I'll be there."

CHAPTER 6

ext, Lucy went to work on her landlord.

"Please Mr. Wells. Mrs. Cole is gone and Berry has no one to take care of him."

"What's that got to do with me?"

He was short and Lucy was sure, jealous of everything that could possibly be as tall as him. Which was why animals were a problem too. Their character was greater than his height.

"If you could bend the rule on pets in the building just this once, I could bring Berry here and take care of him until I can make arrangements with Mrs. Cole's family."

"Absolutely not. If I bend it for you I have to bend it for everyone, and then my entire building is overrun with furballs and fleas. No thank you."

"It won't be like that," she assured him.

"My answer is still no."

"Won't you reconsider - please? It's Christmas," Lucy asked, but the look on his face made her stop.

He wasn't changing his mind for her or anyone, no matter what time of the year it was.

She'd just have to find another way.

Berry was too large for her apartment anyway. He deserved a big house and garden, like Mrs. Cole's, where he could run around and have space.

She went to pick up Berry at seven just as she promised.

Mrs. Stillman looked frazzled.

She informed Lucy that Berry had whined all night and she'd hardly slept a wink.

Even worse, it had upset all of her six cats and they'd done a number on her couch in response.

Lucy couldn't apologize enough as she took the leash from her and led Berry away. The further away they both were, the better.

She'd figure something out.

SHE THEN TOOK Berry and her other charges for their usual walk to McGivney Park.

It was one of the few places they could be off their leashes, and all the dogs loved it there.

Once they arrived, Lucy unhooked their collars and let them run around and have fun while she sat on a nearby bench watching.

The only one who wasn't allowed off leash was Pegasus. The black and white Japanese Chin had a habit of running away.

She didn't like playing with the other dogs and Lucy was convinced that it was because Pegasus thought herself better than running around in a park.

She looked at the other dogs with such an air of condescension it was always better to keep her close.

She and Perdita, Mr. Cross's Dalmatian, were always yapping at each other. Perdita didn't like Pegasus one bit and more often than not, Lucy had to act the go-between.

Now, she put her phone to her ear again as she tried to sort out her most pressing problem.

"Hello? Is this Joy?" Lucy had called every Joy Reese she could find in the directory, until she finally reached the right one.

"Yes."

"You don't know me, but I'm Lucy Adams. I take care of Berry the dog, for your aunt, Mrs. Cole." She nodded solemnly as Joy explained that her aunt had passed away. "Yes, I know. That's why I called. You see, Berry is going to need someplace to live and I was hoping that you could take him."

"I can't," the woman replied quickly.

Lucy's heart sank. "May I ask why not?"

"Look, my aunt loved that dog but I don't. I don't do pets and I have no intention of taking on such a responsibility. And that dog is HUGE."

"I know he's on the bigger side, but truly, Berry is such a sweetie that you'd have no trouble at all."

"I don't think you understand. I don't want to try. I just don't want a dog. It doesn't work for me, or my lifestyle."

Lucy's heart was plummeting rapidly every second that went by. "So what should I do with him?"

"I don't know to be honest. Sorry, but I have my aunt's funeral to prepare for at the moment. I can't deal with what's going to happen to some dog. I'm sorry, but I can't help you."

With that, the line disconnected and Lucy stared blankly at her phone, shocked. She couldn't believe the stance Joy had taken to the idea of caring for Berry.

He was such a wonderful dog. How could she feel that way about him - how could anyone?

Lucy knew that the woman's feelings were shared by many others in the world, but she'd never personally experienced anyone express such outright dislike before.

She was quite stunned, frankly. But still the problem remained. What was she going to do now?

There was no choice.

Clearly it was up to Lucy to find Berry a new home, and soon.

CHAPTER 7

*L*ater, she took the other dogs back to their owners, and then
took Berry along to Toasties.

They had free wifi and Lucy used that and Betsy her PC
to make up some fliers. It took her several tries to get the wording
just the way she wanted, but in the end, she was pleased with her
efforts.

"What do you think?" she asked as she turned the screen for
Berry to see. He raised his nose and sniffed the laptop before losing
interest. "What? You don't like it?"

Lucy finished her snack and then emailed the flier to the print
shop, ordering up a batch of thirty.

She'd pick them up and plaster them around town.

Hopefully, some prospects would give her a call and Berry
would have a new home sooner rather than later.

The print shop had her copies ready by the time she arrived.
She'd used festive graphics and snapped a cute picture of Berry,
wanting the flier to stand out.

No one was going to miss it.

Lucy began to staple fliers on every pole and post in town she could find. She asked a few store owners if she could post some in their windows and they allowed her to do so.

"Hey, what's that?" a boy asked as she stapled her last to a lamp post.

"It's a flier."

"For what?" He had to be about five. A curious age.

Lucy stooped down to his height.

"It's to try and find a home for this dog," she explained as Berry moved closer.

He stretched his head forward to sniff the boy but the little kid recoiled.

"Don't worry. He won't hurt you," Lucy assured him.

"He's so big," he gasped in wonder. "He must cost a lot of money."

"Actually, I'm not selling him; I'm giving him away to whoever can give him a good home," she explained.

"Why?" the boy asked. "Don't you like him?"

She chuckled. "I like him a lot, but he's not mine. The lady who owned him sadly died so now he needs a home. I have to find a new owner for him in time for Christmas."

"That's sad. My dog Ruffles died too. What's his name?"

"He's Berry," Lucy continued as she patted his side gently. "He's a Labradane."

"A what?"

She started to laugh just as a tall blonde woman called out. "Tobey?"

"Is that your mom?" Lucy asked gently. The smile was still teasing her lips.

He nodded.

"I think she's calling you. You should probably go to her."

The boy smiled. He was missing a front tooth. He took off running.

"Mommy! Mommy! That lady over there is giving away a dog for Christmas. Can I have him?"

But by the outright horrified look on his mom's face at the dog's size, Lucy was certain little Tobey, and unfortunately Berry too, was on to a loser.

THE FLIERS DISAPPEARED FASTER than expected and soon, Lucy was exhausted.

"Let's see how it goes overnight," she told Berry as he trotted skittishly beside her. "You never know who might see them. If we don't have any luck, then I'll order up a few more and head further outside of town."

Berry barked happily and Lucy wished it was because he agreed, but she knew it was probably only because he wanted the snack in her pocket.

She took one out and tossed it to him when her phone rang.

Lucy didn't recognize the number. "Hello? Yes, this *is* who you call about the dog," she repeated cheerfully, giving Berry an excited smile. "Yes, of course, you can. Are you free now?"

The call was short, but to the point. The Emersons from Crichton Corner were looking for a dog and saw her flier in one of the shop windows just now. They were interested in Berry.

Excitement filled her chest as she began to walk in the direction of Taylor's Arts and Things.

The family had been buying supplies for their daughter's school project when they saw the flier. They were a young couple with a child, which was perfect. Labradanes were family dogs and great with children.

Lucy was very hopeful that the Emersons might be the answer to her prayers.

She saw them immediately as she approached.

Mrs. Emerson was a few inches shorter than her husband. They were both blondes, fair skinned and wrapped up snuggly in matching plaid scarves.

"Mr. and Mrs. Emerson," she greeted with a smile as she got closer.

"Lucy?"

"Yes. And this is Berry," she said as she and Berry got closer.

Mrs. Emerson's eyes grew to twice the size.

"This is … it?" She looked at her husband.

Lucy frowned. "Is something wrong?"

"Not really, it's just … we thought he would be smaller," she said. Her speech was stilted and Lucy was confused.

"Haven't you ever seen a Labradane before?"

"No, we just saw the picture on the flier and thought he looked sweet," she explained. "I'm sorry. We live in a small house with no backyard. We don't have the space."

"We're really sorry to have bothered you," her husband added, smiling pitifully. "Thanks for coming."

Lucy's hopes were falling off a cliff, and that was all he had to say?

It wasn't his fault though, she thought disheartened.

Maybe she should've put something in the picture to give people an idea of his size.

Sadly, Lucy couldn't think of anything that could convey the dog's big heart too.

*T*wo more days passed and still Lucy had no luck in her quest, other than getting a break from Mrs. Stillman who'd agreed to let the big dog stay with her a little longer, but only at night.

It wasn't long before more people noticed the fliers though.

The town was small and some already knew Berry as being Mrs. Cole's dog, and were keen to take him in given his sweet temperament, but once Lucy met with such prospects she realized that the trouble wasn't him, so much as it was them.

Most didn't have the space for a dog his size. Others weren't up to his care, or they couldn't afford the cost associated with such a large (and hungry) breed.

She was surprised that there was even one who had an issue with Lucy not being able to provide papers to ensure the purity of Berry's parents.

Others were like Mrs. Cole, older and infirm. Not ideal.

She'd endured repeated hopes and repeated let-downs, and was beyond frustrated by the time she finished talking to the Ruprechts.

They were really nice people, but were planning a move in a few months, and given they were relocating to Denver city, it didn't make sense.

They'd merely find themselves in the same position Lucy was now. Such a temporary arrangement wasn't fair to Berry.

Now, Lucy was dreading having to go back to Mrs. Stillman to ask for even more time, but she had no choice.

Mrs. Cole's neighbor was waiting for her when she arrived. The look on her face was laced with disapproval.

"I take it that you still haven't found a place?"

Lucy shook her head despondently. "No. I tried. They were good people, but just not the right fit."

"I can tell you what's not the right fit – that dog in my house. I've lost two lamps already. I'll have to remove the carpet in the back room where he sleeps, and honestly my cats are so unnerved that it's driving me nuts. I can't keep him anymore, Lucy. I'm sorry. I really am, but I can't do it anymore. Christmas is on the way and my house is a disaster zone. I can't clean it because of that … *beast*, and my family's going to be arriving for the holidays soon. He has to go."

"Please Mrs. Stillman, just give me a few more days. Like you say, Christmas is the on the way and Berry needs a home in time for then - the right home. I still have a few more leads," she pleaded.

"This is it, Lucy. Absolute last time. You get three days, and then he's out of here, or I take him to the shelter myself. I mean it." She took the leash from Lucy who watched as a sorrowful-looking Berry disappeared inside.

Clearly he was enjoying his stay here just as much as Mrs. Stillman.

Three days?

Lucy couldn't - *wouldn't* - consider the local shelter. It just wasn't and had never been an option. She loved the big guy too much and could never abandon him that way.

But what was she supposed to do?

Lucy was fast-becoming all out of options.

CHAPTER 9

*S*unset Trail was the most picturesque spot in Whitedale and perfect for dog-walking.

It was why Lucy liked going there so much. Lots of quiet space and room to roam between the trees, along the meandering landscape and with a view of Treasure Lake that was unsurpassed.

Sunlight reflected on beautiful blue water like diamonds and gold, which was how it got its name.

Set on a gentle winding slope, the trail was a criss-cross of paths along Lonesome Ridge, Whitedale's diminutive mountain.

Every day she took the dogs there, weather permitting; the park being for days when the forecast wasn't so great or the likelihood of rain was imminent.

Though right now Lucy felt as if she was walking under a cloud, but at least the weather was clear.

There was absolutely no one left on her prospects list.

Mrs. Stillman was adamant that Berry was going to have to leave soon and there was no place else for Lucy to put him.

She'd gone back to her landlord again, begging him, but that was a waste of time. The local vet couldn't help either; none of his regulars were looking for a new dog and he wasn't prepared to even temporarily house an animal of Berry's size.

She was well and truly stuck.

Oscar, Mr. Reese's Alsatian was trotting beside her. Perdita was jumping all over her new boyfriend Pongo. Mrs. Cross figured her precious lady was lonely and thought it a good idea to get her someone to play with. She needed to hold back a little on the whole *101 Dalmatians* thing.

Lucy's mind was so cluttered. She wanted to keep Berry in town, someplace he knew, someplace where the landscape was familiar.

There had to be *something* she could do to help.

Her thoughts were so scattered that she didn't realize she'd wandered off their usual path. It was only when snowflakes began to fall that she glanced up to see that it was darker than it should be.

The trees seemed much closer now, and the overhanging foliage thicker; blocking out the light.

It was then Lucy realized that she was on unfamiliar terrain. With all her musing, she'd allowed the dogs to lead her deeper into the woods.

A sense of panic began to rise up in her stomach now, as cold wind sliced through the trees, making her shiver a little.

"Where are we guys?" she mumbled.

Lucy looked in every direction, but nothing seemed familiar, and she couldn't tell which way the lake was, finding it even harder to get her bearings.

The dogs hovered around her. They wanted to keep going but she didn't know which direction they should turn.

Maybe if we just go back the way we came?

She turned to do so, but at this point couldn't figure out which direction they'd come here from.

This was … not good.

"Keep calm Lucy. Nothing to worry about. You just need to keep walking. You'll find something," she told herself.

Trying to use her cellphone was pointless; there was no signal on this trail - another reason it was so perfect. You could escape the outside world while you were there, and just enjoy the scenery and the quiet solitude.

But of course that wasn't much help to her now.

She was at a loss, when Berry suddenly turned to the right and barked.

Lucy's gaze snapped in the direction he was looking.

"What? Is there something over there?"

The big dog barked again and began to pull away from her, his tail wagging rapidly now.

Well, if there was something over there that had him reacting in that way, then like it or not, they were going in that direction.

Lead the way, Big Dog.

CHAPTER 10

The snow began to fall harder as Lucy and the other dogs hurried along with Berry leading the way.

The older ones were amusing themselves by jumping on one another and sniffing the unfamiliar territory.

All Lucy wanted was to see something she recognized. Once she did she'd feel as happy and carefree as they were.

She checked her watch. If she didn't find a way back soon, the owners would be unhappy. She was always right on time dropping back their pets. Timekeeping was important to her, and them.

If she was very late dropping them back today, how was she going to explain it? What effect would it have on her business?

When Lucy was scared of one thing suddenly there seemed to be a million more things to worry about as well.

She was still following Berry when something glinted in the distance.

Lucy squinted and tried to make out what it was. It took her a minute to realize it was the sun reflecting on a window.

Relief swept over her. If there was a window, then there was a house. If there was a house, then maybe there was someone home.

Someone who could point them in the right direction.

The second the house came into view, Berry began to bark more. He ran toward it as if it were calling him.

Lucy couldn't hold on to him and all the others too.

The dogs' combined strength was a lot to deal with, especially when Berry was so eager. He'd excited the pack, and the task of calming them all wasn't something she needed right now.

Besides, she could see where he was going, so she figured she might as well just let him lead the way.

Releasing him off the leash, Lucy hurried the other animals along behind Berry. The snow was really coming down now. At least the house would be a good place to shelter for a bit, if nothing else.

They broke through the trees into a clearing around the property. The first thing that struck Lucy was the state of the building. It looked abandoned, though the house itself wasn't dilapidated.

Why would anyone leave a nice place in such a gorgeous location unattended?

The site had an uninterrupted view of the lake, and there wasn't another home to be found as far as the eye could see.

It was double-height, lodge-cabin style; a combination of stone and wood. A gabled roof and huge window panes maximized the natural light and the beautiful surroundings.

The land around it was cleared, as if the owner intended to put in a lawn or maybe a flowerbed, but there was nothing there now.

To one side was a deck that extended out into a jetty on the water.

It was Lucy's dream house.

She walked closer and quickly realized that the place wasn't abandoned, like she'd first thought. It was in fact, under construction. The roof on the far side of the porch was half completed.

And perfect for sheltering beneath out of the snow, at least for now.

"Come on guys," Lucy urged as she began to jog to the house.

The dogs followed happily as they tried to keep up.

By now she was cold and her breath was coming out as white mist with every exhalation.

"Berry!" she called as she got closer. "Wait, hold on!"

Of course, the big guy didn't wait, and instead raced around the side of the house.

Lucy safely secured the other dogs to a nearby post before going in search of him.

There was construction material lying around everywhere, stuff that she didn't have the first clue about, but her primary focus was finding Berry.

"Berry, come here boy," she called out again.

Then a sound from somewhere nearby caught her attention and she walked around the porch to find Berry standing over someone lying on the ground; the dog's face buried in their neck, and his tail wagging a mile-a-minute.

"Berry!"

For a moment she was horrified, but then realized that the person's hands weren't fending the dog off, but rubbing his coat and scratching his fur.

And when that person turned in the direction of her voice, Lucy realized to her surprise that she recognized who it was.

CHAPTER 11

"Scott?'

The same dazzling eyes that had so befuddled her that first day they met, now turned in Lucy's direction, having the same effect on her as they did the first time.

Berry noticed her then too, and the big pooch came bounding back to her.

She laid a calming hand on his back as he panted by her side.

Scott pushed up from the ground, covered in what looked like sawdust and with a big smile on his face.

"Lucy, what are you doing here?" he asked as he dusted himself off.

"I could ask you the same thing," she replied reattaching Berry's leash and keeping a firm grip on it.

Scott's presence explained at least why the big dog had been so drawn to the house. He'd obviously picked up the scent of his friend from the trees.

Thank goodness.

"I live here," he answered and chuckled when Lucy glanced skeptically at the house. "I know, it's a mess. Who could live here, right? I mean, it's my place, but I haven't moved in permanently -

not yet. The house is still under construction as you can probably tell. I've been working on it for about a year now."

"By yourself?" Lucy couldn't betray her surprise. The thought that he'd done all this on his own was impressive.

"Yes. I started the construction as a pet project and I'd hoped to have it done a long time ago, but business picked up and I had so much work backing up for other people that it sort of got put on ice." He looked at the house and gave a rueful smile.

"It's a really beautiful place. Anyone would love to live here."

"You think so?"

"Definitely. I would for sure," she added with a nervous chuckle, then coughed when she realized how weird that may have sounded.

Thankfully the sound of the other pooches' impatient whining drew their attention.

"Do you have more dogs with you?" Scott asked as he and Lucy moved back toward the porch.

"Yes. I'm really sorry to intrude. I·was walking them in the woods and we got lost. Berry is the one who led us here. I tied the others to the porch so I could go look for him," she explained.

The snowfall was thickening quickly as they stepped back on to the porch and the dogs were circling around agitatedly. They could feel the bad weather coming, Lucy suspected.

She needed to get them home.

"Could you tell me the fastest way to get back to town from here?" she asked Scott, as he headed toward the others and stooped to greet them, patting their heads and rubbing their coats.

They were all friendly dogs who welcomed strangers and seemed *very* pleased with Scott's attention.

And by the delighted look on his face, clearly the feeling was mutual.

He glanced up at the sky. "There's no going back to town until the weather clears, and certainly not on foot," he stated. "This isn't going to let up anytime soon."

Lucy looked pained. "So we're stuck?"

"Looks like it," he replied. "Weather changes quickly up on the trail. Usually doesn't last long, but a cold snap can lead to some serious snowfall, and it is that time of year. You guys are welcome to stay here until it passes, though."

"Oh no, we couldn't impose ..." Lucy protested.

"Don't be silly, it's no imposition. If anything you'd be doing me a favor."

"How so?"

"If you stay and shelter here, you make me feel better knowing that guys are safe. Plus, if you do, I can give you a ride back when the worst clears."

The proposition was tempting, and the thought of making their way back to town in this snow wasn't one Lucy relished.

Chances were there was cellphone reception at Scott's house too, so she could keep the owners informed of their pets' whereabouts.

Plus Lucy kind of wanted to see what the inside of the house looked like.

"Okay," she conceded, smiling gratefully. "Thank you."

CHAPTER 12

Scott welcomed them all inside the house, leading Lucy to an enclosed rear room that was unfinished, but insulated from the outside.

She settled the dogs there before following him in to the kitchen which was partially furnished, but seemed fully operational.

"Hot chocolate?" he asked as he approached the stove. He turned on a burner and placed a small pot over the flame.

"Yes, please. I love hot chocolate."

She watched as Scott poured heavy cream into the pot and dropped several chunks of chocolate into it. He added several other things too but she couldn't tell what they were.

"Please don't go to any trouble - I actually thought you meant the powdered kind," she insisted, watching him work.

"Not in this house. My mom was the kind of woman who liked to make things from scratch," he smiled as he stirred the contents. "She taught me well. Marshmallows?"

Lucy couldn't help but smile. "Is it even hot chocolate if there isn't?"

When the chocolate was ready, Scott poured it into two large mugs and set one on the table in front of her, adding several huge marshmallows on top. "Enjoy."

She sipped the warm, creamy liquid and hummed her approval. "It's delicious."

"Thanks. Mom's recipe."

"So is she going to live with you here too?" she queried conversationally.

"No. She died a few years ago."

"I'm so sorry."

"It's OK," he assured her easily. "How about you? Does your family live in town?"

"No," Lucy confessed. "It's just me. I don't have any family."

"I know how that is." He raised his mug to her and winked. "I guess here's to us loners then."

"Cheers."

"How is Mrs. Cole?" he asked, as he sipped his chocolate. They were sitting facing each other at the table and Lucy almost spit out her chocolate at the question.

"You mean you haven't heard?" Sadness reared up inside her afresh.

"Heard what?" Scott asked with a hint of alarm.

"Poor Mrs. Cole died last week."

The expression on his face was nothing short of stunned.

"I … had no idea. I was supposed to come back but I've been working flat out nearly every day coming up to the holidays. I was actually planning to go see her tomorrow. I can't believe it."

"She actually passed the day I met you," Lucy informed him. "An aneurysm, apparently."

"I can't believe it. She was such a sweet old lady and so tough. I kinda thought she'd live forever."

"I know." Lucy felt fresh tears brim at the corner of her eyes.

"So what's going to happen to Berry?" he asked, and she wished he hadn't reminded her of that all too pressing problem.

"I have no idea," she said sighing. "I've been trying so hard to find someone to take him since then, but I've run out of options. He's been with Mrs. Stillman up to now, but she can't handle him anymore. She says I have a couple more days and after that, he's out."

"No one wants to adopt an awesome dog like Berry?" Scott asked, surprised.

"No, that's just it. There were some people interested, but they weren't suitable. They didn't have enough space or they were too old, or simply hadn't thought it through."

"You really care about him."

"Of course I do. He's a great dog, and such a sweetie too, as you know. I love taking care of him. Mrs. Cole loved him, and that's why I need to make sure he goes to someone she'd approve of. I can't just give him to anyone. I need to make sure he'd be happy."

She'd run off on a tangent. It happened sometimes. Now, Scott was just staring at her with a thoughtful look on his face.

"So no one's good enough," he said as he sipped his chocolate again.

Lucy blushed. "I guess so. It's just, I'd hate for him to go to someone who wouldn't love him as Mrs. Cole did. Someone who wouldn't treat him right. I haven't been successful yet, but I'm sure I'm going to find someone, the perfect someone for him."

"I understand. I have a few rescues myself I'm hoping to rehome with the right people, but I haven't had a chance to start looking yet."

Lucy looked up, interested. "Rescue dogs?"

"Yes, four little guys I came across while on the job. Lou Lou, I found down on Weston. She's an American English Coonhound I saw wandering the woods a few weeks ago. She didn't have a collar or any way to identify her, so I think she may have belonged to some hunters who left her behind. Some people just don't care for their pets the way they should."

"I know. I can't stand it. I just don't understand how you can treat any living thing with such disrespect." Lucy smiled then. "That breeds's a really sweet animal too. Very amiable."

"I know," Scott grinned. "Whenever she sees me, it's like coming home to a friend."

"She's here?" Lucy asked, surprised. She hadn't seen any animals when she came in and wondered where they were.

"I have a kennel out back. I built it because I hope to one day get some Leonbergers, or maybe a Neapolitan Mastiff."

Lucy's heart was backflipping in her chest. Neapolitan Mastiffs? They were such huge, beautiful animals. She'd always wanted to see one up-close but had never had the chance. They were also very expensive dogs and required a lot of care.

"Well, whenever you do get them I'd love to be your walker," she offered genuinely.

"I'll keep that in mind."

"So, you were telling me about Lou Lou?" Lucy got back to the topic at hand. "You know, in terms of rehoming her, a dog like that needs someone who can help stimulate its hunting nature. It wouldn't be fair to have her cooped up in a house. You wouldn't want a novice having her either. Breaking her in, if she's not already broken, will be a lot of trouble for someone who doesn't know what they're doing. Coonhounds are stubborn and tenacious. They take a little working with, but once they're settled they're just perfect."

He grinned. "You really know a lot about dogs, don't you?"

"Yes," she chuckled bashfully. "I once thought of studying to be a vet when I moved back home from the city, but I gave that idea up pretty quickly. Being a dog walker works best for me right now, but once I get everything in order you'll see. I have big plans for 12 Dogs."

Scott chuckled. "I don't doubt that for a second."

"So what else are you keeping out there?"

"Well there's ET, a male Kelpie."

Lucy tried not to laugh at the names Scott had given his rescues.

"A good dog, but they get lonely very quickly. Needs someone who can be with them as much as possible. It's a working dog, bred to be active. Shouldn't be kept inside, and needs to get lots of exercise. I mean *lots*."

Scott kept grinning at her as she espoused the traits of each breed, and who would be the most suitable owner for them.

"You're really good at that you know, matching dogs to the right kind of people."

Lucy shrugged. "I guess. I just know my breeds."

"Have you ever heard of a place called Lisdoonvarna?"

"No. Where is that? Slovakia?"

"Ireland. They have a festival there every summer called the Lisdoonvarna Matchmaking Festival. It's apparently Europe's biggest singles event. Great fun."

"You've been?" Lucy asked, mostly surprised that Scott might be single.

"Yes, earlier this year. Some friends and I were there for a vacation and heard about it. It's been going on for over a hundred and sixty years."

"That's a long time."

"It is. They have this matchmaker guy who, the myth says, if you touch his book with both hands you'll be married within six months." Scott chuckled and drained his mug. "I don't know about that though."

"What? You don't believe that stuff like that can happen?"

"Not really. It's nice to think and to hope for, but I think you and I would have better luck hitting one of the bars." He grinned.

Lucy was intrigued. Then her eyes grew wide. What was he suggesting? Was Scott implying that she needed to go out and get matched?

Suddenly she was embarrassed and uncomfortable again.

"So what does that have to do with me?" she asked hesitantly.

"You could be Whitedale's matchmaker. But instead of people, you could match dogs to potential owners. Turn it into something fun."

There was a novel thought. A dog matchmaking service? It would certainly be a unique addition to her business. And unlike her matchmaking neighbour Eustasia, Lucy understood her customer at least.

Also felt nice that Scott thought she had a talent.

The problem was, Lucy thought ruefully, at the moment she couldn't seem to utilise it for poor Berry.

Or could she?

"So how do you think I should I go about something like this ... for Berry, I mean?" she asked thoughtfully.

She liked what Scott was saying, but the mechanics of it was the question.

"Well," he sat forward in his seat. "I guess you begin like you've just done verbally with me - come up with a kind of ... profile, like a dating profile, listing Berry's canine personality traits, and a corresponding list of preferable qualities in an owner. And maybe my brood too, if you wanted to make a thing of it."

She nodded. "But how do I let people know about it?" She didn't relish the idea of posting up more fliers all around town.

"Well, Christmas is the perfect time to get the whole community interested and involved. You could maybe even open a booth or something."

"12 Dogs of Christmas..." Lucy's brain suddenly kicked into high gear.

"Yes, perfect. I love it! See, you *are* good at this stuff."

Suddenly, she was on a roll. "We can clean Berry and the dogs up, maybe put a bow and some festive ribbons on them and take some photos for their profiles? Set up a doggie matchmaking service to find them their forever homes in time for Christmas. A booth at the Christmas fair would be perfect."

"Yes," Scott was nodding enthusiastically. "All those people in one place all at once. If not from here, then maybe even McKinley? Every year people come over for the tree lighting ceremony. Lots of potential matches. Our own matchmaking festival here in Whitedale, except for dogs."

The grin on Lucy's face wouldn't subside. She *loved* this idea. And, most importantly, it truly could be the perfect opportunity to find Berry *his* perfect match in time for the holidays. Scott's ingenuity had once again set a fire under her and motivated her to keep going.

But what was she going to do with him in the meantime? Lucy remembered then, suddenly crestfallen once more.

The Christmas fair was days away, and she still needed somewhere to keep him.

"Sounds great in theory, but what do I do with Berry until then?" she mused out loud.

Scott shrugged. "Why don't I keep him here?"

"You?"

"Yes, why not? I have plenty of space, plus I already know Berry. And I think he likes me. We get along pretty well, don't you think?"

She smiled. "That you do."

"Can I get you a refil?" he asked, as he got to his feet with his mug in hand.

"No thanks, I'd better get going," Lucy looked at her watch, suddenly realizing the time. Scott was so easy and interesting to talk to the time seemed to have just flown by.

She looked out the window; the snowfall had eased, but the sun was disappearing fast. "I really have to get the dogs home ..." She jumped to her feet.

"Right," Scott replied. "That's a shame. I almost forgot you were on the job."

"Me too." She gave him a rueful smile. "It was really nice of you to let us stay this long."

"My pleasure," he answered as he washed the mugs and set them on the drainer. Then he shook the water from his hands and grabbed a towel to dry them. "Let's get you guys home."

Before they left, Scott took Berry out back to the kennel he'd told Lucy about, and to introduce her to the other dogs he'd rescued.

It was a big area with plenty of space for them all to run around in, and the kennels themselves were heated and spacious. It was perfect for the big dog and a lifesaver for Lucy. And Mrs Stillman too, no doubt.

She stooped down beside Berry to say goodbye, and he licked her face happily.

"I've got to go now buddy," Lucy said hugging him gently. "Scott's going to take care of you for a little while, but I promise I'll come back to visit you," she said, then looked up at Scott, a little embarrassed for assuming. "If that's OK?"

He smiled. "I wouldn't have it any other way."

CHAPTER 14

The following morning, Lucy woke with sunshine on her face.

Not literally, but it felt that way.

Thanks to Scott's idea and his kind offer to help Berry, she had a spring in her step and a huge weight off her mind.

She bounded out of bed, did her stretches and never had a better tasting bowl of cereal. She finger-combed her hair into a high ponytail, and brushed her teeth while dancing to cheery Christmas songs on the radio.

As expected, Mrs. Stillman was over the moon to learn that Berry would no longer be an occupant in her house. The timing was perfect too because her family had called to inform her that they'd be coming for the holidays a day earlier, leaving her with no choice but to boot him out.

Disaster averted, just in time.

LUCY PICKED up her usual charges for their walk and the morning seemed to go by quicker, but that might've been because she was so inspired and eager to get cracking with Scott's dog matchmaking idea.

It really was such a brainwave, and sure to be fun, too.

By lunchtime, things were already started to fall into place. She called the town's fair committee and spoke to Mary Winter, the overly enthusiastic community organizer who loved all things Christmas.

Mary was always the first one in town to hang out decorations, and she prided herself on having 'the best' Christmas Cookies on sale at the fair. They were, too.

Lucy was over the moon at her response to the idea of the matchmaking booth. She also happened to be one of the world's biggest dog-lovers, so the idea of helping some down-on-their-luck pups find a home for Christmas was something Mary was deeply enthusiastic about.

"12 Dogs of Christmas is a *great* name for a booth, Lucy. I love it!" she cooed delightedly.

So, she had the permission she needed. But now, Lucy had some groundwork to do.

Berry would be happy at Scott's place for a couple of days, a fantastic temporary solution.

She was determined to have a happy home for him soon, and was also enjoying the prospect of helping Scott out in return.

You really had to love dogs to pick up and take care of strays, not to mention assume the responsibility of rehoming them.

And Lucy really wanted to help him find his rescues their forever homes. He'd already done a lot for these pups by taking them in and caring for them.

It showed real heart.

Once she'd dropped all the dogs back that afternoon, she picked up her cell and dialed the number Scott had given her the night before, giddily pacing her kitchen as she told him about her progress thus far.

And when he suggested she come by his place to plan things further, visit Berry and take him for his walk, Lucy couldn't deny that she was equally enthused about seeing them both.

It took her a little while to find her way back to Scott's this time, which was around the back of Lonesome Ridge.

Lucy still couldn't believe she'd wandered so far off the path as to find her way to his house in the first place.

Thank goodness for Berry and his sensitive nose.

The house was even more stunning in full daylight against a clear blue sky.

Scott had finished a project earlier that week thus was home again, working on the house.

"Hey there," Lucy called out as she got out of her red Chevy pick-up. He turned and waved at her from the roof, a bright smile lighting up his handsome features.

"I see you found your way back on wheels this time."

"Yep, better prepared," she chuckled as she watched him climb down a ladder.

"You want to see Berry and the others first?" he asked. "Give you a chance to get to know them a little."

"That'd be great."

"So how's your day been?" he asked as they walked side-by-side to the rear of the property.

"Couldn't be better," Lucy replied. "I was out earlier and my thoughts were going a mile a minute. I really can't thank you enough for suggesting the matchmaking idea. It's genius."

"Don't mention it. You're helping me too, so it's a win-win situation. I can't keep my guys here forever, and until the house is done I can't give them the attention they deserve. They need more than just visits to feed and walk them. They need a home with someone who loves them and can give them what they need. Just like you said."

He led her to the kennels where Berry, Lou Lou and ET were happily running around the holding area.

As they drew closer, Lucy thought she could hear the faint sound of yelping.

"What's that?" she asked. "Did you get puppies?"

"Found them on my way back from work earlier. A box left on the side of the highway on my way back from McKinley. "Akitas."

"Someone just left them on the road to die?" Lucy exclaimed, appalled.

"Looks that way. I almost ran over the box. I drove around it, but something told me to stop and take a look."

She had to repress her anger, not at Scott but the culprits. How could anyone do that? It was winter, and yes maybe the dogs had a thick coat of fur but that was no excuse. It was *cruel*.

She refocused her thoughts. "So, we have some more recruits for our new enterprise."

He bit his lip. "Looks that way. Sorry."

"Don't be. Just makes me even more determined to get this right."

LUCY AND SCOTT played with the dogs a little, before taking them out all for a walk and run around the woods before darkness fell.

It gave her a chance to really get to know them.

ET was the most excitable. Lou Lou sniffed around a lot; Lucy could tell she wanted to be out on the hunt.

She was otherwise content, but she wasn't going to be happy being trapped behind a fence for long. She needed more space and attention.

Berry was perfectly happy though. He had space, shelter, the open woods and two very familiar faces. Plus, he was getting all the food he wanted. He was in heaven.

The abandoned Akitas were a different story. Their fur was dirty and they were thin; clear signs of neglect.

A few more days with good food and some loving care and attention would perk them right back up though.

Now Lucy picked up one of the little furballs. "Does this guy have a name?" she asked Scott, as she cradled the pup who wriggled about as she scratched his stomach.

"I haven't had a chance to name them yet. I figure whoever gets them might want to do so themselves."

"Good point." Lucy nodded determinedly. "OK, let's get you guys all prepped and ready for a brand new life."

They returned to the house; Lucy more eager than ever to get started on working to match all these great dogs with the perfect person.

"What do you think about this?" she asked Scott, a little while later, reciting the profile she'd just created.

She cleared her throat.

"Single, rambunctious three-year-old Kelpie named ET, phoning home. Gentle, peaceable and hard-working. He loves long walks, exercise, chasing balls, discs and playing hide-and-seek. Needs love from someone who is active and involved, and who wants a dog to put to work. Give him a job and he'll give you more than enough love in return."

"Sounds great!" Scott replied, shaking his head in admiration. "I knew you'd be amazing at this."

She smiled, thrilled with the praise. "I'll get right to work on one for Lou Lou."

"Can I make you something?" he asked as he stepped away from the table. "I haven't eaten all day."

She looked distractedly up from her notebook.

"You know, neither have I. Not since lunch anyway. That'd be nice. Thanks."

"You really are doing a great job *and* you're a natural," he commented as he walked over to the cupboards and began to collect items to prepare something.

Lucy wasn't used to hearing so much praise and she wasn't sure how to respond to it. She never did anything for recognition really; it was always passion that drove her.

And this time she had a dual reason. She wanted to help the dogs first and foremost, but helping Scott was also very satisfying. He worked hard. He cared. He wanted to do right by these animals, and she was going to see to it that he got his wish.

"I hope you like French food," he said as he began to chop some vegetables.

"Never had it," she confessed.

"Never?"

She shook her head. "I don't really go out much."

"None of your boyfriends ever took you to a French restaurant? That's a travesty."

Lucy began to fidget. "Umm, well, I never really had that many boyfriends."

"How many have you had?" he asked casually.

She hesitated. What would he think if she told him?

"I don't know if I should answer that."

"Why not? It's just a number."

"Fine. If it's just a number, how many girlfriends have you had?" she retorted.

"Three," he replied nonchalantly.

"That's all?" Lucy was surprised.

He smirked. "Yup. I was fifteen when I started out with Linda. We were together for three years. Broke up because of college. Susan and I got together my junior year of college and were together for six. Then I met Hailey when I was twenty-six or seven and we were together for five. I've been single ever since."

Lucy blinked. She realized she didn't even know how old Scott was. "How old are you?"

"Thirty-three. Why?"

"Nothing," she said with a shake of her head. "Was just asking."

"So I answered your question. Now answer mine."

Discomfited, Lucy took a deep breath and sighed. "One."

"Really? Only one?"

She could hear the disbelief in his voice. "Yep. Just one."

"That's strange. I would've thought you'd be fighting them off," he stated as he continued to chop.

"Why would you think that?" she asked honestly.

"Why wouldn't I?"

Where did he get those eyes from? Whenever Lucy looked directly into them her stomach flipped about, her mind boggled and her tongue got twisted.

He was so much easier to talk to when he wasn't looking right at her.

He wouldn't be single for very long though. She could think of at least three women she knew who would be perfect for him. Tall, beautiful, intelligent and who could actually hold a conversation while making eye-to-eye contact.

"Well?" he urged.

"Well, what?" she replied, coloring.

He turned back to what he was doing. "So why haven't you dated more?"

Lucy leaned forward on her elbows and clasped her hands under her chin. "I've always been ... shy," she admitted. "Painfully so, sometimes. Doesn't really work well when trying to communicate with other people. Especially guys."

"You're shy?" He seemed surprised. "I wouldn't have thought so. You're so happy and chatty in my eyes."

"That's because of the dogs," she admitted. "I'm better with them than people. They don't disappoint."

"Ah OK. So, someone disappointed you," he stated perceptively.

"I guess you could say that. My dad walked out on my mom when I was eleven. She died a year later and I got sent to live with my Grandma."

Scott stopped to look back at her again. "I'm really sorry to hear that."

"It's okay. It was a long time ago." She sighed. "I started seeing a guy when I was eighteen, but he was just playing with me. I thought he was serious. I guess I didn't know any better at the time."

"He was an idiot," Scott said with feeling. "Anyone who wouldn't take someone like you seriously could only be one."

When she looked up, he was still watching her, those eyes boring into her gaze.

But this time Lucy didn't blush. She simply smiled. "Thank you."

CHAPTER 17

*V*isitors from all around the area flocked to Whitedale for this year's Holiday Fair and tree lighting ceremony.

Grant Square was the center of Whitedale; a large roundabout with a grassy middle, it was the heart of the town. And at Christmas, it was the yuletide epicenter.

White and colored strings of twinkling lights crisscrossed the square from one corner to another. Large wreaths decorated with white lights, red ribbon, and pinecones hung at the entrance from every access point.

The tree itself, erected at the center and surrounded by decorative gift boxes, was the final touch.

The official lighting ceremony occurred exactly one week before Christmas every year. Twelve feet of Douglas Fir stood fully adorned in silver, white and royal blue.

There were ribbons, balls, icicles, and the remnants of snowfall from the night before. Even without the lights, it was beautiful.

This evening, the entire town was out in force, and Lucy was loving the holiday atmosphere.

For her 12 Dogs of Christmas matchmaking booth, Mary had

given her a spot close to the Christmas tree to maximize foot traffic.

Now, standing at the booth surrounded by festive profile photos and cute bios for the dogs, it was the first time since her grandmother's death that she remembered being happy at this time of year.

"Hey Lucy," Mary called out, as she approached her with a smile. "Merry Christmas."

"Same to you. Great turn out," she commented.

The other woman looked gleeful. "Isn't it? I think it's the best we've had since I became head of the committee."

"You're doing a great job," Lucy stated as she rearranged some of the profiles out front.

Mary smiled at the presentation. "This looks great. How has the response been so far?"

Lucy beamed. It was like the sun was inside of her trying to get out. "Amazing actually," she told her. "I already have a dozen or so prospective families. I'll vet them over the next few days and hopefully have these pups cosy in their new homes in time for Christmas."

She couldn't believe the response already. So many potential families! She was sure that among them was the perfect home for each of her and Scott's furry friends.

"Keep it up," Mary encouraged. "I've got to go. It's almost showtime."

"Hey there," Scott called out then, approaching.

"You brought them!" Lucy exclaimed happily, realizing he had Lou Lou, ET, and Berry with him; their tails wagging merrily when they saw her.

"I couldn't leave these guys home, especially today. The perfect real-life canine additions."

He got closer and smiled at the display. "Wow, you really did a great job with this. It looks spectacular." He picked up the flier for Rex and Roza, a couple of Border Collies he'd found in Gafferton.

Their owner didn't want them and was going to put them down if no one took them, so Scott did.

"Tenacious twins Rex and Roza, six-month-old Border Collies, are looking for an active owner," he read aloud. "Energetic, intelligent, agile and balanced; they need a home where they can have lots to do. Perfect for farmers and an ideal work dog, these pooches love a cuddle after the workday is done. Both means double the love."

Lucy smiled. "Like it?"

He grinned. "It's perfect. Did you have any takers?"

Lucy grabbed the sign-up sheet and held it out to him in giddy triumph. "Four already for these two alone."

"I knew you could do it," he encouraged, as the dogs milled around, sniffing the foreign scents filling the square.

"I haven't done it *yet*," she reminded him, trying to rein in both their enthusiasm. But she couldn't deny she was very hopeful.

"You will. I'm sure of it." Scott smiled. "Have you had a chance to look around the other stalls yet?"

"Not really. It's been so busy already. Oh hello big guy," Berry came up her, his huge tale almost levelling the booth, and she reached down and scratched him round the ears.

Lucy was so completely dedicated to her task she sometimes got tunnel vision. Today was one such occasion. She really wanted to find these animals a home and that had been her foremost thought. Especially when it came to Berry.

She'd already talked to some people who were potentially great matches and hoped his new owner was amongst them. She also hoped it would be someone in, or close to town so that she could keep walking him.

She'd miss him if he wound up in a different county where she couldn't see him anymore. She couldn't be selfish, however. If the perfect home for Berry was far away, then she'd have no choice but to say goodbye.

"Well, why don't we grab a quick bite and take a look around before the ceremony starts?"

Now, Lucy looked at the big, happy dog as he wandered around the area, glancing curiously at the lights and festivity.

No, she couldn't imagine not seeing him every day. It would be a hard thing to get used to.

"Lucy?"

Her eyes snapped up at the sound of Scott's voice, and she realized she hadn't replied. "Sorry. Yes, good idea.I was just thinking."

"About Berry?"

She nodded. "I just realized that I'm really going to miss him."

He looked at her thoughtfully. "I think maybe you should cross that bridge when you come to it."

"You're right. No sense crying over spilled milk when the carton's still in the fridge."

Scott chuckled. "A ... different take on it but yes, I guess."

"I'm a bit corny," she admitted, embarrassed. "My Grandma always said if it was something out of the way and a little bit odd, I'd probably say it."

"I think I would've very much liked to have met your grandmother," Scott stated and she smiled, realizing that Grandma in turn would have liked him a lot too.

Now he held out his arm to her. "Shall we?"

She smiled hooking it. "Let's."

$\mathcal{T}$he lighting ceremony was spectacular.

The children's choir sang *Silent Night* beautifully, before Mary made her introduction to the Mayor, who duly flipped the switch and lit up the massive fir in beautiful, twinkling splendour.

Lucy and Scott watched it all as they stood side-by-side with steaming hot chocolate in hand, the dogs between them.

Scott lingered on at the booth a little after the ceremony, and when the time came for the fair to close, he stepped behind the scenes to help tidy-up, settling the dogs by a lamppost nearby.

Lucy smiled at his gallantry. "Thanks."

"My pleasure." He began to collect the fliers and place them into one of the boxes she had stored underneath the countertop.

"You know, Berry really seems to like it a lot at your house," she commented, as she cleaned up. "And tonight, he behaved like a dream in your presence. Have you ever thought of taking him in yourself?"

Scott paused a little, and all of sudden Lucy worried that she'd overstepped.

He sighed. "Berry is a great dog. We both know that. I just think that maybe there's someone else out there who'd be a better person for him."

"Really, who?" she asked, intrigued. If Scott had an idea of someone in particular then she wanted to know.

He smiled a little. "I can't say yet. I just know that I'm not the right one, sorry." He stepped closer then, and Lucy's stomach fluttered as he gently brushed a stray tendril of hair behind her ear, as if by way of apology.

She sighed and bent down to pick up a box, now feeling bad to have assumed.

"You're right, I was just reaching, and I met some really good prospects today already. It's just ... I really don't want to have to send him away."

"I know. But when the time comes, I know you'll do what's best for him. So, all done?" he asked as he stacked up the final box.

"I think so." All of a sudden she felt exhausted. "Man I'm beat."

"You're like me," Scott chuckled. "Once I get my teeth into something I can't stop until it's done. I'll skip meals and even showers."

Her face wrinkled. "That's gross."

"No, that's manual labor. When I want to get work done on the house I get up, put on some clothes and get to it. I can shower before bed. I just need to get going."

"I hope you don't plan to do that when you find your next girlfriend," she commented. "I'm sure she wouldn't find you nearly as appealing."

"Trust me, if I had a girlfriend, there would be a lot of different things in my life."

She turned to look at him, wondering what he meant. What would he even need to change?

"So - see you tomorrow?" Scott enquired, as he closed the door of Lucy's truck once they'd got everything back inside.

"I could maybe stop by after I finish following up with some of the families. We could discuss the options? I've got a lot to get through over the next few days."

"Great. I can make you dinner and you can see Berry of course," he added with a grin.

"Sounds great to me. See you then," Lucy turned her key in the ignition, and glanced back at the twinkling Christmas tree, the backdrop to a waving Scott and his waggy-tailed companions.

And as she drove away, she couldn't help but smile.

Despite her tiredness, tonight had been the nicest time she'd spent in ages.

*D*ays passed and Lucy went about her dog-walking duties as normal, but as soon as she dropped her charges back, off she went to visit prospective owners for the rescues.

The very first day, she found a home for two of the Akita puppies, and was over the moon when she went to Scott's that evening to share the news and see Berry.

Day after day, the process went pretty much the same. She walked her dogs as usual, then afterward visited prospective owners before meeting up with Scott and Berry.

Some days she had good news to share and others, she just went to see Berry, enjoy Scott's company - and not having to go home to an empty apartment.

"I really think ET's going to be so happy," she told Scott now, excited to have found a match for his rescue pup. "Joseph Steinbeck is perfect for him. He's a fireman and trains every day, so taking ET for walks and getting him exercise won't be a problem. Plus, he said they're looking at adding more dogs to the rescue team and ET would be ideal for that. Yes, he's a bit on the older side to start training, but from what I've observed he's very compliant and with the right trainer and some patience, could make a really great rescue dog."

"You're really excited about this," Scott mused as he brought a platter of pizza over to the couch.

Drinks were already on the coffee table and Lucy was curled up on the couch with the remote in her hand surfing Netflix for a movie.

"Aren't you?"

"Of course. And I knew you'd be great at all this, I just never thought it would all happen so quickly. You know, I think we really are going to get all these guys re-homed in time for Christmas."

"Of course we are," Lucy said satisfied. "Once I make a plan I execute it."

"Good to know."

Scott settled on the couch beside her. Lucy wasn't sure what she was in the mood to watch tonight. TV could be a wasteland; you could get lost and never actually find that one thing you really wanted to watch. It was the ultimate 'too much choice' dilemma.

"Having trouble deciding?" he asked as she continued to skim through titles.

"I don't know what I feel like tonight," she admitted. "You pick."

He took the remote from her as Lucy pulled out a slice of meat lover's pizza. Scott had doubled every topping, making it the most loaded pizza she'd ever seen.

When she looked back at the screen, she laughed out loud at the title he'd highlighted.

"OK. *Lassie* it is."

CHAPTER 20

*I*t was now only three days til Christmas and Lucy was still on the hunt for a home for Berry.

Lou Lou, ET and the Akitas were gone. A farmer named Jasper Tucker had taken Lou Lou. He liked to go on frequent hunting trips, was in his thirties and active. He was perfect for a Coonhound.

Now, she was personally delivering Rex and Roza to their new owners.

"Now, dogs are fun, but a really big responsibility," she informed the Dickersons' two small children.

"Can I ride on their backs?" four-year-old Billy asked. "I saw it on TV."

Lucy smiled indulgently. "That's actually not so good for the dogs. They weren't built to bear weight on their backs like that. You could hurt them."

"Then why did they do it on TV?" Five-year-old Sydney wanted to know.

Their parents smiled. "They're just curious," their mother commented.

"That's good, means they're interested," Lucy replied. She turned back to the children. "They probably didn't know better, but you do now, so you can take even better care of your new furry friends. That's what you want, right?"

The children chorused a happy yes.

"Now Rex and Roza aren't like your toys, OK? You have to help your mom and dad take care of them." The children were too young to take care of the dogs on their own, but it was good to have them help so that one day they could take more responsibility.

Good pet ownership started when kids were small, Lucy believed. Not that she thought they'd have any trouble here. The Dickersons owned a ranch, and animals were everywhere.

Rex and Roza would have work to do once they were older, but for now, they were a great addition to the family.

Lucy left the children to play with their new pets while she turned her focus to the ones who'd really be taking care of the dogs, their parents.

"So I know we went through everything before, but I just wanted to emphasize a few things. When it comes to their diet, make sure you watch them carefully. They do a lot of exercising, but you have to be wary of overfeeding them. Treats will help you to train them, but too many can affect their weight. Here are a few."

She handed over the bag of treats she usually bought for her charges. "You'll want to use a pin brush once or twice a week to keep their coat free of mats, tangles, and debris. You'll need to do that more frequently during shedding season."

"Shedding season?" Lynda Dickerson asked.

"Yes. It gets pretty hairy then," Lucy mused ruefully. "But you'll be fine. You're just going to need to brush them more. You can make it something fun for the kids to do. Speaking of the children … collies tend to want to lead those smaller than them, animals and children. Your two are a bit older, and you've said they're well-behaved so that shouldn't be a problem, but I'd still keep an eye on them just for the initial phase, as both the kids and the dogs adjust."

"Thank you," James said. "We've had dogs before but we've

never had anyone do what you've done in making sure we got the right animals for our family, and for our family's needs. Plus, you really seem to care about the well-being of these animals. There should be more like you."

Lucy could feel her cheeks getting hot with the compliment. She wasn't used to them and it only made her social discomfort even more apparent.

Still, she couldn't deny that all of this was making her feel good. "Thank you."

BUT AT THIS POINT, everyone had a home but Berry.

Lucy had met with several families who were interested in having the big dog as an addition to their family. They'd made it on to her list, so they had the basic requirements, but once she met them was when she saw the faults.

"I'm sorry Mr. Chase, I just don't think Berry would fit here," Lucy stated as she sat in the living room of Simon Chase's house.

"Why not?" he asked. "I have space outside and I can afford the cost of his care."

"Yes, that's true," she replied. "But he doesn't like staying outside all the time. His previous owner, Mrs. Cole, kept him exclusively in the house at night. Your house is a great size, but you have a lot of stuff in here and I can tell some of it is expensive. Outside just wouldn't work with Berry. He likes to be where the family is and he can't do that in here."

Simon nodded. "It wouldn't matter to me much. I'm sure I could get it done. Maybe move a few things around?"

"You could try, but it might just make you and Berry uncomfortable. Truthfully, I think another type of dog would suit you best."

"I see. Thank you for your honesty," Simon said as he extended his hand to her.

"I'm really sorry to disappoint you," she continued as she got to her feet and took his hand.

"It's quite alright. Thanks for coming out."

But as Lucy left yet another fruitless prospective match for Berry, she had to wonder if maybe the ultimate fault lay with her.

She ambled back to her truck, unable to shake the thought. Simon Chase would've been a great match for Berry, albeit not for the inside of his house.

What was she saying? She could've let it slide and let him have Berry. Did it really matter that he wouldn't be living the same way he did with Mrs. Cole? He was out of the house a lot with Scott now as it was.

And if Simon Chase was willing to risk his property, who was she to say otherwise?

"You have to stop being so particular," she told herself as she got back into the vehicle. She sat behind the wheel and stared out at the slowly falling snow.

Berry was special to her though. She wanted him to have the perfect situation.

OK, so her apartment was small, and obviously her landlord wouldn't let her have a dog, but Lucy couldn't help but think that he still would've been happiest of all with her.

She certainly would've felt better. She wouldn't need to worry about him. She could take care of him just the way Mrs. Cole would've wanted.

She could do it.

So maybe she should think about getting a different apartment?

It could work, she realized excitedly. She could look for someplace else to live. Someplace big enough for her and Berry, with a landlord who didn't mind pets.

Lucy started the truck. She'd bounce the idea off Scott and see what he thought.

"I THINK IT'S ME," she sighed, when later, she flopped down at a chair around Scott's makeshift kitchen table.

"What is?" he asked, as poured kibble into a bowl for Berry.

"Not being able to find a home for this big guy. Maybe I'm too picky."

"Not necessarily. You just know Berry so well and who'd be right for him. Look what you did for my rescues. Every last one of them has the perfect home now, and that was all you."

"So why not Berry then? Why is it so hard?"

"I don't know," he said. "Why don't you tell me?"

"I was thinking about it while I was leaving the Chase house. Maybe I keep finding faults in every prospective pet owner, because deep down inside I don't believe anyone would take care of Berry as well as I would," she admitted.

Scott turned to her with raised eyebrows. "Keep going."

"You aren't going to say anything?"

"Not right now. I'd rather hear where else you're going with this."

"Well," she said, continuing. "I know I don't have the perfect place to keep him right now. My apartment is small, but I could change that. I could get a new place. It might take a while, but I could do it."

"What would you do with him until then?"

She grimaced a little. "I was kinda hoping I could leave him here with you, if you'd let me?" she asked hopefully. "It wouldn't be for long. I hope. Just until I found a bigger place that would suit both of us."

"A different apartment?"

"No other choice. Besides, it's not as though he'd be home alone when I'm working, because I'd take him on all the walks with me as normal."

"True."

Scott put the dog food away and handed Lucy the bowl. They walked to the holding area together where Berry was running around the enclosure and came bounding up to the gate the second he saw them.

Lucy smiled, she would never get tired of the sight of him running towards her, his large ears flopping on either side of his head, tongue hanging out as if he was smiling.

They opened the gate and stepped inside. Lucy walked to the kennel, but Berry was already trying to get his head into the bowl.

"Hold on a minute," she giggled as she gently pushed his head away and set the food down. Berry bounded over and dove right in the second she stepped away.

She stood staring at the big dog with her hands stuffed in her pockets, then looked at Scott. "I'm being silly, aren't I?"

"Why would you say that?" he asked.

"To think I could honestly do a better job taking care of him than people who have the space, and are willing to compromise their lifestyle to have him." She sighed heavily.

Scott's hand moved to rest gently on her shoulder. "I don't think so."

Lucy turned to look at him, surprised. "Really?"

"Really."

"So you think this could be the right thing?" she asked, hopeful.

"I think you've finally realized what I've known all along," he said gently and turned her to face him. His hands were on her arms, holding her gently. "Lucy, you *are* his perfect person."

She couldn't describe what it felt like when she heard those words come out of Scott's mouth. Deep down inside she'd always known she didn't want a dog *like* Berry. She wanted *him*. She wanted the big guy as her pet, her trusty companion, but was content to just help Mrs. Cole.

Then, the more time she got to spend with him, the more she realized how great it was to have him with her all the time.

"Thanks for that," she told Scott as she smiled up at him.

"For what?"

"For saying that. I needed to hear it."

"Why?"

"I guess I needed to know someone else besides me thought it was a good fit," she admitted bashfully. "I may not have everything he needs right now, but ..." She shrugged.

"I agree. Sometimes you don't have to have everything perfect though, Lucy. Sometimes you just have to have the heart. That's enough for now. The rest will come. And you have the heart," he continued. "I've known that for ages. It's why I wanted to meet you."

His confession took her by surprise. "You - meet me?

"Yes. Mrs. Cole told me about this wonderful woman who came to walk Berry," he chuckled. "She raved about you."

The sentiment made Lucy's heart sing. She'd never told Mrs. Cole how highly she regarded her, so it was nice to know that the older woman felt the same way about her.

"That day we met was purely coincidental, but the second I saw you running behind Berry, I know you were the best person for both of them," Scott continued. "Mrs. Cole needed someone to help, and Berry needed someone who could give him what she no longer could."

Lucy was beaming now.

"Since then I've watched you go all out for him. Persuading people to take care of him. Trying to find a home day after day. You were relentless, and the person who loved him enough to do all of that could only be the best one for him." He looked directly at her, those eyes boring into her gaze again. "You're the perfect match, Lucy. I've just been waiting for you to realize it."

*L*ucy hadn't really been able to enjoy Christmas since her grandmother's death.

But this would be the first time in years that she wasn't going to spend the day alone.

Instead, Scott had asked her over. She brought a homemade pecan pie with her and a bottle of mulled wine that she'd bought at the fair.

He was waiting on the porch when she arrived; Berry beside him. The big dog ran to her the second she got out of the truck, and immediately tried to stick his big head in the pie.

"Oh no you don't," she chided gently. "This isn't for you."

The dog snorted and walked away.

"For the first time ever, I think you disappointed him," Scott commented as he leaned against the post watching her. She had a red wool hat on her head and a cosy matching peacoat.

The snow that morning was heavy and the wind icy in every direction.

"Aren't you cold?" she asked him as she approached the entry-way. Though he was wearing a cosy sweater that looked like it could be cashmere.

Having only ever seen him in work shirts and jeans, it was a nice change.

"I have the heating on," he said with a smile. "Besides, I wasn't out here long. Berry let me know you were on your way."

"He must've heard the truck coming down the road," Lucy mused as she stepped inside.

However, the sound of another vehicle approach from behind drew her attention and she turned back to see two cars and another truck making their way up the driveway. "Who's that?" she asked a little unnerved.

"Just a few of my friends," Scott said casually.

"Your friends?" Lucy almost shrieked. She'd come over today thinking it was just the two of them, a casual thing as always. She wasn't ready to meet strangers.

"Don't be scared," he chuckled, reading her mind. "They won't bite. I promise."

"Why didn't you tell me though?"

"I didn't actually know they were coming until this morning. They wanted to surprise me and drove all the way here from Denver. I couldn't tell them no." He gave her a big smile and then took the pie from her hands. Why did he have to smile like that? It made Lucy forget about her shyness. "Besides, I wanted them to meet you," he added mysteriously.

"Me ...why?"

"Is there something wrong with wanting my oldest friends to meet one of my newest?" he responded.

"What if they don't like me? You know I'm not great with strangers."

"Who is?" He shook his head. "It doesn't matter anyway. I've already told them all about you."

Lucy's eyes widened. "What did you tell them?"

"Just that I met this crazy woman who loves dogs and smiles like sunshine," he commented offhandedly.

Her heart fluttered, but she dismissed it with a scoff.

"So you made me sound way better than I am."

"I don't exaggerate, Lucy. If I say you're wonderful, it's because you are."

Then, before she could react, Scott winked and hopped down off the porch to greet his friends.

CHAPTER 23

"*M*erry Christmas!" a cheerful female voice called out.

It belonged to a lithe blonde. She ran to Scott, threw her arms around his neck and smacked his cheek with a kiss. "You big lug. How've you been?" But didn't give him a chance to reply before she turned to Lucy. "And you must be Lucy. So nice to meet you finally," she said moving to embrace her too.

Finally...? Lucy was completely off-guard but did her best to return the welcoming gesture.

"Ted, could you get those things in here pronto?" the woman asked, turning to a man getting stuff out of the car behind her. "Kids, come on in out of the cold." She looked to Scott again. "Where's the bathroom these days?"

"Through there, just past the kitchen," he indicated with a roll of his eyes. "Same as last time."

"I'll drop this off on the way," She grabbed the pie from Scott's hands and hurried on her way.

Lucy watched her go. "Who was that?" she laughed.

"That whirlwind is Roxanna. I've known her since I was in high school. She's a bundle of energy and the friendliest person you'll ever meet."

"Uncle Scott!" a chorus sounded as three children, two girls and a boy came running in their direction.

"Hey, here comes trouble!" Scott declared as he stooped to hug them.

"We missed you, Uncle Scott," said the oldest girl. She was blonde like her mother and cute as a button.

"Me or my hot chocolate?"

"The chocolate," they answered in unison, and Lucy had to smile.

"At least you're honest," Scott turned to introduce her. "This is Lucy. And this is Jennifer, Morgan, and Tyler."

"Hi!" they all chorused together. They were adorable and he was adorable with them.

"Hey kids," she answered with a small wave. "Merry Christmas."

"Get inside and take your jackets off. The TV's that way," he added and they scampered off immediately.

"And this is Roxy's husband Ted," Scott supplied, as a tall, slightly balding man approached the house.

"Don't tell me. Lucy," he commented with a smile. "I'd give you a hug but as you can see I'm the bag man for this trip."

She laughed. "Would you like some help?"

"Love some to be honest."

"I can get it," Scott interjected.

"No, you have more guests to greet. I can help," Lucy insisted as she grabbed a few of the packages Ted had in his arms.

Soon the other guests arrived. Anita and Paul, two of Scott's friends from Ireland who were staying with Bryan and his sister Lydia in Denver, and had chosen to tag along when they heard of their impromptu plan to surprise him.

They had come prepared too. They brought turkey and stuffing, sweet potato pie, macaroni and cheese, salads, garlic bread, and wine.

Along with the roast ham, potatoes, candied yams, green beans and pumpkin soup Scott had already prepared, they had a true Christmas feast to look forward to.

THE FOOD LASTED ALL the way through the afternoon, with Ted then whipping out some beers.

The men set up in front of the TV, while the women chatted in the kitchen and the kids preoccupied themselves with the gifts their parents had brought, but mostly with Berry.

The big dog was a huge hit amongst the guests.

They each took turns scratching behind his ears and commenting on how amicable he was, surprised that a dog that big could be so gentle and easy with children.

"So Lucy, we've all heard tons about you, and now that it's just us girls here," Roxy grinned, indicated the guys who were enthralled in a game on TV. "What's the deal with you two?"

She looked up in slight alarm. "Me and Scott?"

"Yes," the other woman pressed. "Spill."

They were standing around the kitchen island staring at her, as Lydia washed the dishes and Lucy dried.

Roxy was responsible for packing them away.

"Oh yes, do tell," Lydia urged. "We promise not to say a word." She grinned and continued to scrub the remnants of the turkey roast from the pan.

"Well, Scott's my friend obviously. He's … nice," Lucy replied nervously.

She hated being put on the spot at the best of times, but this was even worse. They were questioning her relationship with Scott and she wasn't entirely sure what that was. They'd become so close this last while, but that was it. Wasn't it?

"That's it?" Anita scoffed. "Please, anyone can tell that guy is falling *hard*."

"You think so?" Lucy questioned uncertainly.

"Definitely," Roxy agreed. "When a guy talks about a woman as much as he talks about you, there has to be more to it than he's saying."

"So he said something to you?"

"Of course not," Lydia replied with a roll of her eyes. "He denies there's anything, just like you're doing," she grinned. "Thing is I don't believe either of you."

"Don't believe what?" Scott's voice interjected suddenly.

"That there's nothing between you and Lucy, that's what," Roxy stated.

"What's between him and Lucy?" Bryan asked, going to the fridge for another beer.

Scott looked at Lucy and she looked back at him, her cheeks reddening.

"See, look at them," Roxy reiterated. "Why don't you two stop playing coy and just admit it?"

"Rox ..." her husband warned.

Scott cleared his throat. "If there was something to say..."

"... then we would," Lucy put in quickly.

Lydia chuckled. "They're even finishing each other's sentences already."

"Definitely something there," Bryan teased.

"Why are you all so eager to make Lucy and I into something?" Scott asked nonchalantly.

"Because it's painfully obvious there *is* something," Roxanna tut-tutted. "We'd all like to see you happy, and I'm sure I speak for everyone when I say that from what we've heard and seen today, we all give you two a big thumbs up."

Despite herself, Lucy smiled brightly. "You guys are great too," she said.

"See! Perfect! She fits naturally into our ragtag bunch," Roxanna continued as she draped an arm around Lucy's neck. She looked at Scott. "So why not just come right out and say it?"

"Rox, if I had something to say, I assure you it would not be public," Scott replied firmly. "And when I do have something to say, Lucy will be the first to hear it."

His gaze met hers as she spoke and she found her breath catch in her lungs. This was incredibly ... awkward.

What did he mean?

"Forgive my wife," Ted demurred, as he came over and hugged Roxanna from behind. "Once she gets something into her head, she doesn't let go."

"Got that right. That's how I snagged you." Roxanna planted a light kiss on his lips, and they all laughed.

"Way to change the subject," Bryan commented with a chuckle. "Now is there anymore beer ..."

It was after eight that evening when the group decided that it was time to leave. It was starting to snow again, and they needed to get going if they wanted to make it back to the city before the worst of it.

Lucy and Scott stood on the porch and waved goodbye. He draped his arm lightly around her shoulders and she leaned against him as the snow fell gently all around.

It was the kind of warm, cosy, *homely* holiday moment she'd only ever seen on TV.

And she couldn't believe it was real.

This Christmas had yielded more than she could ever expect. Not only did she have a new friend, but friends plural.

And lately with Scott, a real sense of companionship; something that she'd been missing for far too long.

"So, what do you think? Not a complete disaster, right?" he asked as he closed the door behind them.

"I think they're wonderful," she admitted. "I really liked them all and the kids are so sweet."

"So I hope you're not going to leave me now too?" he asked, as he turned to her.

The cars were almost out of sight.

She shook her head. She'd just had the nicest Christmas Day ever and she didn't want it to end just yet. "Why do good things always go by so quickly though?"

"So we can have more of them," Scott shivered. "Let's get back inside out of this cold. Feel like some hot chocolate?" he suggested, leading back inside.

"I'd love some. Though I truly didn't think I could fit in anything else after all that food."

The kitchen was immaculate now, with little to no remnants of the humongous feast that had been enjoyed earlier that day.

"Go find a movie. I'll bring the chocolate," Scott stated as he began pulling out ingredients.

Lucy wandered into the living room.

Berry was nestled by the fireplace snoozing contentedly, and she had to smile.

Like it or not, the big dog had pretty much already made this house his home.

Scott came in a few minutes later with two steaming cups of his famous homemade hot chocolate. His was plain but there were marshmallows on hers, just as she liked it.

He stretched out on the couch and Lucy adjusted herself on the opposite end, with her feet towards him.

"*It's a Wonderful Life* is on. Do you want to watch it?" It was her all time favorite Christmas movie. She could never get over James Stewart's characterization of George Bailey.

Scott smiled. "I love that movie. My Mom liked to watch it every Christmas," he informed her.

They settled down to watch the movie, while the fire crackled lightly beneath the TV screen, Berry asleep beneath it.

Lucy sipped at the warm beverage, feeling more content and cosy than she'd ever been in her entire life.

Scott tugged at her toes and she giggled.

"Merry Christmas Lucy."

She smiled. "Merry Christmas."

THEY MUST'VE FALLEN asleep watching the movie, because when Lucy was awakened by Berry's damp tongue licking her face, the sun was just coming up over the horizon.

Across the way, Scott was still asleep, now hugging a cushion to his chest.

She couldn't help but watch him as he slept so peacefully, properly studying the contours of his face without having to worry about him catching her.

Berry nudged her again.

"Alright, I get it. You're hungry," she whispered.

She eased herself from the couch and padded into the kitchen. She got his bowl and the dog food and fixed him his breakfast.

Then she had an idea. Scott had cooked for her so many times already; why didn't she do something from him today?

Lucy set to work at making breakfast. She knew where most things were, having watched him prepare stuff for her so many times.

Soon, she had everything she needed to make them something delicious.

He kept a well-stocked pantry and everything was there to make sweet crepes, sausages, eggs and biscuits.

It had been a while since she'd had a reason to make a big meal like this, and wouldn't bother for just herself, but for Scott it was no trouble.

The smell must have awakened him because he walked into the room just as Lucy was plating the eggs.

"Morning," she greeted cheerfully.

"Good morning," he replied with a grin. "What's all this?"

"This is what I like to call breakfast," she replied. "Have a seat." She brought the plates and cutlery to the table, along with the pot of coffee she'd brewed. "Bon appétit."

They talked and laughed and ate. She couldn't remember ever feeling so at ease with anyone.

Scott was special, that was clear, but the problem was the more Lucy spent time with him and the more they shared, the more she realized she wanted.

CHAPTER 25

*S*cott cleaned up after, protesting that the cook didn't clean where he was from.

Lucy appreciated the sentiment, but she was happy to do it, after all it was his house and she'd made the mess.

But he wasn't hearing of it.

Berry began to bark at the door. He'd been pacing back-and-forth for a few minutes.

"I think he wants a walk," Lucy said.

"Let's take him then. I'll get our jackets."

He returned a few minutes later with both of their jackets and helped her slip hers on.

Berry was already gone, bounding off into the woods ahead of them.

She laughed as she watched the big happy dog running around in the snow chasing his tail.

"Look at him," she said with a chuckle. "He just loves it here."

"He does. It's really good having him here too," Scott replied. "How do you like it?"

"What're you talking about? You know I *love* this place. It's amazing," Lucy gasped. "The kind of house anyone would be excited to come home to."

"That's why I chose this spot. I used to love coming here to fish as a kid, so when I heard that it was up for sale I had to grab it."

"Good thing. If I could afford a place like this I would too. It's perfect for dogs and to relax amongst nature. The human company isn't so bad either," she teased with a smile.

"I could say the same about you."

Scott was looking directly at her now, and Lucy's heart was beating faster. "Your friends seem to think there's something more," she said boldly, surprising herself by being so direct.

But she needed to know.

"Do you think there is?" he asked, as they ambled out onto the wooden pier.

The sun was now peeking up just over the mountains.

"I don't know. Is there?" Lucy's heart was beating so fast, she didn't know how she got the words out.

She caught sight of Berry out of the corner of her eye and her heart steadied again as it always did.

He was occupied looking down at his reflection. He loved to look at himself. Mirrors, water, you name it. The big guy loved his own image.

"What do *you* think?" Scott repeated, still not answering her question.

His eyes were still locked on her face.

Lucy sucked in a breath. It was now or never.

"There is for me. What I want to know is -"

She didn't get to finish her sentence. The second the words left her mouth Scott had closed the space between them.

It was so quick that Lucy hadn't a chance to think about what to do before his lips pressed against hers, and her body was pulled flush against him.

Thankfully, she didn't need to think.

What she was feeling was enough. Her senses were reeling, but her fingers still worked. They curled into the lapels of Scott's jacket and held him. It wasn't enough though. A moment later her hands slipped up from his chest and encircled his neck.

His lips moved over hers like silk over skin.

When they finally parted, she was breathless. It took her several seconds to open her eyes. She didn't want to break the spell she was under, but she had to. She had to look at him.

"I've wanted to do that for a long time," he confessed. "I was waiting."

"I'm glad you didn't wait any longer." She chuckled. "I guess Roxy was right."

Scott laughed. "She's always right."

"I'm glad," Lucy stepped toward him again. She raised her chin and pressed her lips to his lightly. "I think I wanted to do that for a long time too."

"Why didn't you?"

The fact that they were having this conversation at all, was still something Lucy was trying to process.

It was made difficult with him looking at her as if she was the most beautiful person he'd ever seen. She'd only ever seen that look in movies. Never directed at her.

"I didn't realize it before," she admitted. "I thought we were just friends. The only thing between us was our love of dogs," she continued. "The jittery feeling in my stomach whenever I was around you was just because of my shyness, I told myself."

"But it wasn't?"

"No," she replied with a small shake of her head, amazed at her own certainty and the fact that she was confident about admitting all this to him. "It was telling me what I hadn't figured out yet."

"I'm just glad we both got the same feeling."

"You know, this stuff doesn't happen to people like me," Lucy laughed softly, and tucked her hair behind her ear.

"People don't fall in love where you're from?" he teased.

Her eyes must've looked like saucers.

"What did you say?"

He smiled. "I said I've fallen in love with you Lucy Adams."

Her face lit up at the words. She could feel the heat radiating from her cheeks as she grinned at him.

CHAPTER 26

*L*ucy hadn't truly realized she'd fallen for Scott.

It was all so subtle, like the mist rolling in on the surface of a lake. It crept in and before she knew it the house of her heart was entirely filled with it. Pillar to post. Roof to basement.

"I think … I love you too," she whispered.

He reached for her hand and pulled her gently to him. She fell against him, her hands flat against his chest.

"You know, watching you blush just makes me smile because I know you aren't a woman who pretends. You call it shyness, but actually I think it's just wearing your heart on your sleeve. I can trust that. I can trust you."

"Scott…"

"Listen. I told myself I wasn't taking another chance on a woman. I'd sworn off romance long before I met you. Even after Mrs. Cole told me about you, I just wanted to meet the person who had come to mean so much to her. Then we met. The minute I saw your smile, I knew there was something about you."

She laughed. "All I thought was that you were the cutest construction worker I'd ever seen."

He laughed. "Thanks."

"I didn't think we'd see each other again after that. I was glad when we did," she admitted. "Berry coming across your house that day saved me."

"Saved us both you mean. After that, when I took Berry in and you started visiting him here, I realized that I wanted more. I wanted a relationship, someone I could come home to and drink my mother's hot chocolate with on cold evenings. Someone who would curl up with me on Christmas night by the fire, while the dog slept on the rug."

"I think we've already covered that bit," she chuckled.

"Yeah, we did, and we weren't even trying," Scott answered. "It just happened naturally, like everything else with you and me."

"And I liked coming here," she admitted after a moment. "I liked driving out here and being welcomed. I liked watching you cook," she said with a smile. "That was a surprise."

"And I like cooking for you."

"I've never felt so comfortable around a guy before," Lucy admitted. "Usually, I can't put two words together, but with you, any nervousness just sort of melted away. One second, I couldn't think straight when you were near, the next I found I didn't want to stop talking to you."

"Feeling's mutual, believe me."

Her skin felt as if a gentle electric current was moving over it. The hairs on her arms stood on end and she shivered.

"Lucy?"

"Yes?"

"I'm going to kiss you again if you don't stop me," he declared.

She smiled brightly. "So what's stopping you?"

He really was the best kisser on the planet.

Tender and warm. His hands were firm but soft against her skin. The cold wind that blew off the water was nothing. She couldn't even feel it. His kiss was dizzying, intoxicating, and she was enjoying every second of it.

Berry must've gotten tired looking at his reflection because a moment later he was back by their side with his head nuzzling at their legs.

He barked low and then trotted around them happily.

"I think he approves," Scott commented.

Lucy looked at the big dog and smiled. "I think so too."

"What do you say about us all getting back indoors and having more of my mom's special hot chocolate?"

"Do you still have marshmallows?" she asked as he took her hand and began to lead her toward the house.

"When I knew you were coming for Christmas I bought two bags when I went to the store."

"I do believe you're getting to know me."

"I look forward to knowing everything about you," Scott replied as he squeezed her hand gently. "The full profile. But we don't need one of your matchmaking cards this time. I want to take my own time."

Lucy liked the sound of that.

Berry trotted up beside them, and she let her fingers rest on his back comfortingly.

"It's nearly finished?" Lucy commented now, as she looked at the house. She hadn't seen it from this angle before, but now she could see that he'd finished the roof above the porch, and a lot more had been done to the far side of the house.

"Just about. I had a lot of motivation lately…"

"Motivation?"

"I thought maybe a certain fellow dog-lover might one day, if things went well …. like to make it her home." He looked hesitantly at Lucy and squeezed her hand as they walked and she couldn't speak for joy. "Only if she wanted to of course," he added quickly. "It even comes equipped with a place for her dog."

Emotion consumed her. She'd always known this house would be the perfect home for Berry.

She'd just never expected it could be the perfect forever home for her too.

She smiled at Scott.

"Sounds to me like a match made in heaven."

CHRISTMAS BENEATH THE STARS

OUT NOW

Cosy up with another heartwarming festive romance from the #1 bestselling author - coming December 2021 as a Christmas movie!

CHAPTER 1

*H*annah Reid loved Christmas.

She loved the cheery feeling in the atmosphere, the twinkling, festive lights and most of all, the sense that at this magical time of the year, anything was possible.

She couldn't add frost or snow to the list though; a born and bred Californian, Hannah wasn't familiar with more traditional wintery Christmas weather.

Yet.

Andy Williams' warm vocals filled the buds in her ears as she reclined in her seat and peered out the window of the aircraft.

Right then, Sacramento lay thousands of miles below in an ocean of darkness and lights. It would be her first holiday season away from home. Her first ever white Christmas.

It was indeed the most wonderful time of the year ...

Hannah hummed the cheery festive tune and glanced down at the cover of the magazine on her lap, a broad smile spreading across her face.

It still felt like a dream.

Discover Wild, one of the biggest wildlife magazines in the country, were sending *her* - Hannah - on assignment.

She ran her hand over the cover shot of a tigress and her cub as they nuzzled together.

It was an amazing photo, one she would have killed to have taken herself.

"Soon," she mused. *Soon it could be my stuff on the cover. All I have to do is get one perfect shot and I'm on my way to a permanent gig with* Discover Wild.

She hugged the magazine to her chest and closed her eyes, relaxing back against the soft leather seat.

IT FELT LIKE JUST A MOMENT, but when Hannah woke it was to the sound of the pilot announcing their descent into Anchorage.

She sat up immediately and looked out the window.

Everything was white!

She'd never seen anything so beautiful. The mountains surrounding the airport were blanketed in thick snow, and a light dusting covered everything else.

She could see the men on the tarmac clearing away the snow, as half a dozen planes in every size - large Boeings to small Cessnas - lay waiting, along with a row of buses to the side.

She wondered which one of those would be taking her to the holiday village she'd chosen as her accommodation while here.

'Nestled deep in the Alaskan wilderness, Christmas World is a true holiday fairytale if ever there was one.

Set amidst lush forest on the South banks of the Yukon River, escape to a magical land where Santa comes to visit every year, and you can find a helpful elf round every corner. Immerse yourself in our idyllic winter paradise and enjoy a Christmas you will never forget ...'

Hannah couldn't wait to experience the true, out and out winter wonderland the online description promised.

Now, the flight was on the ground, but no one was moving. There was a backup of some sort, and passengers were asked to stay on the plane while it was resolved.

Hannah wasn't too bothered; they'd arrived half an hour early in any case, which meant she still had plenty of time before her transfer.

She preoccupied herself on her phone and more online information and picturesque photographs of Christmas World.

The resort homepage featured a group of happy smiling visitors, with various green-and-red clad elves in their midst.

In the background, picture perfect buildings akin to colorful gingerbread houses dusted with snow, framed a traditional town square. It was exactly the kind of Christmas experience Hannah had always dreamed about as a child.

She couldn't *wait* to be there.

CHAPTER 2

Over an hour later, Hannah was still waiting.

In Anchorage International Airport with forty or so other travellers.

Their Christmas World transfer - the so-called 'Magical Christmas Caravan' was late ... *very* late.

"You can't be serious," a fellow airline passenger commented nearby. "How much longer are we supposed to wait? Are they going to compensate us for this debacle? It is the resort's transport after all," the disgruntled woman asked.

She was surrounded by three miserable-looking children, while her sullen husband stood in a long line of people trying to find out what was going on.

Hannah had noticed the family on the plane earlier, but now she was getting a better look at them. They were exactly the type of people you'd expect to find on such a jaunt; happy family, blonde-haired and blue-eyed, with their cute-as-a-button kids giddy with excitement about a trip of a lifetime to see Santa.

More decidedly *un*happy faces surrounded the resort's airport help desk at the moment, but there were plenty of content ones to be found elsewhere too.

A father with his son excitedly perched on top of his shoulders. A serene mother with her sleeping child, and an elderly couple holding hands while they waited for their connection.

It was everything the holidays should be about, Hannah thought; family and loved ones together at the most magical time of the year.

She had been in plenty of airports, but there was something about this one that appealed to her photographer's eye.

The nearby pillars were like pieces of art, almost abstract; though she didn't really know much about art except what she did or didn't like. These were adorned from top to bottom with garlands and white lights. While elsewhere in the terminal, festive wreaths hung on hooks and there were lots and lots of fresh-smelling pine trees.

And of course, then there was the view….

Hannah had taken countless pictures in her life, some to pay the bills and many more for fun. She'd taken portraits, and even the occasional wedding when things were slow between wildlife jobs, but there was something about the outdoors that she loved most of all.

She'd spent her entire life in it after all, had hiked the Quarry trail in Auburn so many times she felt she knew it by heart. Same for the Recreational River, Blue Heron Trail and the Simpson-Reed Trail, and that was just California.

She'd zigzagged her way across America with her collection of trusty Nikon SLR cameras, but she'd never ventured this far north.

The furthest she'd been was Alberta for a wildlife safari last summer. It was those photos that had opened the door to her current opportunity.

And the reason she was in this snowy picture perfect wonderland right now.

. . .

AN HOUR OR SO LATER, and Hannah was peering out the window of Christmas World's transfer coach as Anchorage melted away in a sea of white.

Fresh snow had begun to fall half an hour before, which almost made up for the exorbitant wait.

But at least they were on their way now, and soon Hannah would have a warm lodge, a toasty fire and the most magical Christmas experience awaiting her.

She wondered if there really would be fresh roasted chestnuts available as advertised, and what kind of activities there would be for guests to enjoy when they arrived.

The website listed things like dog-sledding and carolling, plus places to get hot chocolate, Christmas cookies, and a myriad other festive treats.

All of which sounded amazing, especially since she was tired and in sore need of some holiday cheer after such a long travel day.

She imagined the resort town as something like from the movie, *It's A Wonderful Life,* with that close-knit community feel throughout.

Yes, she was here primarily for a career opportunity, but she'd be lying if she said there wasn't the element of living out a fantasy white Christmas too.

Hannah turned back to the window. The snow was falling harder now, and the smile wouldn't leave her face.

She was about to have the best Christmas ever; she could feel it. And she couldn't wait for it to begin.

It's like Christmas morning. The faster you sleep, the faster it arrives. Isn't that what Mom and Dad always said?

END OF EXCERPT

CHRISTMAS BENEATH THE STARS is out now.

ABOUT THE AUTHOR

Holly Greene is the pen-name of USA Today bestselling author Melissa Hill.

Her page-turning contemporary stories are published worldwide and translated into 25 different languages. Her titles are regular chart-toppers in Ireland and internationally.

A GIFT TO REMEMBER was adapted as a Hallmark Christmas movie in 2017 (with a sequel in 2019) plus an adaptation of THE CHARM BRACELET in 2020 - with multiple other titles now currently in development for film & TV.

Printed in Great Britain
by Amazon

69386423R00220